ALPHA

THE ALPHA ELITE SERIES

USA TODAY BEST SELLING AUTHOR

SYBIL BARTEL

Cover art by: CT Cover Creations, www.ctcovercreations.com

Cover Photo by: Wander Aguiar, wanderaguiar.com

Cover Model: Christopher L.

Edited by: Hot Tree Editing, www.hottreeediting.com
The Ryter's Proof Editing Services , therytersproof.com

Formatting by: Champagne Book Design

Warning: This book contains offensive language, alpha males and sexual situations. Mature audiences only. 18+

BOOKS BY SYBIL BARTEL

The Alpha Elite Series

ALPHA

VICTOR

ROMEO

ZULU

The Alpha Bodyguard Series

SCANDALOUS

MERCILESS

RECKLESS

RUTHLESS

FEARLESS

CALLOUS

RELENTLESS

SHAMELESS

HEARTLESS

The Uncompromising Series

TALON

NEIL

ANDRÉ

BENNETT

CALLAN

The Alpha Antihero Series

HARD LIMIT

HARD JUSTICE

HARD SIN

HARD TRUTH

The Alpha Escort Series

THRUST

ROUGH

GRIND

The Unchecked Series

IMPOSSIBLE PROMISE

IMPOSSIBLE CHOICE

IMPOSSIBLE END

The Rock Harder Series

NO APOLOGIES

Join Sybil Bartel's Mailing List to get the news first on her upcoming releases, giveaways and exclusive excerpts! You'll also get a FREE book for joining!

ALPHA

Billionaire.

Mercenary.

Navy SEAL.

The Teams trained me to be a killer. War taught me to be ruthless. Then an ill-fated mission proved I was human. Combat wounded, cut loose by the Navy, I had a choice. Fade into obscurity or use the skills I had.

Alpha Elite Security was born, and three years later, my company was the most sought-after security contractor in the world. Five global locations, ten company jets, every one of my employees military trained—we were the best of the best. Overseeing operations, I didn't have time for women or anything other than growing my company. My success rate unmatched, I'd never lost a client.

Then I got a call, the only call that would get me back in the field. She was missing. The woman I'd left behind seven years ago. Now I had one objective.

Code name: Alpha.
Mission: Extraction.

For my beloved son, Oliver.
You are still, and will *always* be, my entire world.
I love you, Sweet Boy, and I miss you beyond words.

Oliver Shane Bartel 2004-2020

PROLOGUE

Two months ago

MY ATTENTION ALREADY SHOT, THE VIBRATION AGAINST MY LEG was only an excuse. Discreetly reaching into my pants pocket, I slid out my cell and read the text.

Calling in ten seconds. Answer.

I glanced at my friend and employee, Zane "Zulu" Silas, and tipped my chin toward the door.

Speaking to three executives from a Fortune 100 company that was having supply issues with one of their manufacturing facilities because it was in a hot zone, Zulu didn't falter in his assurance that we could eliminate their problem as he nodded at me.

"Gentlemen, if you'll please excuse me, an urgent matter has come up." I stood. "Mr. Silas will be able to answer any of your questions and give you a schedule of our fees. Thank you for reaching out to Alpha Elite Security. We look forward to your business."

My cell already buzzing with an incoming call, I walked out of the conference room on the forty-seventh floor of AES's Manhattan headquarters.

Striding into my corner office, I shut the glass door and answered the call. "What's up?"

"I'm your best fucking friend is what's up," Vance Conlon, my first hire, boasted.

My best friend was dead. "Because?" I demanded.

"Because I'm having fun with your newly updated proprietary face-recognition software."

Staring at a skyline I hated, I didn't bite.

"You going to ask how much fun?" he taunted.

"No." He'd tell me. Vance never called unless he had something to say. "And it's not proprietary. We're testing it for the military, and you're not supposed to have access to it yet."

"Okay, Alpha, you win, I give." Vance chuckled. "I found her. Twenty-five minutes ago, she walked out of JFK and got in a cab. And for the record, I don't give a shit whose software it is. If you didn't want me using it, you shouldn't have put it on the servers."

The air kicked out of my chest, and I leaned against my desk for support. "What else?"

"Right, you knew I wouldn't stop there." I could practically hear him gloat before his tone turned all business. "Anyway, speaking of software, I hacked the cab company and tracked her. The driver has his GPS set for a small grocery mart near her co-op. If you leave the office now, you can get there before she's done shopping for cheap white wine—Californian at least—dark chocolate, and mild salsa. Which if you ask me, the latter is sacrilegious and the first is just in poor taste."

"Do I want to know how you know her shopping list?"

"Do you want to know how I know you're leaning against your desk looking like you've just had your ass kicked?" he countered.

Goddamn it. Glancing up, I scanned the bookshelf in front of me. "I'm sweeping my office after we hang up."

"Yes, do that," he replied absently as he typed on his computer from wherever the hell he was today. "Check the lobby and the conference room while you're at it. Let me know what you find."

"I'm going to regret introducing you to November, aren't I?" Nathan "November" Rhys was the best cybersecurity specialist I knew. The Air Force's loss was my gain when he went civilian.

"No, but you're going to regret not grabbing a car in the next three minutes if you want to stalk that market and see her."

I didn't comment. Vance knew the drill. I didn't see her, ever.

I looked out for her, kept tabs on her travel, and occasionally checked her bank account balance to make sure she didn't need anything—but I purposely never crossed paths with her.

Vance gave me an exaggerated sigh. "Right. No contact. And why is that exactly?" The question rhetorical, he didn't wait for an answer. "Oh, that's right, because you have no balls."

I stared out at skyscrapers and miles of grayness. I didn't want to admit my control was slipping. It'd been years. Her life was different. Mine was... *fuck*, really different.

Except it wasn't.

I was still flying in jets, chasing down bad guys and collecting a paycheck for people shooting at me. I just wasn't doing it for the Navy as a SEAL anymore. Regardless, Vance had a point. Time had passed, and seven years of hard-practiced resolve was wearing me down.

"Tell you what," Vance continued, "I'm going to read into your silence, and...." He trailed off as he typed. "There. A service not affiliated with AES just had a drop-off at your location. The driver's swinging around, and he'll be downstairs in thirty seconds. Since this isn't one of our own, no one will be the wiser. Go lurk in the shadows. You're good at that. Or walk the fuck up to her. I don't care, just lay eyes on her. For all we know, it'll be three weeks again before I spot her, and maybe seeing her will change your attitude."

I didn't say no. I hesitated.

Then I was walking.

The phone still to my ear, my feet moving, I hit the call button for the elevator before I could tell myself everything I'd built wasn't for her or the opportunity of this moment. "I don't have an attitude."

"Yes, you do." Vance chuckled as the doors opened immediately. "You have an attitude that says you haven't been laid this side of the decade. Also, you're welcome for the waiting lift."

Christ. "Did you hack the building's security for this or call in a favor with the guys in the command room?"

"Unlike sailors, a Marine never tells."

Ignoring his Navy versus Marines jab, I stepped into the elevator that I normally would've had to wait for. "This is a mistake."

Vance's usual casual tone turned somber. "We've all made mistakes. Walking into a grocery store in Manhattan doesn't come close to making the list, but regret does. Go see this woman, Trefor. It's time." He hung up.

Adrenaline filled my veins like a fix. A fix I only got from two things in life. But it'd been years since my last HALO on the Teams, and even longer since I'd seen her. Two addictions, and neither one curable.

I'd left the Teams, but I'd never left her.

Impatient, I watched the last few floors tick down on the display, and a moment later the doors slid open to the busy lobby. Stalking across the polished floors and out the revolving doors, I made my way to a black Town Car double-parked in front of the building.

Opening the rear passenger door, the driver, an older gentleman, smiled. "Good evening. Mr. Adam Trefor, I assume?"

I nodded in acknowledgment even though after years of being a civilian, it was still odd to hear people call me Adam instead of Alpha. "Do you know where we're going?"

"Yes, sir."

"Hurry," I demanded.

"Of course, sir." He shut my door, but he didn't hurry. He couldn't. It was fucking Manhattan at eighteen hundred hours on a Thursday.

Thirteen punishing minutes later, he pulled in front of one

of those small, overpriced delis that doubled as a grocery store for basic needs that Manhattan was infamous for. Before I could get out of the car, my cell vibrated with a new text.

Perfect timing, she's still inside. Last aisle by the white wines. But grab the Peju Province. You can thank me later.

Vowing to find a new assignment for Vance the second I was back in the office, I glanced at the driver. "Can you circle the block until I come back out?"

"Of course, sir. Take all the time you need."

"Thank you." With a nod, I was out of the car and buttoning the jacket of my custom Ermenegildo Zegna suit as I aimed for the front door of the market.

Ignoring the glances from women shopping by themselves, I cut across the front of the store and rounded the corner on the last aisle.

Then I stopped dead in my tracks.

Jesus.

Blonde, ethereal, delicate, and more beautiful than I remembered, the only woman I'd ever loved stood mere feet away from me in a pale green dress.

Staring, my heart pounding, the air in my lungs nonexistent, all I could think was how unforgivably selfish I'd been on the worst day of her life.

I deserved her hate, but I told myself that was seven years ago. Time was on my side, and it'd been long enough. She had to forgive me.

Move, Trefor.

Make the move.

As if sensing my presence, she suddenly looked over her shoulder, her gaze landing exactly where I stood.

But she didn't look up at me.

Not all the way.

Her head slightly dipped, her gaze cast down as if staring at my legs, her emerald green eyes didn't meet mine.

Fuck this.

I stepped forward.

The man came around the corner from the opposite end of the aisle. Dark haired, bearded, he smiled wide and kissed her cheek. She looked surprised, but she let him take the basket that was perched on top of her small rolling suitcase and the bottle of wine from her hand.

Turning to the shelves of red zins in front of me, I tried to ignore the strike to my chest that wasn't at all like the goddamn kick I'd felt in my office. This was a full-blown, direct hit IED.

Leveled to nothing but shrapnel, I stood there.

I just fucking stood there.

Rooted like a coward, I watched the asshole put the wine back on the shelf and dump the basket on the floor. Taking her suitcase and smiling again as he spoke to her, he nodded toward the front of the store.

She said something I couldn't hear.

He threw his head back and laughed.

Not even cracking a smile, she listened as he spoke again.

Then she nodded, and they both turned toward my position.

I didn't hesitate.

I turned the corner, crossed the front of the store, and walked out.

My nerves shot, my light jade Armani wrap-front dress wrinkled from too long of a day, I stared blankly at the bottle of Californian sauvignon blanc in my hand. The hair on the back of my neck prickled, and adrenaline coursed through my tired body.

I was being watched.

I could feel it.

The small market in upper Manhattan was packed right after the workday ended, but it wasn't that. This was something else.

Someone else.

My shopping basket perched on top of my small rolling suitcase, I held both handles in one hand as I stared at the familiar wine I would buy, open, pour into a glass, then not drink.

Maybe have a few sips.

But I didn't really drink.

Not that I couldn't hold more alcohol than most men twice my size, I could. Genetics and being raised by a father and brother who thought a key component of self-defense was learning how to hold hard liquor without getting alcohol poisoning had only been the beginning. I'd been initiated to a state of drunkenness by age sixteen that I never wanted to repeat again, but go figure, I liked the taste of white wine. For a few sips. Maybe my father and brother should've included wine in their initiation and I wouldn't be standing here staring at what bottle I least wanted to waste.

Mentally shaking away thoughts of my past, I focused on the tingling sensation that was now stronger than it'd been a moment ago.

Inhaling, I chanced a glance over my shoulder but purposely didn't lift my head enough to meet anyone's direct gaze.

Impatient women in expensive clothes, store clerks stocking shelves… and a man in a suit.

An expensive suit.

Like the ones you saw all over Manhattan, but this suit wasn't covering the underused legs of a business executive who sat behind a desk all day.

No, this suit was barely containing muscular thighs with the impeccable cut of its fine wool.

My breath caught, and I dared to look higher.

An expensive, fine leather, designer belt hugged a tapered waist.

My stomach flooded with a swarm of butterflies, and goose bumps raced across my suddenly heated skin. A rush of warmth I hadn't felt in so long it was no longer familiar settled in my chest like a physical weight.

I told myself I shouldn't.

I forced myself not to.

Do not look up.

This wasn't me. I didn't get these reactions anymore. I didn't have wayward emotions, and I certainly didn't stand in grocery markets and flush over the cut of a man's suit as it hugged his muscular legs.

This was *not* me.

But the sensation of being watched was careening with the riot of physical reactions storming my body, and this was happening.

For the first time in years, I didn't want to be the woman I'd become. I didn't want to stop myself from looking up, only to walk away with a bottle of wine I wouldn't drink and retreat to a rented apartment I hadn't furnished, but I didn't have a choice.

Before I could take that step in the opposite direction, the man's custom-suited legs moved with a step toward me.

Unable to stop myself, I started to look up.

"Ah, my beautiful American."

Cologne swamped me as my head snapped in the opposite direction from the suited man.

Dark brown eyes crinkling with a full smile met mine as the bearded man leaned down to kiss my cheek. "You should not have to do your own shopping."

"Khalaf." I covered my shock, just. He had never kissed my cheek in public. "What are you doing here?" How did he find me? We'd parted ways in London too many hours ago to count.

He tsked as he took first my basket, then the wine. Placing the bottle back on the shelf, he shook his head. "A beautiful woman does not need alcohol to feel good." His warm smile covered the sting of his reproach. "Come, I will feed you. You do not need to be in here alone, looking for your dinner." He set the shopping basket on the ground right in front of us as if it was someone else's problem to pick up.

"Where are your guards?" He never went anywhere without them, and he never did anything as pedestrian as coming into a market.

Khalaf gave me a look of amusement, as if I were ignorant, before taking the handle of my suitcase. "They are in the car out front. I spotted you as you walked in and had my driver pull over. After London, I have been thinking...." He trailed off, but his eyes stayed on mine.

I swallowed. "About?"

"I do not think it was happenstance that we met in the lobby of that hotel."

All the tingling warmth left my body, but I didn't so much as blink. "No?"

"No," he said definitively as he leaned forward. "You may have been in London at that hotel for a work conference, and I for meetings, and now we are both here in New York, but this is not happenstance that is putting us together." He paused for dramatic effect. "It is fate, and it's time we act upon it." He nodded toward the front of the store. "What do you say, my beautiful American?"

Words meant to be a lighthearted dance between flippant and playful dragged heavily across my dry tongue. "I am not looking to get married, Khalaf."

He laughed in earnest. "Oh my darling girl, you are much too beautiful for that." His eyes crinkled again as his voice dipped seductively low. "But a mistress?" He made a low, humming sound as if in delight. "A man should be so lucky. Come. I will feed you, and you will tell me everything you desire. Then, maybe, if you are a good girl, I will take you with me on my next business trip."

Still feeling like I was being watched, taken off guard by Khalaf's presence, my instincts begging me to look toward the suited man but circumstances forcing me not to, I merely nodded at Khalaf.

"Good," he murmured, taking my reaction as consent. "Then it is settled." He turned in the direction of where the suited man had been standing. "Let us make fate happy."

The aisle now void of those muscular thighs in fine wool crepe, an overwhelming sense of loss I couldn't explain settled in deep. My choices stripped long before this evening, I followed Khalaf and his cologne, but as we turned the corner on the last aisle, an entirely different kind of fate mocked me.

A masculine scent ghosted across my senses like a memory.

Cold wind and sharp angles.

It filled my head, and the reaction was instant. Regret mixed with a longing I kept buried deep, and I desperately inhaled.

The scent was already gone.

PART ONE

Seven Years Ago

ONE

Adam

"THIS IS SO FUCKING FUCKED," ZULU MUTTERED.

I didn't say anything. I straightened the sleeves of my full-dress uniform in a useless attempt to cover the bruising on my left hand. The laceration on my cheek, I couldn't do anything about.

I raised my right fist to knock.

"Wait," Zulu clipped.

I glanced at him.

Same dress uniform, similar cuts and bruises, the rage and defeat in his eyes mirroring my own, Zulu looked beat to hell. "You promised him."

I knew what I'd promised Petty Officer Second Class William "Billy" Nilsen. I knew exactly what I'd said before his last mission, what I said to him before every mission. It was a version of the same thing I'd promised before we'd enlisted.

Three days ago, my fist had bumped his and I'd given him the words I never thought I'd have to follow through on. *"I promise I'll take care of her if you kick your last door down."*

Billy had held my stare like he always had and given me the same response he always did. *"You better, or I'll come back and beat your ass before kicking your ass."*

Trying to block the memory, I glanced at Zane. "I know exactly what I promised him." But that didn't alter what we had to do right now.

"We both told him we'd take care of her." Zane jabbed a finger toward the front door of the house I knew better than my own growing up. "We knock now, it's bullshit."

"I know," I reiterated.

"Telling her he's dead, then turning around to catch transport in twenty-eight minutes isn't fucking taking care of her."

Anger, rash and instant, exploded on the only damn friend I had left in this world. "What do you want me to do?" I demanded in a furious whisper. "Call it in and tell them to send someone she doesn't know to do the next-of-kin notification? *He was our brother,*" I spat.

"She's *eighteen,*" he spat right back in a hushed tone, just as angry.

"I fucking know how old she is, goddamn it." I was acutely aware of how old my dead best friend's sister was. She was eighteen going on thirty, because being raised by a widowed father who was a vice admiral in the Navy and having your only sibling become a SEAL before you were a teen didn't leave room for a childhood, let alone innocence. Add in the fact that her father was already six feet under thanks to a fucking aneurism last year, and I didn't want to knock on this door.

Fuck, I didn't want to knock.

I didn't want to break the heart of the only woman who'd ever looked at me like I made the sun set and rise. Except she wasn't a woman when she used to look at me like that. She'd been a child with pigtails and skinny legs and more smile than common sense.

I was the latchkey kid from the wrong side of the tracks with dirty clothes, worn-through shoes and anger always lurking beneath the surface. But her five-year-old self took one look at me the day her brother dragged me home like a stray, and she'd smiled ear to ear.

That was the beginning of the crack in the wall around my sixteen-year-old heart.

Thirteen years later and I was about to destroy her world.

Orphan her.

Make her feel more alone than I did the first day I laid eyes on her.

I didn't want to fucking knock.

But I had to, and I only had a few minutes to do it. Zane and I needed to get our asses back downrange and catch the motherfuckers who'd done this, but first I needed to do the right thing and let her hear the news from someone she knew. Then I needed to get my head on straight and finish the mission.

I didn't have time to stand on a doorstep I'd crossed more than the cracked pavement leading up to the dump of a house I'd grown up in. I was wasting precious time I could be with her. Doing what, I didn't fucking know.

Holding her.

The same way I'd held her last year after her father's funeral once everyone had gone home. Billy had taken a bottle of Jack and disappeared into the backyard, and she'd been standing in the middle of the kitchen looking at all the food. Then she'd burst into tears, and I didn't think.

I was on her faster than I had a right to be. My arms were pulling her against my chest, and my lips were on the top of her head, telling her bullshit lies about how everything would be okay.

It hadn't been the first time I'd hugged her or kissed away her tears like I was her blood brother.

But it was the first time I'd felt the curve of her hips and the swell of her breasts and smelled the perfume she'd taken to wearing that wasn't anything like the strawberry shampoo she'd used as a kid, because at seventeen she wasn't a kid anymore.

She'd had the curves of a woman, and fuck, had I noticed.

I'd noticed so goddamn hard, I wouldn't even admit to myself the reasons why I hadn't touched another woman since that day.

My head fucked, anger warring with grief, I glanced at Zane. "Her age doesn't change what we need to do."

"We'll be back in a week," he argued. "Hell, a few days if the intel this time isn't fucked."

"Will we?" I could be standing on his parents' doorstep next week in my service dress blues.

Zane snorted. "Don't go fucking soft on me now. You know exactly what I'm saying. She's got no one. In a week, we can come back and one of us can stay with her. Billy would be pissed as hell about this. You fucking know it."

"Maybe, maybe not," I lied. My best friend would be more than pissed. His sister was his world. Despite the string of ever-present nannies because their father had hardly been around, Billy'd taken on the majority of the responsibility of raising her since losing their mother when he was thirteen and she was two. In the past twenty-eight hours, I'd thought more than once that some cosmic bullshit had intervened and taken his life first. Had she gone before him, Billy wouldn't have handled it. At all. "I know he wouldn't have wanted her to be notified from anyone other than us." I also knew Zane was right.

We could've waited a week, but I was selfishly standing here because I needed to see her. I needed forgiveness that I didn't save her brother. Not that I deserved it.

Before I lost my nerve, I knocked.

The sound carried through the early dawn as the first rays of the sun caught the neighborhood. A dog barked, and sprinklers turned on.

There was no movement in the house.

I knocked again.

Zane cursed.

Faint, distant, I heard feet on stairs a second before her muffled voice. "Coming."

Adrenaline rushed, the rock in my stomach grew and I hated myself. Her bare footsteps on wood floors echoed in time with the countdown of seconds that was left before I destroyed her life.

The lock clicked.

I fucking held my breath.

TWO

Adam

THE DOOR CREAKED OPEN, AND THERE SHE WAS.

Maila Marie Nilsen.

Emmy for short.

My Emmy.

For a split second, the little girl who'd grown into a beautiful young woman took me in with surprise and the beginning of the smile she always gave me. But then her gaze cut to Zane, our uniforms, and a fraction of a second later, horror distorted her features.

"No." Vehemently shaking her head, she stepped back. "*No.*"

I stepped forward. "Maila."

"No," she shouted, tears already streaming down her face. "Don't you dare." One hand fisting against her mouth, the other lashed out and struck me. "Don't you dare say it, Adam Trefor," she sobbed. "*Don't you dare!*" She struck me again. "NO."

I wrapped my arms around her and pulled her to my chest. The pit in my stomach lodged in my throat. "I regret to inform you Petty Officer Second Class William Nilsen lost his life in the line of duty." My voice broke. "Billy's gone."

"Nooooo!" Her wail filled the picture-perfect morning with the destruction of war as both her fists hit at me with devastation. "No, no, *nooooo*!"

Zane closed the door behind us.

Sobbing, shaking, the force of her assault giving way to grief, her body started to slip as her knees gave out.

Sweeping an arm under her legs, I picked her up. "I got you."

"No, no, no." She choked on her cries.

I carried her to the same leather couch her brother and I had been on over a decade ago when we'd sworn to each other that we'd both pass BUD/S together or die trying. Not letting go of Emmy, I sat.

Her hands over her face, her bare legs limp on my lap, her chest shook with anguish as she cried *no* over and over.

I didn't tell her it would be okay.

I didn't hush her.

I didn't give her the promise her brother made me swear to.

I tightened my arms around her, and I let the shit I'd been holding in for twenty-eight hours go. "I'm sorry, Emmy." Tears slicked my face. "I'm so fucking sorry."

Squatting next to us, Zane held a glass of water for her. "Drink, honey."

I released my hold on her just enough so that she could take the glass.

Her hands shaking, the look in her eyes killing me, her sobs turned to a low keen as she looked from Zane to me. "D-d-did he s-s-suffer?"

The image of the last time I saw her brother both enraged and haunted me.

I would never tell her that the only identifying marker we had once we'd gotten inside the blown-out building was his MK 17 and too many body parts to count. "No." Placing my hand over hers so she didn't spill the water, I brought the glass to her lips. "Take a sip."

Zane grasped her shoulder. "It was instant, sweetheart. We can't give you any more details, but I will tell you this. He died a hero. His actions saved the rest of the team."

She drank, but then she dissolved into a fresh wave of grief.

Zane caught my gaze, then lifted his chin toward the clock on the wall.

I was a selfish asshole, and Zane had been right. I should've waited a week.

Nodding toward the kitchen, I issued Zane an order. "There's a list of numbers on the wall by the phone." I'd written it myself and taped it up the week before Billy and I enlisted. The numbers had changed over the years, some were scratched out, some were added, but the sentiment was the same. It was a list of people to call in case of an emergency. A list of people Emmy could call. People she could rely on. Because even back then, despite wanting nothing more than to be a SEAL, it'd felt like shit leaving her behind.

"Call Mrs. Jansen," I directed Zane. "The second number listed is her cell." The neighbor was the closest thing to a grandmother Emmy and Billy had ever had.

Emmy cried harder as she choked out words through her sobs. "Y-you can't call her. It's too early. She's sleeping."

I threw Zane a look, but he was already moving. Locking down my own emotions, I took her face in my hands and held her broken gaze. "You need people here with you right now. People you can lean on."

She grabbed the front of my uniform as understanding took. "Don't leave me." Fear and desperation mixed with the devastation in her eyes. "You're all I have now, Adam." Her breath hitched on a sob. "You're all I have left." She buried her face in my chest and wept. "Don't leave me. *You can't go back.*"

My chest fucking caved in as impotent anger flared. "You know how this works."

Her head shook violently, her sun-kissed shoulders trembling, her long legs draped over my lap. Wearing only pajama shorts and a tank top, her soft, sleep-messed hair covered my chest and,

God forgive me, I wanted to carry her upstairs, crawl into bed and hold her for fucking eternity.

"*No, no, no,*" she cried, smelling like woman, fresh sheets, and pain.

So much damn pain.

Her grief palpable, I wanted to kiss her as much as I wanted to find the assholes responsible for Billy's death and destroy them limb by limb. But just like on a mission, I had no room for emotion right now. "I have to go back, Emmy," I said quietly, using the childhood nickname I wasn't sure matched the woman she'd grown into but was so ingrained, I said her name in my sleep.

Her sob was as painful to hear as it was to witness. "Billy nicknamed me that."

Guilt crushed me. "I know." Selfish and full of regret, I tried to justify my decision to come here today. "I'm sorry I can't stay, but I didn't want a stranger to give you the notification. We took leave just to get here to tell you in person so you heard it from us, but our mission isn't over."

She covered her eyes and wept with soul-crushing sobs. "Billy, *Billy*."

I wrapped my arms around her, but I was a fucking bastard. I was already scanning the doorway to the kitchen, looking for Zane to come back and put a barrier between me and her. Drowning in guilt that her brother was dead, that I hadn't saved him, I'd thought I needed to do this, but now I wanted an exit strategy.

I was going to kill every last terrorist responsible for this.

Zane walked into the living room with the phone to his ear. "Mrs. Jansen's packing a bag so she can stay, then she's on her way. She wants to know how many days."

"One week," I told him. "Then I'll be back."

Maila's sobs paused, and she looked up at me with a tearstained face. But it wasn't with the innocent face of a five-year-old girl. It wasn't even with the face of the woman who'd answered the door a few minutes ago before I'd destroyed her life.

She looked at me with grief and fear, but then her features twisted with anger. "*You liar*. You don't get to promise you're coming back. I hate you, Adam Trefor, *I hate you*."

Before I could process the Maila Marie Nilsen storm that'd just slammed into me, she was off my lap and aiming for the stairs.

Her slender, bare foot hit the first step, and she paused only long enough to yell at us as a sob shook her slight frame. "Get out, both of you!"

I was on my feet to go after her when a hand hit my chest.

"Brother," Zane quietly chided. "Maybe you should give her a little breathing room. Let her process this for a moment."

We didn't have a moment. We didn't even have a few minutes. I sure as fuck was going after her. "Let Mrs. Jansen in. Tell her to call the other numbers. I want Emmy surrounded by people she can trust. She doesn't deserve to be alone." Not like this. Not orphaned and thrust into a world where she had no blood relatives left. It wasn't lost on me that I was in the same boat, but this wasn't about me. I could handle myself. I always had. This was about her.

For two seconds, Zane leveled me with a look that said exactly what he thought of my decisions, but then he stepped back.

If I hadn't been lying to myself, shutting down every damn thing in my head so I could mission focus, I'd be staring at the naked truth.

It'd always been about her.

Thirteen years ago, I'd walked into this house and a little girl had smiled at me. I didn't know then what that weighted heaviness in my chest was.

But I fucking knew now.

I took the stairs two at a time.

THREE

Maila

No. This wasn't happening. *No.*

My brother.

My only brother.

With sobs stealing my breath and tears blinding me, I ran up the stairs.

I'd lost everything.

Everything.

Daddy, now Billy.

I didn't even remember my own mother.

I had no one, *no one*, except a stray boy my brother had brought home, but he wasn't a boy anymore. Adam Trefor hadn't just grown into a man, he was a Navy SEAL. A cold, calculating, impenetrable SEAL who was going back to the very same place that had killed my brother, and I couldn't breathe.

First Daddy, then Billy, and now Adam was going back to the same world full of war and danger that had killed every man I loved?

Why, *why*?

A fresh wave of tears mixed with anger, disbelief and so much grief that I couldn't do this.

I wouldn't.

I would not stand here another minute drowning in memories and wishing for a life I would never have again. I couldn't wait for another visit from a uniformed man telling me Adam was dead, if I even got that, because who knew who Adam had listed as his next-of-kin. He didn't have anyone.

Adam was just like me, or I was like him. What did it matter the order? It changed nothing. Adam had been where I was now for years already. Hell, maybe his whole life. Alcohol and hard living took his mama years ago, but she'd never been a mother to him.

Once, we'd all been a family. The Nilsens and a stray boy. Four souls brought together by life's shitty circumstances but forged by need. My mama had been long gone, and Daddy was always halfway around the world on deployments or hiding in his study when he was home. It was always just me and Billy and whatever nanny we had at the time. I loved Billy more than words, and I knew he sacrificed his whole youth to take care of me the very best way a young boy could, but sometimes I was ashamed to admit, I'd felt like something was missing.

Maybe I had more love to give, maybe I was missing a mama I couldn't remember, or maybe I just needed more love.

I was only five years old, I didn't know.

But then Billy came home with a quiet boy with black hair and blue eyes that were so stark, they were almost haunted. He was so broken but so beautiful, I couldn't help the smile that'd spread across my face. I knew that very instant that nothing would ever be the same again, and I'd been right.

Everything changed.

Suddenly, there was a teenager around who knew how to make grilled cheese sandwiches and put Band-Aids on my skinned knees, and who was so reserved but so very capable he'd acted more like an adult than a sixteen-year-old. But he also had just enough impressionable youth left that Daddy started coming out of his study to give all the advice he'd already given me and Billy another go around.

Adam was drawn in by Daddy's attention, Billy and I loved

having Daddy out of the study, and the next thing we knew, Billy's room got a bunk bed and Adam stayed over anytime his mama wasn't *feeling good*. Which was a lot. But I selfishly didn't care.

Because the Nilsens became a family.

What'd always been me and Billy and a revolving door of nannies became me and Billy and Adam and a father who started sending the nanny home when he wasn't on leave. What used to be me and my big brother and a man I called Daddy but hardly ever saw, became something so much more.

We became a four-person unit that laughed around the dinner table on holidays and shared milestone events. My heart had been full. So full that I didn't want our happiness to end. I wanted it to last forever, and that forever started to look a whole lot like piercing blue eyes and dark, unruly hair as the boy Adam grew into the man Adam.

I couldn't pinpoint the very moment I fell in love with Adam Trefor, but I knew one thing for sure.

I'd loved him from the second I'd first laid eyes on him.

I knew he saw me as a child, as the younger sister of his best friend. But I saw him as more, and I'd had a plan. Then Daddy died.

Now Billy was gone.

I couldn't do this.

No escaping the sobs, no way out, my mind disconnected from my body, and suddenly my suitcase was on the unmade bed and I was ransacking drawers.

"Maila."

I didn't want to hear my name spoken with concern by not a Navy SEAL but the man I'd fallen hopelessly in love with. A man who'd held me so tight after Daddy had died that it'd felt like he loved me as much as I loved him.

"*Maila*."

I didn't want this.

I didn't want to smell the distinct scent of military transport intermixed with a subtle, masculine cologne that was like cold wind and sharp angles, because no matter how many times I'd seen Adam smile, the starkness that never left his eyes was a part of every single thing about him.

I couldn't do this.

I couldn't breathe in my favorite musk that was mixed with starched uniform.

I couldn't stand here and pretend I wasn't losing everything.

So I hopelessly, frantically threw clothes into the suitcase.

"Stop." The quiet command came a second before huge, muscular arms wrapped around me from behind. "Stop, Maila."

I sucked in a sharp breath.

Before today, the last time Petty Officer First Class Adam Michael Trefor called me by my full name, his arms were around me. Except he hadn't said my name. He'd breathed it on a hoarse whisper as he'd buried his face in my hair and surrounded me with his huge arms and unwavering strength.

My stomach didn't bottom out like it did a year ago, because the ground underneath me was already gone. But an ache I knew well, one I'd been harboring forever, grew, and I hated myself.

My brother was dead, and I was thinking about his best friend.

Anger surged, and I twisted away from him. "Let go of me."

He did the opposite.

Quick, commanding, he grasped a handful of my hair and yanked both my head and my body.

My neck arched, my head fell back, and my chest landed against his impossible strength. I gasped.

"*Stop*," he ordered, fury contorting his features.

A hundred words pushed at my mind as tears leaked from my eyes. Stop what? Stop crying? Stop running, stop grieving, stop living, stop loving? Stop *what*? I didn't have anything left to stop, because my world had already stopped the second I opened the front door.

But I didn't say that.

I didn't say anything. There weren't any words left. Billy was gone, Adam was leaving, and my whole family was relieved of this pain crushing me from the inside out, but I was left here to endure it. By myself.

A new kind of sob, one full of a self-loathing survivor's guilt that piled on top of the isolating grief, broke free, and I couldn't hold back the single question swirling in my head anymore.

"WHY?" My fist pounded against his chest. *"Why me?"* I hit him again. "I did everything right. *Everything*. I never complained. I never begged Daddy or Billy or you not to serve. I never did anything wrong. I was a good girl. *I was a good person.*" Why was this happening?

His nostrils flared, his eyes turned to a storm like the ocean at night and he pulled my hair even tighter. "You did nothing wrong, and none of this is your fault. You hear me?"

"I did everything wrong." I cried harder. "Billy's gone, and it's all my fault. I didn't ask him to stay after Daddy died. *Why didn't I ask him to stay?"*

"Do not do this," Adam ordered in a lethally commanding tone I'd never heard from him. "You know what your brother would want. You know he wouldn't want you to think this. He did exactly what he was trained to do, what he loved to do. His actions saved the team. He didn't hesitate, he didn't falter. He fought with courage." Adam shook me. *"Honor that."*

My mind, my thoughts, my heart, they all fractured. "I was four years old." Another sob escaped. "Four. When Daddy told me the only honorable way a man dies is for his country." I hated my father in that moment. I hated every single breath he ever took for his country because it was a breath he didn't take for us. "He told Billy that. He *trained* him to think like that. He drilled it into him. He drilled it into you. He forced his beliefs on all of us, and now look what's happened." Both my fists hit his chest. "They're dead, and you're going back to the place that killed them!" I burst into tears.

Before I took my next breath, Adam Trefor, the Navy SEAL, the unwavering, unfaltering stoic man, he was on me.

Fisting two handfuls of my hair, his lips crashed over mine.

With the force of a violent tempest, he angled my head and thrust his tongue into my mouth.

Everything I had ever wanted came to fruition and crashed into my worst nightmare. I couldn't breathe, I couldn't think, I could only feel. Every fiber of my being wanted to drown in Adam's angry, desperate kiss. I wanted to bury myself in his dominant grip. I wanted to disappear into his strong arms and too-tall frame and forget every single moment that'd led up to this.

I wanted to be his because I didn't want to be me.

I wanted to be Adam's and nothing else.

Not the girl who lost her entire family. Not the orphan at eighteen. Not the girl who was waiting for bad things to happen, only to have them come true.

I just wanted to be his and live in this possessive, dominant, demanding kiss forever.

I wanted to be the woman who deserved the hunger he was devouring my mouth with. I wanted to be the woman who elicited this response from a man like Adam, a response not conditioned by grief and backed by pity.

I wanted to be whole.

The thought no more than materialized, and his grasp on my hair tightened, only to use it to pull me away from him.

His lips wet from our kiss, his eyes a lethal cocktail of fury and desire, his expression was more stern than I'd ever seen it. Holding me like he possessed every inch of my body and mind for his dominant will, he laid down words like they were an unbending order. "You will stay here, and you will wait for me. One week. Once I'm back, we'll bury him together. Then we're going to talk about this. Understand?"

Bury him.

Two words and my loss came crashing down around me all over again as if hearing it for the first time, but worse. The impossible reality of this hit me like a freight train. My throat tried to move with the reflexive response of a swallow, but nothing could push down the pit of despair that'd come roaring back. "He's here?"

Adam's piercing stare with his blue eyes that were the color of the tropical ocean right before the sun rose and gave it depth held me captive for three impossible heartbeats. Then, ever so slightly, his head lifted in acknowledgment. "We brought him home."

I had to know.

I didn't want to know, but I needed to. I knew myself. I knew how I processed grief. I knew the questions and regrets and guilt I would face in the coming days and months. Hell, I was already there. It was a place I knew intimately but never, *ever*, wanted to be. But that place was my cross, and I had to ask what I knew my soul would need to know. If I didn't, I would forever wonder, and asking now before he left may be the only opportunity I'd have.

Fighting the unending tears that did nothing to ease the grief, I asked, "Is he… in a casket?" Was his body in one piece?

Studying me like he always had, except looking at me different than ever before, Adam's gaze didn't falter, but he said nothing.

"Don't sugarcoat." I needed to know. "Tell me the truth."

"There was an explosion." He paused. "Suicide bomber."

My breath hitched, then everything went still.

A clarity I never wanted or asked for suddenly became a part of my being as much as my own name.

I knew what I had to do.

Turning away from Adam, I picked up a shirt I'd haphazardly

tossed in my suitcase and carefully folded it with shaking hands. "You can go now."

"Alpha," Zane called as his footsteps sounded on the stairs. Stopping at my doorway, he eyed me, then Adam. "Time."

I focused back on my suitcase and tried not to lose myself in hopeless tears.

"Give me a minute," Adam clipped.

"We don't have a—"

"*Now,*" Adam cut him off.

Ignoring Adam, Zane walked into the bedroom and silently pulled me into his arms. His huge muscles no less impressive than Adam's or Billy's or any of their other team members, he hugged me tight. "Love you, girl. You were his reason. Know that. Know that he didn't go down without a fight." He pulled back to look into my eyes. "He'd expect the same of you." His lips touched my forehead for longer than a normal kiss, then Zane retreated.

Adam watched him walk out of my bedroom, but then he pushed my suitcase across the bed in disgust. "Stop packing."

"Go save the world." I hated myself the second the words left my mouth.

Adam didn't deserve those words, but I was angry, at him, at my father, at the world and even a little bit angry at Billy. I knew three days ago that something was wrong. I didn't want to think about it, so I'd ignored the growing concern. But each day that it grew farther from the seven-day mark since I'd last heard from Billy, I knew something bad had happened, because my brother had made me a promise.

Billy and I had a system, and despite all the obstacles that came with his promise because of what he did and who he was, he'd never broken it. Every week since he'd passed BUD/S and gotten on the Teams, he'd managed to get word to me that he was okay. Occasionally it was a phone call, sometimes a text, usually an email, but a lot of times it was from one of the guys on another team, telling me everything was status quo and Billy would be in touch when he could.

But three days ago, no call, no email, and no text from Billy or anyone else had come.

Frustration crossed Adam's sharp features. "This is not me abandoning you, and this isn't about saving the world, because you know that's a bullshit remark. I'm doing my job, Maila. I'll be back in a week. Wait for me, and we'll do this together."

Together.

I couldn't stop the tears dripping down my face any more than I could the anger. What kind of together would we ever have now? He was offering me everything I'd ever wanted but at a price I could never afford or want to pay. "And then what? You stay a day, a week, then you kiss me again and tell me what to do like you have a right?"

His nostrils flared, and the sixteen-year-old boy who'd had a temper from circumstances beyond his control made an appearance before Adam quickly masked it with his Navy SEAL-trained, locked-down expression. "I'm sorry. That shouldn't have happened."

The hit to my heart would've destroyed me yesterday.

But today?

It didn't even touch me. I was already so devastated, there was nothing Adam Trefor or anyone else could do to me.

Not now.

Not ever.

Because I was never going to love again.

Ignoring the man I used to idolize and love, desperately trying to ignore the images my mind kept conjuring of all the horrific scenarios that could've happened to my brother, I pulled my suitcase back across the bed.

Zane appeared in the doorway again and knocked twice on the frame. "Alpha. Go time."

"*Emmy*," Adam clipped.

The tears coming faster, everything getting harder and harder to hold in, I said nothing as I blindly threw shit in the damn suitcase.

"Alpha," Zane quietly commanded.

Two paces and Adam kicked the door shut. Then his huge, overmuscled, war-hardened, six-and-half-foot-tall body that was all sharp angles and cold wind was between me and the bed as his rough hands gently took either side of my face. "Say the word and I will miss that fucking transport, Maila."

The tenuous dam broke, and I choked on grief and impossibilities.

So many impossibilities.

And yearning.

A yearning that cut so deep, it was bleeding me out, but I couldn't stop it. I had no control over any of this. Not my life or Adam's or what had happened to Billy, and all of it was too much. I didn't start to crack, I was already fracturing. My legs shook, my body trembled, and I had to reach for him to keep from falling into nothingness.

But my fingers weren't long enough to encircle his thick wrists, and I couldn't stop any of this.

I couldn't tell Adam to go AWOL, I couldn't bring Billy back, I couldn't save my father and I couldn't remember the woman who gave me life.

Everything breaking, every part of my mind and body wanting to give in and give up, I did the only thing left in my power to do.

I held my tongue.

Killing me as sure as if I'd pulled the trigger myself, I kept my mouth shut and didn't say the one thing I'd wanted to say since I was five years old.

FOUR

Adam

FOUR HOURS INTO DEBRIEFING, FOUR HOURS AND FIFTEEN MINUTES since my boots had touched American soil, thirty-nine hours since I'd slept, and five days since I'd showered.

I stared, unseeing, at the intel projected on the screen.

Lieutenant Commander Davis was still yelling about casualties and cleanup and countermeasures, but I didn't give a single fuck. The HVT was dead, his security detail were all dead, and I'd spared the HVT's asshole adult son only to bring him back for interrogation.

But none of it brought Billy back.

None of it erased the same image that'd been cycling on repeat in my head for six days.

"Say the word and I will miss that fucking transport, Maila."

Except she hadn't said the word. She hadn't said a damn thing.

I'd stared at her eyes and saw the one thing I couldn't undo.

Despair.

"Alpha," Lieutenant Commander Davis barked. "Anything to add?"

"No, sir."

"Dismissed," Lieutenant Commander Davis grunted. "Nilsen's funeral is tomorrow at thirteen hundred hours, so get some rest, clean the fuck up and let's pay our respects."

I didn't say a word to my teammates. Bypassing Zane's knowing stare and the lieutenant commander's concerned expression,

I skipped the showers on base and headed for my truck. Twenty minutes later, I'd showered at my apartment, grabbed my go bag and service dress blues, and was already on my way to the civilian airport.

I was pulling into short-term parking when my cell rang.

Glancing at the screen, I sent Zane's call to voice mail. A second later, he called back.

I answered on the first ring. "Busy."

"Doing what?" Zane asked. "Roark's taking us down tomorrow."

I wasn't waiting for Zane's former Marine pilot friend who was flying the team down tomorrow in his private aircraft. I'd booked this flight a week ago, and if I hauled ass through the terminal, I'd still catch it.

"Hanging up now." I pulled into a parking space. "I've got a commercial flight to catch."

"Christ," Zane muttered. "Just do me a favor."

"What?" I got out of my car.

"Don't scare her."

Fuck him. "I've never scared her," I lied, knowing full well I had. The guilt for kissing her at that moment had been eating at me for seven fucking days, but like a selfish dick, I didn't regret it. My only regret was letting Billy die instead of me. And not waiting a damn week to tell her, but I knew I couldn't have waited. My best friend had called his sister every single week since we'd earned the Trident. The day I told her, I knew he was three days past due.

Zane snorted. "Right, keep telling yourself that."

Ignoring his bullshit, I locked my truck. "See you tomorrow."

"Alpha—"

I hung up and sprinted to the terminal. Getting through TSA relatively quickly, I checked the monitors for my gate, then hustled.

Making it to the gate right as the gate agent was about to close the door to the jetway, I held my ticket up. "Ma'am, please wait."

A smile spread across her face as her gaze cut from my face to my biceps. "Of course, sir." She scanned my boarding pass. "Have a nice flight."

Muttering a thanks, I jogged down the jetway.

The gate agent must have warned the flight attendant I was coming because the second I ducked my head and stepped on board, he stopped me with a polite smile. "We're about to taxi out. If you're quick, I have vacant seat in first class. Three B."

"Thank you, I appreciate it." And I did. The leg room in first class was double that in coach.

The flight attendant nodded. I stowed my bag, took my seat, and a few minutes later we were taxiing toward the runway.

Glancing at my watch, I leaned my head back and exhaled.

Two and a half hours flight time, half an hour to grab a rental and another twenty minutes to get to the house would put me at twenty-one hundred hours.

I hadn't warned her I was coming tonight. In fact, I hadn't texted her once in six days. If I wasn't dead on my feet, I maybe would've thought twice about it, but ten minutes after takeoff, I was out. My next recollection was the seat belt warning ding going off and the captain telling the flight attendants to prepare for landing.

I glanced out the window at the sparkling lights of Miami proper below us and the ocean in the distance. Then, for just a single moment, I allowed the thoughts I kept buried deep to surface.

Me, Emmy, the house she'd grown up in—a house that felt more like a home than anywhere I'd ever listed as my address—and the end of my current deployment. I never allowed myself to think that far in the future, let alone about her in that light.

Emmy.

The girl with the smile who was now a woman with grief.

Ten days ago, I was ready to re-up. Ten days ago, I wasn't thinking about the best fucking kiss I'd ever had or the soft curves on a barely legal woman who was all but my sister.

Ten days ago, my best friend was alive.

A wave of guilt hit.

Then, like a selfish prick, I rationalized it.

Billy had told me to take care of her. What better way than to be with her? I could get out, get a civilian job, make house, be there for her every day. I didn't know what the fuck I'd do, but I had contacts and skills. I'd figure something out.

The main thing was that I would be there for her.

And I wouldn't have to see that look of despair in her eyes ever again when I walked out the fucking door.

By the time the plane had taxied to the gate, I'd convinced myself that she wasn't too young, that I wasn't a complete dick and it was a viable plan despite shit timing. I had a week of leave. We'd lay Billy to rest tomorrow, and I'd hold her until her tears eased. Then I'd give her a few days before persuading her to give me a chance.

More convinced by the second that life was finally throwing me and her a bone, I breezed through the terminal, grabbed a rental and sped toward the house.

On edge with nerves I never got, not even on the worst missions, I shoved down grief for the loss of my best friend and pulled into the driveway.

Checking the time on the clock on the rental's dash, I frowned at the dark house with no cars in front. Maybe she was asleep at twenty-one hundred hours, but I'd never known her to turn in early, not even when she was a kid. She used to say she wanted to stay up as late as me and her brother. It drove Billy mad, but I'd never minded.

Grabbing my bag and pocketing the keys to the rental, I

strode to the front door, but before I knocked, I noticed the drawn curtains on all the downstairs windows facing the street.

Instinct catching my nerves, I glanced at the windows again, then knocked.

Nothing.

Turning, I scanned the street, but everything looked like it always did.

Debating whether I should text her, I knocked again.

After another thirty seconds of no sounds coming from inside the house, I grabbed the spare key hidden in a fake rock in one of the front planters and let myself in.

The second I pushed the door open, my earlier instinct turned into alarm and hit me square in the chest.

Still air, faint scent of mildew and deafening silence.

My hand went to my empty hip for a weapon I didn't have on me.

"Emmy?" I reached for the light switch near the front door that turned on the lamp that was older than me.

Nothing.

Dropping my bag, training my eyes to adjust to the dark, I moved toward the short hall next to the staircase and swept my hand across the original plaster, aiming for the light switch I knew was near. My hand connected, the hall light kicked on and I strode back toward the living room.

Then I stopped dead in my tracks.

Every piece of furniture was covered in sheets.

Whipping out my cell, I couldn't dial her number fast enough.

My heart racing, adrenaline pumping, I waited for the call to go through, but it never did. Three tones and a recording told me the number was no longer in service.

Anger surged with fear, and I was rushing to the kitchen to the piece of paper next to the house phone.

I dialed Mrs. Jansen.

Five rings later, a tired-sounding elderly woman answered. "Hello?"

"Mrs. Jansen, this is Adam Trefor."

"Hello, dear. I am assuming you're calling because you're in town?"

Biting down my frustration, I spoke with a feigned calmness. "Where's Maila, Mrs. Jansen?"

The old lady inhaled deeply. "I do believe she left you a note, dear. She said you would know where it is."

What the fuck? "She's gone?"

"I believe so, dear. She said I didn't need to sit with her until you came back because she had something to do."

"Where did she go?" I demanded.

"She didn't say, and to be honest, I was a little concerned." She cleared her throat then her voice turned thick with unshed emotion. "Considering the circumstances… with Billy, with everything." She paused then inhaled again. "She just seemed a little too calm. That child has been through so much." Sniffling, her breath hitched. "I'm so sorry, dear, I know you don't need me crying on you. Please, find the note. That's the message she said she wanted me to pass along to you in case you called."

Anger coursed through my veins. "Her brother's funeral is tomorrow."

Deep sorrow laced the old woman's next words. "I know, dear. I know."

Nostrils flaring, directing all my frustration at a reckless eighteen-year-old instead of at myself, I snapped out a command to an elderly woman who didn't deserve my wrath. "Get a pen, Mrs. Jansen, and write this number down."

"Yes, dear. Hang on." She set the phone down and, a long moment later, picked it back up. "Okay, I'm ready."

I recited my cell phone number. "You call me immediately

if she gets in touch with you." I scanned the kitchen, looking for a damn note.

"I will. Would you like me to ask her to call you? I can give her the number."

"She has the number." She fucking left. *Without telling me.* "I have to go, Mrs. Jansen. Let me know the second you hear from her."

The old woman sighed tiredly. "I'm not one to run my mouth, dear, and I certainly don't put myself in other people's business. You know this, but we've known each other now since you started coming around the Nilsens when you were still growing into those big dreams of yours, so I feel like I can say this to you." She took a steadying breath. "That sweet girl has had puppy dog eyes for you since the moment you walked into her life. I saw it. Her father saw it, and her brother saw it. We all knew. But what I saw was the way you looked at her too. You were too old for her back then, but she's not a child anymore."

"Your point?" I ground out.

"My point is she's a woman who lost everything that meant anything to her, and if she didn't wait for you to come back, then I would imagine there's a very good reason for it."

My back teeth clenched, my jaw ticked.

The elderly woman dropped the final blow of her truth bomb. "You're a Navy SEAL, dear, and there's only so much heartache one woman can take."

"Message received." I forced the fucking polite response when all I wanted to do was climb through the phone and throttle the messenger. "Call me if you hear from her."

Silence.

I didn't have time for this. "Mrs. Jansen," I snapped, wondering where the fuck Emmy would've left a note.

"I heard you, dear, but please know that my first alliance will always be to her. That said, if she is in any danger or I think she needs help, even if she doesn't want me to, in that type of situation, I will call you myself."

"Understood." Losing my fucking mind, I checked the junk drawer in the kitchen.

"See you tomorrow," she replied sadly before quietly hanging up.

I slammed the phone in the cradle and stalked into the living room, but every damn thing was covered. Desperate, I pulled the sheet off the coffee table, but all that was under it was old magazines.

Standing in the middle of the living room, I spun in a circle.

"What the fuck, Emmy?" Where the hell would she leave me a note? Nothing in the kitchen, nothing in the living room, and the dining room was a fucking sheet tent over the table and chairs.

Out of options down here, I took the stairs two at a time. When I reached the landing, I paused at the door to the master suite that was cracked open. Vice Admiral Erikson Nilsen had been religious about keeping that door closed, and after he'd passed, Emmy had kept up the tradition. But now it was cracked three inches.

I pushed the door open.

Shocked, I fucking stared.

Gone was the old, heavy wood furniture set Nilsen'd had since I'd met his son. Gone was the bed he'd used to sleep in with his wife. Gone was the solid desk with locked drawers and a wall of framed accolades. No lamps, no mementos, not even the carpet remained.

In the center of the gleaming hardwood floors and freshly painted white walls was an entire home gym with a standing mirror in the corner and some free weights on the ground, and that was it.

Not knowing what the fuck was going on, the pit in my stomach growing bigger, I left the master and strode toward Emmy's room. Throwing the wall switch, my moment of relief that the light was still working was short-lived as I took in the scene before me.

Desk bare, bookshelf empty, nightstand void of anything except the lamp, closet door open to empty nothingness, the bed was the only piece of furniture that held any indication that someone had lived here as recently as last week.

Perfectly made with her white comforter and too many pillows, the corners were tucked in military neat, but there was no note.

Dread mixing with the adrenaline coursing through my veins, I turned and forced myself to walk toward Billy's room. Hesitating like a pussy, my hand on the door, I inhaled before I pushed it open and hit the light.

Nothing was touched.

Neatly stacked paperwork on the desk, clothes hanging in the closet, shelves full of a mixture of teenage shit and remnants collected from our years of service. A huge TV on the dresser with a gaming console, a half-drunk bottle of water on the nightstand—it all looked like he'd been here yesterday, with one exception.

In the middle of his king-size bed that he'd swapped out for bunk beds after I'd gotten my own place near base was a folded piece of paper.

My heart fucking pounding, not sure I wanted to read what was written on that goddamn note, I picked it up anyway.

Adam,

If you're reading this, then you came home alive. For that, I'm grateful.

There are no words that can explain why I had to leave, or maybe there are too many. Either way, it doesn't change the fact that I'm gone. Please give Billy the send-off he deserves. He would want that from his team, and I would appreciate it.

Respectfully, I'm asking that you do not come after me, even if you think it's the right thing to do. It's not. If I wanted to be found, you wouldn't be reading this. I know you're probably upset with me for not waiting to say this in person, but I needed to start making choices for myself. I hope you can understand that.

And lastly, in case there was any doubt, I loved you from the moment you walked into our lives thirteen years ago. I know I was only a little girl, but I knew enough to understand what I was feeling, even back then. You made my life full. You were the missing piece, but I never wanted to burden you with that truth because I didn't want to be an obligation to you. I just wanted to be free to love you and think that you loved me back.

Then, somewhere along the way, that all changed and I fell in love with you. Maybe it was in the kitchen after Daddy passed and you were there for me when no one else was. Or maybe it was long before that. I don't know, but it doesn't matter now. I'm done losing pieces of myself, and I'm done loving. I have nothing left. Not even the best kiss of my life can change that.

Stay safe,

Emmy

I sank to the floor and broke.

PART TWO

Present Day

FIVE

Adam

I DIDN'T KNOCK.

Ruthlessly pressing my hand to the scanner, I assumed he hadn't changed my access status. Not that he should've given it to me in the first place. This wasn't my residence.

The scan took, and the lock clicked.

No hesitation, I pushed the impact-resistant, bulletproof metal door open and immediately realized my mistake.

Classical music blaring, his naked ass in full view as sweat dripped down his scarred back, Vance Conlon thrust into some chick on her hands and knees on his coffee table.

"Perfect timing, Trefor." Shameless, Vance Conlon, didn't even pause as he fucked the naked woman. "We were just getting started. Weren't we, pet?"

The woman glanced at me and gasped.

I should've fucking knocked.

"Urgent matter." Ignoring Vance's bullshit and his latest conquest, I strode to his desk and flipped open his laptop. "Finish that later."

Brazen and arrogant, he laughed. "Lauren is no *that*. Are you, princess?"

"Um. N-no?" Wide-eyed and looking between us, the woman stuttered.

A slap echoed through the dimly lit loft, and the woman yelped.

Vance's demeanor did a one-eighty. "Are you questioning my judgment?" he barked.

"No," she squeaked.

"No what?" he demanded.

"No, sir."

"Better," Vance mused, his tone casual again. "Marginal, but better." Another slap echoed through the cavernous space, and he issued a command. "Get up."

I opened the program I needed.

Vance reached for a pair of jeans on the couch and stepped into them as the woman got off the coffee table and crossed her arms over her breasts. Her head down, she aimed for the bathroom, but Vance was quicker.

Casually fisting a handful of her hair with one hand, he grabbed his drink off a side table with the other and walked the woman over to the desk. "Darling, meet my boss, Adam Trefor." His gaze intent on me, Vance took a swallow of his drink. "Not a *that*, now is she?"

On the surface, everything about Vance Conlon was controlled. But the look in his eyes was another story. I'd known Conlon since my first deployment, and there were two things that made him tick. Money and sex. You fucked with either of those, you were on his shit list. Except Conlon didn't openly hold a grudge, and he sure as fuck didn't forget a slight any more than he'd announce his intentions. Vance Conlon remembered every move of every person who'd ever gotten in his way, and he kept score. Eventually, he got even.

It was why I'd hired him.

Conlon wasn't a team player. He didn't have a moral code, and with the exception of his twin brother, he wasn't loyal to anyone. All of which made him predictable and perfect for what I needed.

Leveling him with a look so he knew exactly what I thought

of his current stunt, I then turned my gaze to the woman. "Nice to meet you."

Barely legal, her hair a mess, she nervously nodded as she hugged herself tighter. "Same to you, Mr. Trefor."

I was pissed Conlon had given her my name, not that I actively hid my identity, but I didn't advertise it either. "Apologies for the interruption."

Heat covered her cheeks. "No big deal."

Still holding her hair, Vance chuckled before sipping his drink. "Oh, it's a big deal, darling, but I'll work that out with you later." He winked and let go of her. "Go freshen up."

She scurried off.

I waited until the bathroom door closed, then I pulled a cell out of my pocket and tossed it on the desk. "Track the text."

Vance smirked. "A text."

Three words. "Sent anonymously," I clarified.

Less than impressed, he raised an eyebrow. "That's what you interrupted me for?"

I crossed my arms.

"Right." He nodded and took another swallow before setting his glass down and picking the cell up. "And why exactly are you bothering me with this?" He glanced at the text but didn't comment on it. Syncing the phone to his military-grade, encrypted laptop, he leaned over and typed a command. "You know how to do this yourself."

He was right, I did. I could do this in my sleep, and I had traced the text, a dozen times already, but the answer kept coming back to the same thing, and I didn't trust myself. "Check it," I demanded.

The same number with a Miami area code I'd seen on my laptop popped up on his screen before the trace pinged from it to a number in the Bahamas, then one in Venezuela, another in Cairo, and finally a number in Iraq.

"What the hell?" Frowning, Vance typed the command to repeat the trace, then braced his hands on the desk to wait.

The proprietary software I'd had specifically created for AES did its thing, then gave the exact same information again.

The text had been sent from Iraq, and someone had gone to a lot of trouble to disguise it.

SIX

Quinn

His drink in his hand, Khalaf leaned back in the leather club chair of the hotel bar. "Do you know what I think I enjoy most about you?"

The trick question sent pinpricks of awareness across my exposed arms. "It would not only be unladylike and presumptuous of me to assume but unseemly to ask."

His expression serious, he didn't give me his usual smile. "That is it, right there." Lowering his voice, he leaned forward. "Your submissiveness, my dear, is alarmingly attractive."

Dipping my head, I took a sip of my drink but said nothing.

"Yes," he mused, staring at me a long moment. "Just like that. Obedience suits you, Quinn Michaels."

This time I didn't dip my head, I volleyed. "Obedience is usually a word reserved for canines."

"Not when I use it. It is a high compliment, and that is how I intended for you to take it." He took a sip of his scotch and changed the subject. "Do you like your dress?"

I glanced down at the red silk. "It's lovely." I feigned shyness. "Thank you for taking me shopping today."

His smile appeared, and it was full of warmth. "You quite enjoyed yourself, didn't you?"

A four-thousand-dollar dress followed by two-thousand-dollar shoes? No, I didn't enjoy myself. I thought of the battered car I'd had when I was sixteen that cost five hundred dollars, but one I'd bought with my own money. Of course, the moment I'd pulled into the driveway, my father'd had a fit. In front of my brother and his best friend, he'd forbidden me to drive it. I thought I was going to cry from embarrassment, but before I could shed a tear, my brother's best friend had stepped forward and said it wasn't that bad, only needed a little TLC and new tires. My brother had agreed. My father wouldn't listen to me, but his son and his son's best friend, on a short leave from the Navy, he'd listened to them. Told them if they could fix it up before they had to go back in forty-eight hours, he'd let me drive it.

My brother had bought the tires, then promptly found a girl to spend the night with, but his best friend? He'd stuck around.

All night.

By morning, I'd had new tires installed, an oil change, something fixed with some hose or other, and the car sounded almost like new. I'd sat on the driveway all night with my brother's best friend, bringing him Cokes and regaling him with stories about the stupid girls in my class and even stupider boys—boys who weren't twenty-seven-year-old Navy SEALs who'd passed BUD/S.

But my brother's best friend was more than a SEAL.

He was a man who'd worked all night, patiently listening to a teenager's stories, never once making me feel less than.

By the time the sun was peaking and my brother rolled up in the same outfit from the night before with a sloppy smile, I didn't know if I was more in love with my new-to-me car or the man who'd spent all night fixing it.

Actually, I did know.

But I'd never admitted it.

Because as much as I was in love with the boy my brother

had brought home so many years ago that I no longer remembered a time before him, I knew I wasn't supposed to.

I was never supposed to fall in love with my brother's best friend.

His eleven-years-older best friend.

Now here I sat, across from a man almost twice my age, in a posh hotel bar in London wearing a dress that could have bought eight versions of my first car. But the dress would never outclass the best night of life, sitting on a driveway in southern Florida heat as a sixteen-year-old.

Shoving down memories and focusing on what I needed to do, I lied. "Thank you. I did enjoy myself."

"I could tell." Khalaf winked with confidence before leaning forward. "Which is why I have a proposition for you."

"You already had a proposition for me a couple weeks ago. Come to London with you on business and keep you company while you have downtime between meetings." I pretended to pout over the rim of my martini glass that had some overly sweet, nonalcoholic drink Khalaf had ordered for me. "But I hardly see you except for dinners and shopping."

"You are bored then?"

Suspicious an affirmative answer would be too obvious, I lifted a shoulder. "An intelligent woman is never bored."

He threw his head back and laughed as if I'd said something humorous.

I drank again.

Composing himself, he straightened his tie. "Oh, my beautiful American, what a challenge you are, but I do enjoy you." He winked again. "Maybe too much. Which is why it's finally time." He stood and held his hand out to me. "Come, *habibti*."

Setting my unfinished drink down, I took his hand and stood on the too-high heels he'd picked out for me.

Pulling me in close while still leaving inches between us,

he carefully never touched me in any way that could be misconstrued in public. The sides of his lips lifted, and he lowered his face just enough toward mine. "I think you need to come to Dubai with me."

I didn't hide my shock. "Dubai?"

"Yes." His eyes sparkled. "You will love it."

"You have business there?" He'd never mentioned Dubai.

"My dear, I have business wherever there is hospitality, but yes, I have dealings there as well as a home."

"I thought you said you were from Saudi Arabia?" None of the intel had mentioned Dubai.

His smile was Oscar-worthy. "I have lived many places, and I have had many homes."

Choosing to ignore his last statement because I'd learned over the past couple of weeks that asking him pointed questions made him shut down, I protested with the first thing I could think of. "But my work."

His shrug was meant to be nonchalant. "Quit. You have not wanted for anything since you have been here, have you? Have I not given you everything you need?"

I tried to lift my lips in the same way he did, but the expression was so foreign and so unused, I gave up the pretense. "No, I haven't needed anything, and you've been more than generous, thank you. But I can't quit my job, Khalaf. I have bills to pay back in Manhattan and an apartment to maintain."

"Do you wish to go back?" he asked as if it were a casual, everyday question.

I gave him the one true, honest answer I could. "No."

This time, the smile he gave me was genuine. "Then it is settled."

"Khalaf." I aimed for a response that wouldn't insult him, but also one where I didn't immediately give in. "It isn't that simple."

"I have already told you, and I have shown you that you'll be taken care of. You don't need to have these concerns or worries about bills and money. You're far too beautiful for that, *habibti*. Besides, I can give you a much nicer place to live than a rented apartment in a filthy city." His hand waved dismissively through the air. "But it is your choice." His smile, while intended to be reassuring, was laced with manipulative control. "Make a decision. I will not offer this opportunity again, Quinn. You come with me now or we part ways." He lowered his voice. "For good."

Picking up on his not-so-veiled threat, I frowned and said what anyone playing the game would say. "Why for good? Why must it be all or nothing?"

He gave me an offended expression. "Have we not gotten to know each other over the past couple weeks? Do you not trust me?"

"I do, but you haven't once come to my hotel room since we've been here." A room he'd booked, paid for, and set up with listening devices I'd found within minutes but left untouched. "You only dine with me or take me shopping, then retreat to your suite. Now you want me to quit my job and… what? Come live with you?"

He threw down more manipulation. "Do you think you will get a better offer?"

"I'm just asking for more details, Khalaf." Walking the line, I tried to choose my words carefully. "A holiday in London is far different than moving into your home in Dubai with you. What if it doesn't work out?"

He bristled at my question but tried to hide his irritation. "I have given you all the details you need, and this *working out* you speak of is insulting. I am a man of my word. If you come with me, as I have already told you, you will want for nothing."

Yes, he'd given me a few particulars, but only the ones he

wanted me to know, carefully hiding the pertinent details. "I did not mean to insult you, I was simply asking why." I knew why. He was doing what he'd been doing all along. Testing me, vetting me, watching me—make no mistake, this was a business transaction, and I was the commodity.

His finger touched the tip of my nose as if I were a child while his smile returned like he was being reassuring. "You are too smart and too pretty for a hotel tryst, my beautiful American. Take a chance with me for a new life. I can see in your eyes that you want it." He squeezed my hand. "So, yes? You will come?"

I hedged only because I needed a little time. "When would we leave?" I would have to set things up.

"Tonight. I am leaving on the jet in half an hour." He glanced at his watch. "That gives you enough time for Amir to take you to your room and pack your new dresses for you."

Shit. *Shit*. "I'm not sure I can fit all the new clothes you bought me in my suitcase." I couldn't pack with a bodyguard in my presence and do what I needed to do. "I might need to get a new suitcase, and I have to make a few phone calls to let work know. I'm sure Amir would be bored. I can do it myself, but thank you."

Khalaf tsked. "It is after business hours, *habibti*." Before I could react, he grabbed my clutch, plucked out my cell, pocketed it and tucked my purse back under my arm. A charming smile spread across his face. "There, I have now solved one of your problems. No work calls tonight." He winked. "As far as your new dresses, leave your old clothes behind. I will buy you anything you want in Dubai." He lifted his head and nodded at one of his three ever-present bodyguards. "Amir will help you pack. I insist. You should not have to do this by yourself." He squeezed my upper arm with a little too much force. "He will even buy you a new suitcase if you like."

The youngest but most personable of all of Khalaf's bodyguards came to the opposite side of where Khalaf stood. "Sir?" Together they caged me in.

"Amir, please take Miss Michaels to her room and help her pack." Khalaf gave the tall, dark-haired man a look I couldn't decipher. "She is coming with us."

"Understood," Amir replied.

Khalaf looked back down at me, but he didn't smile as he squeezed my arm once more. "Hurry. One half-hour." Letting go of me, he turned, and his two other bodyguards, Mardon and Fahad, fell in step with him as he walked toward the lobby.

Amir took the opposite arm Khalaf had. "This way."

SEVEN

Adam

His hands still on the desk, Conlon dropped all pretense and looked at me with concern. "Who is she, and why did they take her?"

"Irrelevant." I nodded at the laptop. "Who do we have in Iraq?"

"Who do we have or who can we trust?" Vance stood to his full height. "And you should know this better than me. You hired everyone on staff."

"You vetted them," I reminded him. "But I'm not talking about AES staff." I'd started Alpha Elite Security three years ago, and we'd quickly become the most sought-after security contractor in the business because I didn't cut corners or make mistakes. Meticulous about everything, I only hired the best special operatives the military had to offer—SEALs, Force Recon, Rangers, Delta Force—elite soldiers who were a cut above. If I wanted them, I recruited them. If they were still serving, I waited, then recruited them.

I paid handsomely for my men, the technology, the weapons, and the equipment. I considered everyone on staff family, which was one of the many reasons I didn't have boots on the ground in Iraq. I wasn't stupid enough to walk my people into a prime K&R target zone. At least, not without a damn good reason and the support of the US Military.

Vance pointed at the geographic image on the screen as he stated the obvious. "That's not just Iraq, that's Baghdad, brother."

"I know."

"Whoever the client is, she's fucked."

Ignoring his all-too-true assessment but not correcting him on his wrong assumption, I asked again. "I need someone on the ground. Who do we know there?"

"That's not active duty?"

"I'm not bringing anyone in on this." I couldn't. It would create an international incident. "I need someone local."

Vance picked up his drink and smirked. "You already brought someone in. I'm standing right here."

Out of patience, I pocketed my phone and turned toward the door.

"Wait, wait, wait." Vance took a swallow of his drink and set it back down. "I'm only fucking with you. I might know someone. A kid."

I'd learned early on that despite talking shit, Vance rarely exaggerated. If he said kid, he probably meant it, and I needed to clarify because that was a hard limit for me. "An actual kid?"

Vance nodded. "I did him a favor once. Well, a favor for his mother before she ate a bullet."

Jesus. "How old?"

He lifted one shoulder. "Sixteen now, maybe seventeen, but finding him will be like looking for a needle in a haystack. Or more precisely, looking for an orphan in a lawless, bombed-out city full of militant and extremist groups who hate Americans like it's their religion."

Fuck. "At this point, it'd be easier if I walked into the middle of the city and tracked the original number myself." It wasn't my first choice, but it wasn't off the table.

"You could try. It's been three years." Vance half shrugged. "Maybe your terrorist friends in Iraq have forgotten all about their bounty on your head or the part about how finding you in-country doubles the payoff."

We both knew they hadn't.

The bounty, a leftover hazard from having been a SEAL, was the only reason I wasn't already in Baghdad instead of here, talking to him. "Any other options?"

"Yeah." Vance casually picked up his drink again. "Dozens and dozens." He nodded at his cell. "Call any of the guys at AES. Every single one of them will do it for you." He leveled me with a look. "Me included."

"No." No fucking way. "I'm not risking it."

He laughed. "Risking what, exactly? A covert op with highly trained operatives that eat this shit up like child's play? Half of those adrenaline junkies would nut themselves just for the thrill of the opportunity." He downed the rest of his drink. "What are you really worried about?"

Making a worse mistake than seven years ago. Letting it get out that this was personal. Actually finding what I was looking for. There were a hundred reasons, none of which I was going to tell him. "I'm not bringing anyone else in, and I'm not risking AES staff."

"Okay." Vance shrugged like he didn't give a shit. "Then it's the kid."

I didn't want to risk an innocent's life, especially not one that was an actual minor, but sixteen was different in Baghdad, and I was desperate. I didn't care about my own safety, I could handle this op in a heartbeat, but I cared about my employees. On the off chance I was spotted, it'd not only cause an international incident, it'd risk AES and too many people's livelihoods. I wasn't stupid enough to make that mistake, but I also wasn't seeing any other options for getting in and out quick before that cell had a chance to grow legs and walk away.

"What's the probability you can find this kid?" All I needed was someone on the ground near the cell phone tower with my equipment. Two minutes, and I could get an exact location.

Then I'd have something concrete to work with.

Vance scrubbed a hand over his jaw as his gaze drifted. "Twenty percent. Maybe. But that's just finding the kid and having him get to where you need him to be. That's not a guarantee you'll actually find the cell."

"With my equipment on the ground near the tower it pinged from, I'll be able to trace its exact location." It was my best shot.

"If it's still on. If it hasn't been tossed or sold. If it's still in-country by the time we get there." Vance eyed me. "You and I both know that's a lot of *ifs*. Not to mention you stepping foot in that sand trap is hazardous to your health."

I had to try. "I'll need a name, description, and last known whereabouts of the kid." I could get as far as the airport in Baghdad. I'd work it from there. Somehow. I had to. This was the only intel I had.

Vance eyed me. "You want to tell me what's really going on?"

"No." Not that I didn't trust him with this, not that I didn't need him if I wanted to double my odds, but I wasn't ready to bring anyone in yet.

He laughed. "Do I get to guess?"

The bathroom door opened, and the woman tentatively stepped out in a towel, looking between me and Vance. "Um, my dress?" She gestured toward the couch.

"Text me the information I need." I turned to leave.

"I bet it isn't irrelevant," he casually stated.

I glanced over my shoulder at the woman, then at Vance. "Not the time."

His eyes on me, Vance issued the woman an order disguised as sexual intent. "Darling, get the shower going and wait for me in there. Get nice and wet."

The woman couldn't retreat fast enough.

I waited until I heard the shower turn on. "She legal?"

"Do you care?"

There were few things I cared out. I'd learned long ago, first in BUD/S, then in the field, that having anything other than the objective on your mind wasn't only a detriment to the mission, it could cost you your life. Worse, the lives of the men standing next to you.

Vance sighed in mock deference. "Yes, she's legal. Deliciously young and submissive but, nonetheless, of age of consent. Now, are you going to tell me who the client is or what this is about? Or should I simply retrieve my gun and follow you blindly into the abyss of self-destruction you seem intent on?"

There were times I appreciated Conlon, times I put up with him, and times I'd had enough of him. Then there were times like this. I despised his arrogance, but I fucking loathed that he was right. I was walking headfirst into the one firefight that I knew I had no chance of winning even if I did find that cell.

This was going to destroy me.

She was going to destroy me.

"You're the one who told me there are two ways to do something," Vance started.

"The right way and again," I finished.

He crossed his arms. "So what's it going to be?"

"There is no right way for this." That was the problem.

"Hasn't stopped us before. Who is she?"

The woman whose life I'd destroyed seven years ago.

The woman I'd cruelly walked away from at the worst time in her life.

The woman who deserved more than to have me as her last hope.

The woman I vowed two months ago to never follow again.

Vance raised an eyebrow.

"It's her," I admitted.

"Her," he stated, his expression locked.

I didn't blink, I didn't nod, I didn't fucking breathe.

I waited.

Because the moment he said her name out loud, this would be real.

In a rare show of emotion, Vance briefly closed his eyes and exhaled a curse. "Mother. *Fucker.*" He cursed again. "*Her*, her? As in the late Vice Admiral Nilsen's daughter, Maila Nilsen, her? The woman you've had me tracking since I came aboard because you're too much of a pussy to tell her you want to fuck her? Then two months ago when I practically hand her to you on a silver platter, you walk away because some bearded fuck smiled at her—*that* her?"

I lifted my chin once.

Vance slowly shook his head. Then he inhaled and grabbed a shirt off a chair. "Right." Throwing the shirt on, he stepped into a pair of boots. "I'm assuming you've already confirmed she's not at her place?"

"Rent's paid, but the doorman hasn't seen her in months. No activity on her bank account or credit card in two months, and her passport hasn't had any hits either."

"Fuck. I knew I shouldn't have stopped tracking her when you told me to after walking out of that market." Reaching under the couch and coming away with a go bag, Vance grabbed his cell and keys. "Let's move. That text is already an hour old."

I glanced toward the bathroom. "What about that?"

Vance slapped me on the shoulder as he walked past. "Already told you, not a *that*." He held his front door open. "And she'll figure it out." He frowned. "Probably."

"Unsanctioned and off the books, this isn't going to be easy. We're going to be on our own," I warned.

"It's like you're trying to get me hard." Vance slung his bag over his shoulder. "But in all seriousness, we need another pilot.

Unless you want me practicing my chopper skills on your sexy new fifty-million-dollar Falcon."

"We're not taking my personal jet." We'd be identified before we could land, if not shot down the second we entered Iraq's airspace, but Vance had a point. My jet, along with all the other company jets, required two pilots. Technically, I could fly my Falcon solo if I had to, but Baghdad was a fifteen-hour flight.

"Okay, one of the sixty-million-dollar company birds it is." Vance winked. "Always wanted to get behind one of those."

"You're not certified on the Gulfstreams."

"I'm not certified for a lot of shit. Never stopped me before."

Fuck. "If one of us is compromised and the other has to fly out solo, that's an unmitigated risk." There was a lot of shit I trusted Vance with, but that wasn't one of them.

"Translation, if something happens to you and I have to get your expensive toy home on my own, that's an unmitigated risk."

I didn't disagree.

Vance shrugged. "Then call Zulu."

Logistically, I should've seen this coming, but just like everything else related to a five-foot-nothing blonde, I was reactionary and had a goddamn blind spot the size of my chest when it came to her.

Besides Zane being my second and him keeping AES running if something happened to me, I had other reasons I didn't want to involve him. Mainly, he was the closest to Emmy after me and I needed him to be around to look out for her if something happened to me. That said, the clock was ticking, and I was out of options.

Pulling my work cell out, I dialed.

"A threesome." The smile that spread across Vance's face should've been concerning. "This is going to be fun."

EIGHT

Adam

FROWNING FROM THE PILOT SEAT OF ONE OF AES'S COMPANY JETS, Zane scanned the apron for the hundredth time. "We're sitting ducks out here."

"At least we're breathing sitting ducks." If we ventured outside the boundary of Baghdad's airport, I could guarantee we'd be in a hell of a lot worse situation.

Zane checked his watch again. "What did Conlon say his drop-dead time was?"

"He didn't." Holding my old cell, checking the battery and signal strength the same way Zane kept checking his watch, I resigned myself and shoved the damn thing back in my pocket.

"Still nothing?"

"No." I hadn't gotten another text on my old number since the single one eighteen hours ago.

"You sure that text was about Emmy?"

"We went over this," I reminded him.

"Tell me again." Zane rubbed a hand over his jaw. "I'm still trying to process this shit."

"Hell of a time to process it after we've already flown here."

"Humor me."

Christ. "Only six people had my cell number back then. You, Billy, Emmy, the vice admiral, Lieutenant Commander Davis, and Mrs. Jansen. Everyone's dead except you and Emmy. I only keep that number active for one goddamn purpose. The text was about her." It had to be. "The only question that's relevant now is who took her, and that's why we're here."

Zane didn't let it go. "So you haven't seen her since the week before Billy's funeral?"

I glanced across the expanse of the Baghdad airport from my position in the copilot's seat before training my military-hardened gaze on him.

When I didn't say anything, he lifted an eyebrow. "Heard from her? Followed her on social media? Kept tabs on her? Run a search? Anything?"

"You've already asked all of that." Several times during the flight here. Other than that, he'd been unusually quiet.

Zane crossed his arms. "And you keep avoiding the answer."

I wasn't avoiding shit except my own damn guilt. "There's nothing to tell."

"Sure." He snorted. "Because you're such a saint and haven't looked for her once in seven years."

I glanced out the side window. "I haven't." Technically, it'd been Vance.

When I'd first recruited Conlon, I'd told him there was a conditional test for hire. If he could find the woman I gave him only a few details on, the job was his. He'd told me he didn't give a shit about the job, but he'd look anyway because, as he put it, I was *full of it*. Telling me with a knowing grin that it wasn't some random missing woman, he'd used every program at our disposal, followed all the leads I would have, and an hour later declared the same conclusion I'd come up with.

She was a ghost.

She'd never come back to the house, at least not for the first four years when Mrs. Jansen was still alive and looking out for her on my behalf. If she hadn't been making annual withdrawals from her back account those first four years, I would've been worried as fuck. Then a couple of weeks after I'd hired Vance, he'd hit paydirt on a random search and found her in Manhattan. He'd kept tabs on her on and off for the next three years until I told him to stop two months ago.

"Okay, what the fuck, Alpha?" Zane threw his hands up. "I've kept my mouth shut this whole fucking flight, but enough's enough. Billy told you to look out for her and you don't even keep tabs with all the spy shit software at your disposal?"

"She told me not to." The worn piece of paper still in my wallet, I knew her last words to me by heart.

"I know what that fucking note said. I also know what I saw the day we did the notification. She'd snapped, man, totally fucking snapped. We both saw it, but you're telling me you were so hell-bent on getting back downrange and taking out those motherfuckers that you didn't even check in with her once? Did you ever stop to think that maybe if you'd done what Billy'd asked, hell, what was decent, that we wouldn't be here right now?"

Every goddamn minute since I'd gotten the text. "Heads up." Two airport personnel bypassed the private jet parked next to us and kept coming. "We're about to have company."

Ignoring what'd I said, Zane brought up what he hadn't mentioned since the morning of Billy's funeral when he'd found me at the house, drunk off my ass, sitting on the floor of Billy's bedroom.

"You fucking kissed your best friend's kid sister minutes after telling her that her brother was KIA. Then, as if that wasn't fucked-up enough, you just let her walk the hell away. I can't believe you, Alpha. You should've fucking called her or at least checked in on her. If I'd known you weren't keeping tabs, I would've done it myself."

The two armed airport personnel looked up at the cockpit and signaled for me to open the door.

"I didn't let her walk away," I lied. "She chose to. And since you know what her note said, then you know what she asked of me. I stuck to the fucking script." Unfolding myself from the copilot's seat, I stepped out of the cockpit and opened the passenger door. Shielding my eyes against the bright sunlight as a blast wave of desert heat swamped the cool interior of the plane, I stepped back.

First one, then the second airport security guard came up the airstairs. The first one glanced toward the empty seats in the main cabin while the one behind him rested his hand on his gun.

"You have now been parked longer than you indicated," the first guard said in accented English.

Zane muttered something about poachers from the cockpit.

"My apologies, gentlemen. Just a little while longer." Conlon had said he'd need two hours. It'd been double that, and he'd gone radio silent. I was giving him another hour before I tracked him.

The first guard, looking put out, glanced at the guard behind him. "How much longer?" He swept his hand toward the runway. "We are a very busy airport. You have refueled. We need the space."

Translation, he wanted more bribe money before he alerted whatever terrorist organization that was the flavor of the month that there was a plane ripe for stealing with a little firepower and a hostile takeover.

"Understood. Allow me to compensate you and the airport for permitting us to stand by for two more hours." I reached into my pocket.

The man behind the first guard raised his rifle.

I held a hand up. "I'm just getting my wallet."

"We do not take bribes," the second guard warned in mock disdain.

"Of course not." I pulled my wallet out and thumbed through the set amount of hundreds I'd placed there after the first guards had shaken us down almost two hours ago. "I'm simply offering a cash ramp fee for another two hours." I took out five bills, leaving the other twenty-five in the wallet.

The second guard held his rifle aimed at my head while the first guard nodded at my wallet. "All of it."

I handed over three grand.

The first guard counted the hundreds, then pocketed them. "You may stay one more hour." He turned to leave.

The second guard behind him held his aim and his glare for a beat then lowered his weapon. Both men walked down the airstairs.

When they reached the apron, the first guard glanced back up. "One hour," he warned.

I secured the door and reached for my phone.

Zane stepped out of the cockpit. "You paid them too much. The going rate on a second bribe here is fifteen hundred, two grand, tops. Which is one of the many things I would've told you if you'd called me before you'd pulled Conlon out of his fuckfest."

"A, it wasn't a fuckfest, it was one woman. And B, I had my reasons."

"Yeah, what fucking reasons are those? Conlon has no self-preservation and zero regard for his own life, so he'd be trigger happy at whatever shit plan you came up with regardless of the risk."

Glad he'd moved on from our previous conversation, I gave him the truth. "You know you're the only one I trust to keep AES afloat if something happens to me." I scanned the airport, then typed a text. "Conlon has plenty of regard for his own life."

Zane snorted. "Operative words being 'his' and 'life.'"

I hit send and pocketed my cell. "How many missions have we all been on together?"

"I don't count, and I doubt you do either, so I'm calling your bluff—or is this a trick question?"

"Countless missions." I looked him in the eye. "And we're all still here."

Zane shook his head. "We've now got fifty-eight minutes. If Conlon doesn't show, you know I have to fly us out of here."

I futilely scanned the airport for any sign of the car and driver I'd had waiting for Vance when we'd landed four hours ago. I knew as well as Zane what the risks were. Our flight plan, aliases, and the tail number of the Gulfstream were already circulating on the streets of Baghdad. If we hadn't been made by now, it was only a matter of time.

"Vance knew the risks going in, and he knows what'll happen if we get down to the wire. If we have to leave without him, we move to plan B."

"Which is?"

I scanned the port side of the plane before glancing at Zane. "Do your preflight checks."

NINE

Quinn

KHALAF KEPT MY PHONE.

Amir had packed my clothes with a quick efficiency like he'd done this exact thing a thousand times. Then he'd taken my arm and my suitcase and steered me toward a waiting limo.

That was eight hours ago.

Five minutes ago, Khalaf took my passport.

Right before his private jet smoothly touched down, Khalaf had leaned over my seat, helped himself to my purse again, and plucked my passport out. With a smile, he told me he'd handle everything.

The jet came to a stop, and Fahad got up to open the passenger door.

Khalaf undid his seat belt, then mine, and stood. "Come." He held his hand out to me.

Tired, on edge, full of a gourmet meal and too many glasses of sparkling water, I took his hand and stood.

My legs stiff, I wobbled in my heels.

Khalaf looked back at me and frowned. "You are ill?"

"No, just tired. I'm all right."

With a stern expression not born of concern, he studied me a moment. Then he led us to the exit and only dropped my hand so we could both walk down the stairs.

The dark navy sky hit me first.

Endless and full of stars, it beckoned with tales of ancient history, and for a moment, I forgot all about what I was doing. Then a breeze swept past me, and I smelled heat, sand and exotic spices, and it was as if I were in a whole new world.

"This way." Khalaf, surrounded by his usual three guards, summoned me without patience toward the first of two waiting SUVs with tinted-out windows.

Amir opened the passenger door, and Khalaf got inside. Then Amir offered me his hand to get in beside his boss.

The interior was outfitted like a limo with two bench seats facing each other, and I slid in next to Khalaf. Amir took the opposite seat, closed us in, and then the driver, who I couldn't see because of a privacy screen between the front and the rear of the vehicle, immediately pulled away.

Khalaf addressed Amir in English, even though he had been speaking to him in Arabic throughout the flight here. "The hotel is ready, yes?"

"Of course, sir," Amir answered in English.

I glanced at Khalaf. "Hotel?" He'd said he had a home here.

He patted my leg. "Your room in my home is not ready, *habibti*. I want everything to be perfect for you, so tonight we stay at the hotel."

With no more of an explanation, he switched to Arabic and had a conversation with Amir. In fact, since getting on his jet, he'd all but stopped speaking English unless he spoke directly to me.

For twenty minutes, I looked out the window.

Dark, inhospitable desert landscape gave way to a bustling city with gleaming skyscrapers and twinkling lights. It almost looked like what New York would look like if it were all brand-new, impeccably clean, ultra-modern and polished to a high shine.

We pulled up to a sky-high hotel on the ocean, and a valet opened our door. The second SUV pulled up behind us, and Amir and Fahad flanked Khalaf.

A hand landed on my elbow. "Wait," Mardon, Khalaf's usually sneering bodyguard, clipped.

Once Khalaf was a couple of paces in front of us, Mardon urged me forward. "Come."

Like a dog, I was guided behind Khalaf, and we went straight to the elevators. Amir swiped a card key once the doors closed and pushed the button for the top floor.

No one spoke.

A dizzyingly swift ride later, Amir and Fahad exited the elevator first into an opulent suite that overlooked a magnificent ocean reflecting the moon and stars. They split up and each walked the perimeter of the suite, in different directions, opening and closing doors while Khalaf, Mardon, and I waited in the foyer.

A moment later, Amir nodded at Khalaf.

Khalaf turned and smiled at me as if all were normal. "This way, my beauty. I will show you to your room." Without waiting to see if I would follow, he crossed the suite, bypassing a full kitchen, living room and dining area. Opening a door to a bedroom on the left side of the suite, he gestured for me to go inside.

I stepped past him, but he didn't follow.

I turned to face him.

"Get some sleep. I will wake you in the morning." He started to close the door.

"Khalaf, I need my suitcase." And my passport. "And my phone."

He smiled like he always did when he was being manipulative. "I already told you, no work tonight, *habibti*. Tomorrow is soon enough."

"And my luggage? I need clothes to sleep in."

He chuckled. "It will be dealt with tomorrow. I am sure you can manage tonight. No one but I will disturb you. I promise." He winked. "Get some rest, my beautiful American. You look tired."

He shut the door, and I heard a lock click.

With nothing except my clutch purse, a wallet with useless currency, and some lip gloss and tissues, I stood there in my dress and heels I'd put on too many hours ago to count.

Glancing out the windows, I didn't go near them. We were so high up, my stomach swam at even the thought of getting near the glass.

"Shit," I muttered barely above a whisper.

Then I dropped my purse, went to the bathroom, and stopped in my tracks. Toiletries of every kind imaginable, along with makeup, hairbrushes and perfumes all neatly lined the vanity.

Ignoring all of it, I turned the water on full blast in the bathtub, then I went back out into the bedroom.

Slow and careful, I looked in all the places I'd looked in the last hotel room Khalaf had booked for me. I found two listening devices, one behind a bedside lamp and another behind a picture frame in the bathroom.

Leaving both, I stripped and got in the hot bathtub. Too tired to soak, I merely soaped and rinsed, then wrapped up in a plush white robe hanging in the closet and crawled into the bed.

I didn't know how long I lay there or how I managed to fall asleep, but the next thing I knew, sunlight was streaming in through the windows and Khalaf was walking through the door.

"Good morning, *habibti*. You seem well-rested." Dressed in a crisp white button-down and drowning in his cologne, he sat on the edge of my bed. "I have something for you."

"Good morning." I blinked back sleep. "You didn't have to get me anything, Khalaf."

He waved a hand dismissively, then reached in his pocket and came away with a small jewelry case. "For you. Open it."

Panic, swift and unexpected, gripped my stomach and rushed up my throat. Choking it down, I opened the box.

Relief that it wasn't a ring made my lungs exhale. "A diamond." A large one.

"Mm," Khalaf made an appreciative sound before running his finger over it. "Three carats for you." He looked up at me and touched the tip of my nose once. "Anything larger would be unseemly in your belly piercing."

The diamond wasn't just a gesture, it was a message. "I never told you I had a belly button piercing."

He smiled wide. "Of course you did, my *habibti*." His hand landed on his heart. "I remember everything you say." He leaned forward and lowered his voice. "And I think it is sexy."

Abruptly, he stood. "Get ready, we are leaving in one hour." He turned toward the door.

"Khalaf, my luggage?"

"Everything you need is in the closet," he answered without looking back before pulling the bedroom door shut behind him.

I stared at the diamond for a moment. Then I took it out of its case.

Sunlight hitting all the facets, it took three turns before I saw it.

Small and nearly invisible, hidden under the setting was a micro-sized tracking chip.

Getting out of bed, I aimed for the bathroom but stopped when a flash of color in the closet caught my attention.

I opened the door wider.

Two dresses hung next to each other. One white, one red, and one slip to go under either. Beneath them, neatly placed, was a pair of brand-new designer high heels in a subtle fawn color.

I glanced at the empty shelves, but that was it.

That was the extent of the clothes Khalaf had left out for me. No bra, no underwear, and all of it placed at some point after my bath last night without me noticing.

Cursing myself, I walked into the bathroom with the diamond.

TEN

Adam

I CHECKED MY WATCH.

Thirteen minutes left.

Scanning the airport, I checked my cell.

Zane, finished with his preflight checks and sitting in the pilot's seat, glanced at me. "Twelve minutes."

Seeing my reflection in his mirrored aviators, I nodded. "I know."

"I should start her up."

I got Zane's logic. I'd texted Conlon, and if he'd gotten the message, he knew the timetable. His radio silence wasn't anything new, nor was it necessarily cause for alarm, but in this situation, in this corner of the world, it wasn't boding well.

I gave Zane the go-ahead. "Do it." Scanning the entrance to the airport for non-commercial travel, hoping like hell Conlon was on his way back, I checked my watch again.

Eleven minutes.

Fuck.

The Gulfstream's engines roared to life and Zane radioed ground control before he glanced at me. "Plan B?"

"Not yet." We had ten more minutes.

Zane shook his head. "Pushing the envelope in this situation isn't a smart call. Waiting until the very last minute of our three-thousand-dollar hour sends a message."

"I know." It told every security guard out there that we were either belligerent, cocky, or waiting for someone who hadn't come back. It was the equivalent of holding up a surrender flag, which only made us more vulnerable. If we didn't leave, the guards would want more than a bribe this time. They'd want a reason. No one hung out at the Baghdad airport for sport.

"Clock's ticking," Zane warned.

"Stand by." Dialing Conlon, I got out of the copilot's chair and stepped into the main cabin. Unlike the last time I called, this time it didn't even ring. A generic voice mail immediately picked up. "Fuck."

"Problem?" Zane asked as he used reverse thrust to back us up.

"Yeah." I glanced out the windows on one side of the jet. "His cell's going straight to voice mail now."

"That's answer enough, and I've got clearance. We're out." Zane turned the Gulfstream around.

I stepped across the aisle and glanced out the windows on the port side of the plane.

A dusty, battered, first-generation Humvee that was missing the top came flying through the service entrance of the airport and barreled across the tarmac, aiming right for us.

Conlon was behind the wheel.

"Stop," I commanded Zane. "He's here."

Zane eased back on the thrust.

I released the hatch, and the airstairs unfolded as Conlon slammed on the brakes and skidded to a stop just feet before the steps.

Jumping out of the Humvee, leaving the ignition running, Conlon took the steps two at a time as he yelled, "Go, go, go!"

Zane was taxiing before I had the hatch closed.

Conlon rushed down the aisle, weapon drawn. Peering out the rear port side window, he yelled up to Zane, "Get this bird in the air ASAP, Zulu!"

"What happened?" I demanded as I watched four Iraqi police cars come speeding through the service entrance of the airport before airport security blocked the first vehicle in the caravan.

"You mean besides the fact that we're Americans?" Conlon smirked as he moved up a window.

My patience having worn thin three fucking hours ago, I snapped. "Answer the question."

"Right." He looked out another window before tucking his piece in his back waistband and glancing toward the open cockpit. "Can you speed this up, Zulu?"

"I'm only cleared for the far runway, and unless you want to draw more heat than you already have, I'm not taking off from the fucking taxiway." Zane turned the plane toward the runway. "Alpha, get up here and handle communications. If shit starts to go down, you can try to talk your way out of it while I do the flying."

"Copy." Eyeing Conlon, I headed toward the cockpit just as air traffic control called our tail number and told us to hold position.

"Keep moving," I ordered Zane as I grabbed the headset and scanned the distance to the runway. Glancing back at the Iraqi police vehicles still blocked by airport security, I replied to the tower and tried to stall. "Baghdad ground, Gulfstream November four zero niner two whiskey, say again?"

"Gulfstream November four zero niner two whiskey, *hold*," the air traffic controller firmly stated.

I nodded at Zane, and he eased us to a standstill.

Conlon appeared at the open cockpit door. "Pretty sure the Iraqi police didn't see me get onto this particular plane, but just for argument's sake, what would happen if we took off anyway?"

"Unbelievable," Zane muttered.

I threw Conlon a warning glare over my shoulder as I hit the talk button on the radio. "Baghdad ground. Gulfstream November four zero niner two whiskey requesting permission to cross runway one-eight right at taxiway alpha and proceed to runway…" I glanced at Zane and he mouthed *two-eight right*. "Two-eight right," I added.

Zane, Conlon and I were all silent as we waited for the tower to respond.

Thirty seconds later, the mic crackled and a different traffic controller's voice came over the line.

"Gulfstream November four zero niner two whiskey, Baghdad ground. Proceed via alpha, hold short of runway two-eight right."

Zane eased the G550 forward on the taxiway toward the runway.

I confirmed with air traffic control. "Roger, Gulfstream November four zero niner two whiskey, proceeding via alpha, will hold short of runway two-eight right."

"We good?" Conlon asked.

"Not yet." I glanced at Conlon as Zane lined us up for take-off. "What the hell happened?"

Conlon chuckled as he rubbed a hand over a bruise forming on his jaw. "Long version or short version?"

My Sig Sauer P226 on my waist, I knew from experience that I could draw and put a bullet between Vance's eyes in one second flat. In that moment, I fucking thought about it. But I needed his intel, and I'd been at this game too damn long to hope for a single second that we would've extracted Emmy from whatever hell she'd gotten herself into. Let alone have done it in one of the most terrorist-riddled cities in the world with no previous intel, no team on the ground and nothing more than the M45 Conlon carried and the laptop he'd had when he'd gotten off the plane but didn't have now. Therefore, I wanted to know what the fuck Conlon had found out.

"Sitrep," I demanded. "Now."

"Right." Conlon tilted his head from one side to the other,

cracking his neck before rubbing his jaw again. "Long story short, she's not here."

Glad she wasn't in-country, but also pissed we didn't have her, I took it out on Conlon. "What the hell took five hours?"

Conlon shrugged. "Took awhile to find the kid, let alone convince him to stand in the middle of an open-air marketplace with a laptop and initiate the trace while I stayed the fuck out of sight." He glanced out the windows behind him. "But we got it done, and I found out who the burner belonged to."

The mic crackled and air traffic control came on the line. "Gulfstream November four zero niner two whiskey, Baghdad ground. Line up and wait."

"Roger, Baghdad ground," I confirmed.

Conlon walked to the back of the plane. "We're cutting this close."

"Gulfstream November four zero niner two whiskey over to tower on eighteen thirty-five," replied Baghdad ground control, telling me to switch to tower control.

"Tower, it's Gulfstream November four zero niner two whiskey with you on runway two-eight right," I told air traffic control before releasing the talk button and glancing back at Conlon. "Correction, *you* cut this close."

Baghdad tower control came over the radio. "Gulfstream November four zero niner two whiskey, taxi into position."

I clicked the talk button as Zane pulled us forward and readied us for takeoff. "Gulfstream November four zero niner two whiskey, roger into position."

"Oh fuck." Conlon rushed from the back of the cabin to the front as he looked out the aft side windows. "Zulu, get this bird up now or we're going to have a problem."

I glanced out the side window as the police cars sped toward our side of the airport. "Start fucking talking, Conlon."

Air traffic control came over the radio. "Gulfstream

November four zero niner two whiskey, cleared for takeoff runway two-eight right. Contact departure in the air."

Zane thrust the engines, Conlon fell into a seat, and just as the Iraqi police surrounded the Humvee, we were wheels up.

I glanced over my shoulder.

"Close calls." Conlon grinned. "A rush almost as good as sex."

"Departure," Zane spoke into the radio. "Good afternoon, it's Gulfstream November four zero niner two whiskey with you out of one point three for five thousand."

"Gulfstream November four zero niner two whiskey, good afternoon," Departure replied to Zane. "Radar identified. Climb to flight level..."

Once I heard we were in the clear, I took off my headset and climbed out of the copilot's seat.

Conlon held his hands up before I sat next to him. "Don't shoot the messenger. You came to me, remember?"

"Whose burner was it?"

Leaning back in his seat, his usual custom suit replaced with a dusty T-shirt and ripped jeans, he glanced out the window.

"You're stalling." Which only meant one thing. He knew who was on the other end of the cryptic text I'd received on a cell phone that hadn't been my number for seven years. "Who was it?"

Vance's green-brown eyes met mine with a wariness I rarely saw in him. "Not exactly a who." He inhaled, then let it out slow. "The burner cell was a decoy, but it traced back to a what." He pulled a crumpled piece of paper out of his pocket. "I checked it three times, which apparently tipped off the unwanted company on my six. It's partially why I was late. I tried to evade them." He handed me the paper.

I looked down at the ten scribbled digits.

Digits anyone in my line of work knew by heart.

"Langley," Vance calmly stated as if shit hadn't just gone

FUBAR. "CIA headquarters." He paused as if waiting for an explanation.

I didn't have one.

I was thinking.

No. Wracking my brain. But every damn scenario I was coming up with was worse than the last, and none of it bode well for Emmy.

Vance pointed out the obvious. "Someone went through a lot of trouble trying to cover their tracks when they sent you that text."

"Fuck." *Fuck.*

"Any idea who?"

"No." Possibly.

"You going to call it?" Vance asked.

"No." I was going to do one better.

I stood and went back to the cockpit. "Zane, we're changing course."

ELEVEN

Quinn

I GLANCED AT THE TALL MIRRORS IN THE OPULENT MARBLE BATHROOM, then at the vanity that was littered with all the same makeup, toiletries, brushes, perfumes and hair products from last night. Some of which I'd used.

I looked back at myself in the mirror.

Oppressive desert sunlight streaming in from floor-to-ceiling windows, it was more than obvious I was naked under the soft cream, spaghetti strap silk slip.

My white-blonde hair hung in perfect waves down my back, and my heavy charcoal eye makeup stood out even from five feet away. My skin was buffed smooth, my perfume was designer, and my heels were five inches. The only mar in my flawless image was the fingerprint bruises on my arm and the silhouette of a three-carat diamond in my belly button piercing.

Staring at my reflection, I turned to my side and studied the quarter-inch bump outline the diamond made in my silk slip. I glanced at my upper arm. The piercing was a relic of my freshman year in college, but the jewel and bruises were new.

I was wondering if I should cover the bruises with makeup when the bathroom door burst open.

Khalaf's razor-sharp gaze found mine in the mirror, and the smile that spread across his handsome face was cunning. "Beautiful."

In his custom suit, designer shoes and wearing his expensive watch I couldn't pronounce the name of, he waltzed in. His impeccable appearance was the same as in London, but everything about him seemed to have changed the moment his private jet had touched down in the United Arab Emirates.

Stopping one inch behind me, Khalaf turned me toward the mirror as the heavy, signature cologne he told me he had made especially for him swamped my own scent.

Lowering his head but keeping his eyes on me, he let his lips touch the bruises on my upper arm that he'd given me. "Always so beautiful," he whispered before straightening to his full height. "But I will have to be more careful with you." His thumb coasted over the bruises.

"*Shukran*," I replied, purposefully mispronouncing thank you in Arabic.

His chuckle was deep as his hands slid down and grasped the outside of my thighs. "You are worth every penny I have spent on you, *habibti*, but your Arabic with an American accent?" He shook his head slightly. "Not your strong suit. Stick to English, my beauty."

I gave him the almost smile I'd perfected. "I think you need to give me lessons, and a moment alone to finish dressing."

"Oh, you will get lessons." His laugh deep and provocative, he ignored my last comment and grasped the delicate fabric of the slip. Using his fingers as if this were a game in seduction, he walked the material up my legs. "But first I want to see what I gave you."

Unwelcome panic threaded through my chest and gripped my lungs. "What are you doing, Khalaf?" He had never touched me like this. Not that I hadn't been expecting it, but my stomach still knotted, and I reached for a way out. "You can already see it through the slip you gave me to wear."

His tone immediately changed. Stern, almost menacing, his eyes narrowed. "Are you saying you do not trust me? It is just you and me in here, none of my guards."

Which was exactly the problem, but precisely should have been my goal. "We're usually never alone. In private," I amended.

"What did you think would eventually happen, *habibti*? That you would remain untouched with a man's money supporting you and never have to be unaccompanied with him?"

This time, when he used the term of affection, there was no warmth behind it. In fact, he'd practically spit it out with disgust. "I thought we would talk about this first." Or not at all, because this was way past where I ever thought it would go.

"Then let us talk." He didn't let go of the hem of my slip nor stop his movements. "Are you nervous because you are untouched? Inexperienced?" His posture turned rigid in warning, and he lowered his voice. "Or perhaps it is not the act of touching at all but the very man standing behind you who has showered you with gifts." His voice dropped even further. "Are you ungrateful, American Quinn?"

Willing my breathing to remain even and my expression submissive, I ignored the churning in my stomach and forced myself to lean back into him. "Of course not."

His demeanor immediately reversed, and his voice softened. "Ah, *habibti*. Always wanting more of what I have, aren't you?"

No. "Maybe."

Chuckling as if he hadn't just flipped his attitude toward me, then flipped right back, he casually lifted my dress to above my waist as if he had seen me naked a hundred times and we were intimate lovers. Exposing both my bare pussy and the new diamond glinting in the sunlight that dangled on the gold ring hanging from the bottom of my belly button, he made a sound low in his throat. "Exquisite."

"What are you doing, Khalaf?" Tamping down erratic emotions of anger and fear I no longer had use for, I asked the question, but my quivering voice betrayed me.

"Looking at you." He brought the slip higher, exposing my

breasts, and made a noise low in his throat again. "Do not think I did not notice you avoided my question. So I ask again. Are you a virgin, American Quinn?"

My nipples tightening from the cold and indignity, I bristled both with anger and nerves. "Why do you ask?" I knew why.

His gaze, assessing but not starved like a man drowning in desire, raked over my body. "I need to know how to treat you."

Fighting to keep from grabbing the hem of the slip and pulling it down, I dug my nails into my palms. "You treat women differently based on their level of experience?"

Missing nothing, his gaze shot to my hands before meeting my eyes in the mirror again. "I will treat *you* differently based on your level of experience, *habibti*."

This time he managed to make the pet name sound almost sincere, but I knew how this game was played. I gave him a half-truth. "I am not untouched."

His eyebrows drew together. "Your barrier is broken?"

My throat moved with a swallow as errant fear leaked past my compartmentalized barricades and snaked up my spine. Shoving it down, I made a calculated decision.

I pushed a single word out. "Yes."

"Hm." Pensive, still holding my slip up with one hand but letting it drop back down far enough to cover my breasts, he fingered the diamond as if he were fingering a woman's clit. "Thank you for telling me." Making slow circles over the jewel, he held my eyes in the mirror. "Do you know what this is for?"

Yes. Tracking his property. I'd found a small nail file in the bathroom and already used it to gently push the device out. Then I'd slipped it into the inside lining of my left shoe in a tiny cut I'd made.

I feigned shyness. "A gift for coming here?"

"Mm," he responded, neither confirming nor denying while he kept rubbing the jewelry. "And why would I give you an expensive gift such as this, my American beauty with the harsh name, just because you came here with me?"

Instead of looking at him in the mirror, I tilted my head up to meet his gaze. "Because you want to believe in love." I didn't know if my response was the best acting of my life or sheer projection.

His dark eyes studied me, and for a brief second, I didn't know what was real.

"Do you wish to be loved?" he quietly asked.

Softening my stance, I leaned more into him and recentered my weight. The move was calculated, but then I did the last thing I thought I was capable of. Unguarded, I touched my mouth to his neck as if I were giving him the kiss of death, then I told him the absolute truth. "No."

He stiffened at my response, or my forwardness, maybe both. Either way, I knew the moment his body language changed the impact I had made. I'd broken the rules. His and mine. But his rules were arbitrary, unstated, and expected to be followed without hesitation, yet subject to his mood and agenda. They were always the wild cards. But my rules? I only had one.

Never show true vulnerability.

Which was exactly what he thought I'd just done by giving him a truth he could use against me. A woman without hope was a woman without boundaries.

Now he thought he knew me.

Like a lion stalking its prey, his inhale was slow, but then his punishment was swift.

Dropping my slip to fist a handful of my hair, whipping my head back, he dangerously grasped my throat with his other hand in a punishing grip. "Did I give you permission to touch me?"

I breathed in.

Deep.

Then I exhaled.

If I remembered how to smile, I would have.

This was in my comfort zone.

The opposite of panicked, I carefully took in every nuance of his body language, words and hold on me.

I had two choices.

Submit or fight.

I'd been submitting for months.

Two long months of relentless grooming, sloppy conditioning and skillful mind fuckery. All carefully veiled but nonetheless transparent, and all by a man who was nothing close to who he portrayed himself to be.

This was my chance.

This was my opening.

My arms relaxed, my body poised to set off a chain reaction of events, my lips parted to pull the trigger with only one word in warning.

But Amir stepped into the open doorway of the bathroom.

His gaze briefly met mine in the mirror before training on his master. "The car is ready downstairs."

Khalaf ignored his guard and spoke to me as if we did not have an audience. "Do you think you deserve a man to take care of you? Do you think disobedience is worthy of reward?"

My answer was no on both counts, but I wasn't playing the same game as him. "You gave me a diamond," I dared to say.

He let go of my hair and throat and grasped the diamond over the silk of my slip, taking the three carats between two fingers. "I can also take it away." He pulled until the nothing strip of flesh that was pierced through stretched to the point of pain.

Inhaling through my nose, I let it out through my mouth. Then I gave him his win. "I understand."

Letting go of the diamond, he stepped back but didn't retreat. "Get dressed."

I reached for the white dress with longer sleeves.

"Red dress," he barked before checking his watch. "And hurry."

Looking in the mirror, he straightened his tie. "Do you know how to behave, or do I need to end this here?"

Reaching for the red dress, I slipped it over my head. Smoothing my hair, I checked my makeup. Then I turned to him and waited without comment because silence spoke volumes.

His dark-eyed gaze, neither piercing nor kind, took me in from head to toe. Then he turned toward the door and threw a command over his shoulder. "Follow."

I exited the bathroom behind him, grabbed my purse off the dresser, and the three bodyguards fell into line around us. When Khalaf continued through the living area of the penthouse suite toward the front door, I paused.

"I need my passport, please."

Khalaf glanced at Amir as he held the now open door to the suite where two additional guards I had never seen before stood waiting in the hall. "Tell the drivers we are coming down." He looked back at me. "You do not need it."

For a split second, I dropped my guard and let irritation through. "Are you taking me outside the hotel?"

His smile was sinister. "Do you have a problem with that?"

I kept my expression and tone even. "Of course not, but I am a foreigner in this country, and I should carry my passport wherever I go." The identification also had a small, hidden tracking device embedded in the binding, not unlike the one now in my heel.

"You do not need it where we're going." Khalaf nodded at Fahad, his cruelest-looking bodyguard who stood behind me.

A heavy hand landed on my shoulder in warning.

Khalaf's perfectly white teeth gleamed in the desert sunlight streaming into the suite as he smiled wide. "Now, are we ready?"

Five guards and a man with more moods than money—I was ready whether I liked it or not. "Of course."

TWELVE

Adam

As far as I knew, there were only two people in the entire world who knew the protocol.

Two people who could get the attention of the one man every country wanted to get their hands on, including the country that'd trained him, right down to the exact man responsible for pulling him from the Teams and setting him on a course that made him who he was. That man was none other than Vice Admiral Erikson Nilsen, but since Billy and Maila's father was dead, the vice admiral was no longer a threat to Ghost.

Every other government organization in the United States was another story.

Which was why Ghost trusted no one.

Except me and, once upon a time, ironically, Billy. Ghost's reasoning? If Billy admitted to the vice admiral that he knew how to find the most elusive weapon the United States had ever created then lost control of, Billy would be in more trouble than Ghost himself.

Ghost had also said he was indebted to Billy, but I never found out why. All I knew was that there was an elaborate protocol to follow if I ever needed to get in touch with a man who might as well have invented the key to becoming invisible.

Because that's what Ghost had done six years ago.

Before he'd gone off the grid though, he'd given me two explicit instructions. One, never admit to ever knowing him. Two, never look for him, try to contact him, or speak of him—unless, as he put it, an extreme and irrevocably life-threatening situation arose where I could trust no one. And if that happened, I had one shot.

One chance to call for help.

If I fucked up, he wasn't coming. If I was followed, at any point, he wasn't showing. If my death was imminent, I would die. If I was outing him, everyone I knew would die. If I was acting like a pussy, he would beat me, then I would die.

I got it.

Ghost was my one shot at a Hail Mary, and I was using it.

Because of a fucking text.

Praying for the hundredth time that morning that Ghost was paying attention and that I wasn't catching dysentery or who the fuck knew what else, I ordered my third unbottled glass of water from the dirty-as-fuck sidewalk café in the middle of New Delhi.

Then I drank the third glass.

Slowly.

Standing from the exact table I was supposed to occupy and leaving the precise tip amount the protocol called for, I avoided the chaotic traffic as I walked across the street and bought the daily newspaper from the stand I was instructed to purchase it from.

Ten minutes later, the newspaper was folded in thirds, placed in a stamped envelope and mailed from a local post office to a drop across the city. Fifteen minutes after that, I was back in my hotel, rumpling the sheets to make the bed look slept in and wetting a towel before leaving it on the floor. Two flights down a rank stairwell and I was back in the polluted humidity of the city, hailing a taxi to get back to the airport.

An hour later, I was using a fake passport to get through airport security to catch a commercial flight to Istanbul. In fucking coach class. After Istanbul, another café and another mailed newspaper, it was on to Barcelona to repeat the whole fucking process.

Too many hours later, three different fake IDs burned in three different airports on three different airlines, I was back on US soil.

I'd followed the protocol exactly.

Now I was sitting with a new burner, the number having been written in reverse order on a stamped postcard and left at an outgoing mail drop in the hotel in Barcelona. The address I sent the postcard to was probably another drop, but I wouldn't know because I hadn't bothered checking. Ghost's whole damn protocol was fucking outdated, and I was over his Soviet-era spy bullshit. He needed a goddamn encrypted phone like the rest of us.

Sitting in the dark in my penthouse, staring at the Manhattan skyline from the wall of windows on the thirtieth floor of a building I owned through a shell corporation, I stewed.

Fucking Ghost.

I'd done everything right, but the damn burner wasn't ringing.

Swirling the ice in my tumbler, I downed the rest of my Maker's Mark. You could dress me in a custom Brioni suit, put me in one of the most expensive high-rises in Manhattan, and offer me forty-year-old scotch, but I was still the kid who grew up dirt poor in one of Miami's worst neighborhoods. Maker's Mark was my drink of choice.

Eyeing the bottle on the kitchen counter, refusing to entertain the thought that Emmy was beyond my reach or worse, I thought of Billy and the first time I'd met him.

A gangly kid with a surfboard whose smile was brighter than his sun-bleached hair rode his bike by the bus bench I was claiming for an afternoon after school and stopped. He'd asked if I was the kid in his English class, then asked if I surfed. I'd told him this was Miami, not California, and he'd laughed. Then he'd said I should come to the beach with him. I hadn't had shit else to do but go home to an empty apartment in a condemned building, so I went. A few hours later, sunburnt and exhausted from trying to learn to surf on nonexistent waves, William "Billy" Nilsen dragged me home with him for dinner.

Walking into the nicest house I'd ever been in as the scent of cooking food filled the neat living room, I'd thought I'd hit pay dirt. Then a smaller, prettier, blonder version of Billy came running down the stairs. She'd taken one look at me and smiled like it was Christmas morning.

Emotions I couldn't describe back then, because I'd never experienced them, hit my chest and almost knocked me on my ass. I didn't know how I'd gotten so lucky to walk through that front door, but I knew I never wanted to leave.

Fortunately for me, Billy had already decided we were friends.

Shoving down memories better left in the past, I stood to get another drink when my work cell pinged with a new text.

Vance: *Did you call the number yet?*

Still pissed at him for Baghdad, I shot off a reply.

Me: *Did you tell me why you were being pursued by the Iraqi police yet?*

Two minutes after takeoff, Baghdad traffic control had radioed and told us to turn around because a person of interest had been seen getting on our plane and he was wanted for questioning. Lying to air traffic control and later the Iraqi police who were patched through by Baghdad's ground control, I'd denied we had any passengers. Repeatedly. Which was nothing new in my line of work, but now I was on the police's radar in that corner of the world, and that wasn't good for business.

My phone rang once, and I answered. "Vance."

Conlon chuckled. "I know it's bad when you use my first name." His tone sobered. "But for the record, the less you know the better. You got your information, none of us have any more bullet holes, that particular company jet is intact, so win-win." I heard ice clink in a glass as he paused. "The only question now is why, after all that, you're sitting on your ass in your penthouse doing nothing."

Forty-eight hours ago, I'd made up a bullshit lie about following down a lead and told him and Zane to drop me in Saudi Arabia before heading back stateside without me. Then I'd made my way to India and followed protocol.

Jet-lagged, impatient and pissed off, I turned it around on Vance. "Why aren't you on assignment?"

"Who says I'm not?"

"You're calling me." Vance never called me while on assignment.

Vance chuckled again. "Right." The ice clinked in the glass again. "Good catch."

I didn't bother telling him to pick up one of the dozens of assignments we had waiting to be handled. Vance Conlon did what Vance Conlon wanted to do, when he wanted to do it. I'd long since given up trying to assign him to shit. Truth was, he was more valuable to me than wasting him on ninety percent of the work AES took on. Not to mention, he didn't work as part of a unit. Sure, I'd used him as backup, so had the other guys, but any assignments he chose himself, he flew solo. I'd long since stopped questioning his process or his antics.

"What do you want, Conlon?"

"Remember Peru?" he seemingly asked randomly.

"Which part?" I remembered every assignment. Especially the ones where every single thing that could've gone wrong, did. Since I'd started Alpha Elite Security three years ago, I hadn't lost a single client or had a single fatality of one of my men. But Peru was close.

"All of it." Vance snorted. "K and R's are such a pain in the ass," he mused, pausing as he drank again.

Kidnap and ransoms were an alarmingly increasing percentage of AES's business. "Your point?" I walked to the kitchen counter.

"My point," he drew the two words out with an air of superiority, "is that I think you're forgetting the setup of that particular assignment."

I didn't forget. "The target was behind her own kidnapping." She'd wanted to leave her husband and take his millions with her.

"Exactly," Vance stated, all humor from his tone gone.

With the bottle of Maker's Mark in my hand, about to pour another drink, every muscle in my body went still. Then anger coursed through my veins as I picked up on his insinuation. "She wouldn't do that."

Vance didn't make a joke. He didn't give me his usual pretentious chuckle, he didn't even give me attitude. He calmly, without judgment, asked if I was too close to this. "Are you sure?"

I wasn't sure of anything associated with that damn text, which was why I'd tried to get a hold of Ghost, because he used to have contacts at the CIA and knew the players. As far as Emmy, she'd never been dramatic. I couldn't see seven years changing that, but Vance had a point.

I couldn't bet on it.

"Message received," I conceded.

"I'm not trying to send a message, brother. I'm just asking the question because you would do the same for me. Returning the favor is all."

In a rare show of his humanity, I took him at his word. "Appreciate it."

This time he did chuckle. "No, you don't. You want this woman safe from whatever web she's caught up in, and you want her to be who you once thought she was." I heard him swallow before setting his glass down with intent. "Trust me, I get it. We all have that one." Keys jingled, and I heard a door open. "Speaking of women, I'm out. You need me, you know where to find me."

"Copy."

"One last piece of advice?"

Vance Conlon didn't give advice any more than he took it. Curiosity a bitch, I took the bait. "What?"

"Next time you burn three of your identities, change your clothes."

Goddamn it.

"Right." Vance chuckled when I didn't acknowledge him. "But seriously, in every other way, you were solid. I was only able to track you because I knew the identities."

Motherfucking *shit*. "Do I want to know how you have that information?"

"Probably not," he cheerfully replied.

I'd fucked up the protocol. Majorly.

"Later, boss." Conlon hung up.

Fuck, fuck, *fuck*.

Goddamn Conlon had tracked me. Not to mention, I was now wondering what else wasn't secure in my private safe, let alone the shit I had stashed around this penthouse and half a dozen other properties I used as my personal residences, but all of that paled in comparison to the fact that I'd just fucking blown it.

Not bothering with the glass, I drank straight from the bottle before slamming it back down. "Damn it!" I pounded the kitchen counter with a closed fist. "*God-fucking-damn it.*"

"You always swear at yourself when you drink alone?"

My reflexes still active-duty sharp, I drew before I spun, aiming my 9mm at the dark corner across the living room where the voice had come from.

A voice I should've recognized.

Fuck. "Ghost."

THIRTEEN

Quinn

THE STIFLING DESERT HEAT STOLE MY BREATH A SPLIT SECOND before the punishing sun struck the front of my body like a slap to the face.

Khalaf, surrounded by four security guards, walked in front of me while Mardon, having switched positions with Fahad after we'd gotten off the elevator, followed behind me. If I wasn't so pissed about my passport, let alone my phone, the scene in front of me would be almost comical.

Khalaf had eaten alone with me dozens of times over the past few weeks. First in London, then New York, then back in London.

At any point, I could've picked up a steak knife and slit his throat.

Or poisoned his drink.

I could've even gotten creative and pushed him off a balcony somewhere.

But I hadn't.

I'd worked too damn hard to get here, and Khalaf had seemed to think I was special. Or at least I thought he had when he'd chased me down in New York after a carefully orchestrated meet on my part in London. But the fact that I now only had one security guard while we were leaving the hotel didn't paint a pretty picture.

The only question was how much time did I really have left.

Khalaf hadn't spent weeks grooming me for sport. I knew

the end game. But hoping I was being groomed for his own use, not to show off to buying customers, had been sloppy on my part.

Amir and Fahad got Khalaf situated in the first of his two SUVs before getting in after him. One of the extra guards from upstairs started to close the door.

I didn't dare speak up in front of all the people loitering around the hotel's entrance, but I did manage to step out of Mardon's reach and put myself in front of the SUV's door before the guard closed it all the way. My hand landed on the frame, and Khalaf looked up.

I put every ounce of acting skill I had into my expression.

Take me with you, I begged with my eyes.

Khalaf's chest rose with an impatient inhale. Then he tipped his chin at Mardon, who now had his hand securely wrapped around my upper arm, and spoke in Arabic. "*She comes with me.*"

Mardon all but tossed me into the SUV.

I landed on the bench next to Fahad, who moved over like I was rotting trash.

Khalaf leaned toward the still open door and issued a low threat in Arabic at Mardon. "*You damage the merchandise, I damage you.*"

The bodyguard slammed the door without comment.

The driver took off, and my suspicion was confirmed. I was out of choices and out of time. Speeding through an inhospitable landscape to an even harsher reality, I had one shot.

One last attempt to get Khalaf's attention.

Focusing my gaze on his eyes, I waited.

And waited.

Precious seconds ticked by as the driver put more distance between us and the high-rises of Dubai.

Then, finally, Khalaf looked up from his phone and met my gaze.

Brazen, out of line, and unprecedented, I parted my mouth and slowly, so slowly, licked across my top lip.

Khalaf's sharp intake of breath made both bodyguards turn their attention from their vigilant watch out the window to him.

This was it.

He could kill me for disobedience, or he could react like a man.

I wasn't afraid of dying.

I wasn't even afraid of being sold.

But in that moment, I was afraid Khalaf would not behave like a man.

My breath halted, my body still, I held his stare as he held mine.

The bodyguards looked at me, then looked back at him.

Amir spoke in Arabic. "*What's going on?*"

Both bodyguard's attentions momentarily on Khalaf, I made my last move.

Either sealing my death certificate or making the boldest decision of my career, I pushed my tongue against the inside of my cheek.

Khalaf's reaction was instant and immediate. Fury descended over his features, and he barked orders at his bodyguards in rapid-fire Arabic.

The next thing I knew, I was forcibly seated next to him, Amir and Fahad were on the other bench, and a security panel embedded in the floor of the SUV was going up, separating the two sides as Fahad argued warnings at him.

Ignoring him, Khalaf fisted a handful of my hair, yanked my head back and switched to English. "What do you think you are doing?"

I gave him the truth. "Stopping you from selling me."

Every muscle in his body went still except his hand in my hair. It tightened. "What did you say?"

"Am I wrong?" I challenged.

His nostrils flared. "Maybe you are not obedient after all. Maybe I misjudged everything about you."

My cards already on the table, I played my hand out. "If you are going to sell me, why not see if we are compatible first? Maybe I will surprise you." I planted the seed. "Maybe you'll want to keep me."

"What do you think you are doing?" he demanded.

Stalling, buying time, hoping to get my hands on his cell phone before Amir and Fahad could shoot me. "Making you an offer."

One second his expression was ruthless and cold, the next, he was throwing his head back and laughing.

I eyed his cell tucked into the inside pocket of his open suit jacket.

He stopped laughing, but a sinister smile held in its place. "And you what?" He forcefully dragged his thumb over my cheek until the vulnerable flesh pushed too hard against my teeth and I tasted blood. "Thought your mouth on me would be a good offer?"

I would bite him before I sucked him. "Yes."

His laugh this time was practiced. Leaning forward, he let his beard drag across my cheek before he whispered in my ear. "Stupid American woman."

I should have slit his throat when I'd had the chance.

Grasping my jaw, his fingers dug in on both sides. "Did you think you could get on your knees in a moving vehicle and pleasure me so well I would give up everything for you?" He raised a mocking eyebrow. "That I would marry you? Give you my royal bloodline and implant my seed in you?" He leaned even closer and lowered his voice. "Make you important?"

I'd lost the game, but I didn't let the mission go.

Not yet.

I reached for his Italian-made suit pants. "I told you, I don't want to get married." Daringly, I placed my hand on him.

The intake of his breath was sharp, but his hand flying to my wrist was quicker. His thick fingers wrapped around my small bones and squeezed without mercy. Then he trained his voice to a lulling, deceptive calm. "Do you think I believe your lies, *virgin*?"

It was my turn to stiffen in my seat.

"Am I wrong?" he mocked, repeating my question to him.

I stared at him.

"This is not a complicated question. Yes or no?"

I was fucked. I thought he'd believed my lies, but all along I was the one being played. He already knew the answer to his question. It was the sole reason I was here in this SUV with him and his bodyguards in the middle of the desert.

He knew.

Carefully making my tone submissive, I hedged. "You know the answer."

"You are right." He smirked before his expression hardened and his voice turned spiteful. "So tell me, American whore. Where did you learn to pleasure a man with your mouth when your barrier is unbroken?" His fingers on my wrist tightened. "What makes you think you could begin to pleasure a man such as myself?"

I told him the truth. "I don't."

The bark of his laugh was unexpected and condescending, but it broke the menace in his expression. "Soon enough, you will learn." Releasing my wrist and shoving me away, he pressed the button that lowered the divider between us and his bodyguards. Switching back to Arabic, he barked an order at the two men. "*Do it.*"

Before I could steel myself, Khalaf had switched seats with Fahad. The huge bodyguard flipped me like an insolent child, brought my back to his chest, wrapped an arm around my torso, and effectively pinned my arms. Then he roughly yanked my dress up as Amir pulled out his cell and kneeled between my legs.

Before I could kick Amir in the head, Fahad let go of my dress and jammed the barrel of his gun into my temple.

His hot, rancid breath hit my face as he spoke with lethal intent. "You move, I kill you."

"*Khalaf*," I stupidly cried out as the second bodyguard shoved my legs open, exposing my bare core.

Not even looking up from his cell phone, Khalaf issued a calm order in Arabic to the bodyguard between my legs. "*Make sure you get a good picture. They will want to see proof.*"

To my horror, Amir leaned closer and aimed his cell phone camera at my bareness as his free hand reached out.

Pure, unadulterated rage spread through my veins. "Stop right now!" I was going to kill every one of them.

Amir didn't stop. He didn't even pause. The fucker reached forward, his thick fingers landing on my pussy, and he spread me open.

I bucked like a horse. "NO!"

The fingers left my pussy, the gun jammed harder into my temple, and suddenly, Khalaf was leaning across the space between the seats.

His menacing gaze filled with stone-cold intent, he produced a syringe from his suit jacket pocket. "Since I have a mild affection for your green eyes, I am going to give you a choice." Uncapping the syringe, he pressed the tip of the needle to the side of my neck. "We can do this the easy way and you can spread your legs and hold them open, or we can do this the hard way."

Every single reason why I was here left my head, and suddenly my mind was throwing fractured images at me. One image actually. One I tried to never, ever think about. One with piercing blue eyes, thick, dark hair, and a smile so reserved it shattered my heart to even look at it. The image, the memory, the thought, all of it unwelcome, all of it crushing me from the inside out, I did the stupidest thing I ever could have done.

I lashed out.

My high-heeled foot made a solid connection with Amir's head a split second before the sting of a needle sank into my neck.

My muscles, my coordination, my brain, it all went instantly fuzzy, and I couldn't move as Fahad spread my thighs wide, then reached between my legs.

Thick fingers roughly dug into the lips of my pussy and stretched me open.

Flashes of light went off.

My vision tunneled. My body sank backward.

Weightless.

Floating.

Ocean.

Mediterranean blue.

I slid into darkness.

FOURTEEN

Adam

"You're losing your touch." Stepping from the shadows into the ambient light from the nightscape of Manhattan, a man I had not seen in six years nodded at my piece. "You would've already been dead."

Shoving my piece in my back waistband, I took in Ghost's appearance. Jeans, T-shirt, heavy boots. His hair was longer, and he'd bulked up with twenty-five more pounds of muscle. If it weren't for the six feet and change of height he carried with dexterity, he could've blended in anywhere.

But looks could be deceiving.

"I fucked up the protocol." I knew what Ghost was capable of. There wasn't a living being I knew who was more lethal with nothing except his hands and a pocketknife. His skills so far beyond anyone I'd ever met, it didn't matter that I was one of the few people who knew his birth name. He was no longer that man. He was simply a ghost. One you prayed you never met.

Looking almost casual, he shrugged. "I know."

"Then why are you here?"

"Figured you were going soft in your old age. Forgot what was important." He tipped his chin at my drink. "Case in point."

"Bourbon beats beer any day," I argued, the same argument we'd had countless times when we'd been on the Teams together. Not that I could call Ghost a team player or a Teams man. He and

Conlon had more in common than either of them liked to admit. "For the record, I didn't forget the details."

Ghost moved toward the kitchen without making a sound. "I didn't say you forgot details. I said you were going soft." He opened the fridge and reached into the back left, precisely where I had a six-pack of his favorite beer.

"HALOing into hostile territory and traversing a Fedayeen hotbed in a hundred-and-ten-degree heat in MOPP gear to take out a chem bio target isn't the same as sitting behind a desk, building a company." I poured myself another drink.

Ghost grabbed a beer, scanned the kitchen, living room and entrance in one glance, then twisted off the cap. "You making excuses now?"

Hell. Was I?

I looked out at the cityscape. Manhattan was never pretty. That word wasn't even in my vernacular. But at night, from thirty stories up, when you didn't see anything but the lights, it made a view.

I took a sip of my Maker's Mark. "I got a text."

Ghost had silently moved through the penthouse to stand next to me. His eyes on the same view, he took a pull from his beer. "I know."

"Christ." I shook my head. "Anything you don't know?"

"Victor tracked you by the passports I gave you." Using Vance's call sign from when we all served, Ghost spared me a glance. "His hacking skills are improving."

Fuck me. "It wasn't his hacking skills." I rubbed a hand over my jaw. "It was my own damn stupidity." I needed a shave and a sanity check.

"Hacking skills aren't a one-way street, but for the record, it was both."

I didn't argue. I didn't want to discuss Conlon any more than I wanted to know what Ghost had been up to for the past six years. "You know anything about that text I got?"

Ghost took another swallow of his beer. Then he answered my question with one of his own. "How many of those IDs I gave you do you still have left?"

Before Ghost had dropped off the grid, he'd given me a dozen rock-solid fake IDs with the works. Bank accounts, credit history, fake employment profiles—they were all so legit, even I couldn't find fault with them. He'd told me to keep them active, said it wasn't a warning, but a promise that I'd need them one day. I hadn't questioned Ghost since he'd been my swim buddy in BUD/S, and I didn't question him that day six years ago, but I fucking should have because it was the last time I'd seen him before tonight.

"All the IDs are still active." But I'd burned three getting him here. "Nine are still clean." I glanced at him. "Even though I suspect you already know this."

Neither confirming nor denying my statement, his gaze cut to me, scanned once, then held.

I stared back, but he wasn't looking at me. Ghost was looking through me. I knew the look, and it wasn't good. Ghost was thinking, and if he had to think something through, if he wasn't already ten steps ahead, then the situation was fucked. Royally.

I waited until he turned back to the view. "I know the text came from inside Langley."

"Baghdad's hot for you and Victor now. Zulu as well."

"No shit." Too on edge and too damn tired to play this on his terms, I laid it out. "I'm running out of time. Who do you still know on the inside? Someone I can trust." The question was a fucking joke. Trust and CIA operatives didn't belong in the same damn sentence together, but I had to ask anyway because I was out of options.

Ghost stared at the skyline a beat. "You still got that ID for Adam Hunt?"

I knew the names of all the IDs by memory because I actively checked on them, using them occasionally to keep them current. What I didn't know was that Ghost remembered the names, but I shouldn't have been surprised. Being on the Teams, where we each were now, those were the kinds of details you kept track of if you wanted to stay alive.

"The only ID you gave me that used part of my real name?" I took a swig of the bourbon and let it settle in my mouth a second before swallowing. "Yeah, I still have it."

"Good. You're going to need it." He finished his beer and walked to the kitchen.

I didn't miss the way he casually but thoroughly wiped the bottle with his T-shirt before setting it in the sink without leaving any fingerprints. "Because?"

Ghost strode toward the entryway and glanced at the security panel on the wall that I hadn't heard beep at any time in the past few hours to indicate someone had opened a door or a window.

Using the side of his fist to push the handle down, he opened the front door and looked back at me. "Because you're going to need it to get her out."

Goddamn it. "Out of where?"

"Hire a private jet not associated with you or AES or anyone else that can be traced back to someone on your payroll. Better yet, buy or lease one under Hunt's name and create a history with it. Make sure it holds up under scrutiny. Then beef up Hunt's background. Buy a company or two, stocks, venture capitalist shit. I don't care, make it extravagant and make it solid. Hunt needs to be money."

"Ghost—"

"Don't use Zulu or any of the other AES pilots. Get someone you trust who has an ID they can afford to burn." He scanned the hall. "Have the jet fueled and ready at Teterboro by oh-seven-hundred."

I couldn't believe I was blindly agreeing to this without more intel. "Range?"

"Seven thousand miles. Minimum."

Christ. I glanced at my watch. "That's in eight hours." My mind was running down possibilities, but even for me, getting a non-company, long-range private jet with untraceable pilots, all off the grid, in that amount of time was going to be tight. Really fucking tight.

"Seven hours, fifty-eight minutes," Ghost corrected before leveling me with a look. "If you're smart, you'll walk away from this. If not, you'll be at Teterboro."

Before I could tell him there was no way in hell I was walking away, let alone ask him where the fuck we were going, he was smoke.

It wasn't until after the door clicked shut that I realized it hadn't beeped when he'd opened it.

"Motherfucker," I muttered, pulling out my cell as I walked over to the security panel. Entering my code, I saw the system had been disabled. Resetting it and changing my passcode, I made a mental note to ream my tech team. Then I glanced through my contacts on my cell and pulled one up. Memorizing the number, I walked back to my office and grabbed a clean burner.

Powering it up, I dialed.

After four rings, a deep voice I hadn't heard in years answered. "Hello?"

"It's Alpha." I used my Teams name in case anyone was listening on his end. "I have to ask you something."

Roark MacElheran, a former Marine pilot, paused. Then, "You have the wrong number."

"I'm calling from a burner. It's secure."

He hung up.

I waited.

Two minutes later, my burner rang with an incoming unidentified number. I answered without speaking.

"Where did we first meet?" Roark asked.

If I wasn't so spun up, I would've appreciated his caution. "Technically, we didn't meet the first time you saved our asses in Iraq. You hovered over the hot zone in your Super Cobra, dropped lines, we hooked on. Then you gave us a windy-as-hell ride back to the FOB Sykes where we caught our own transport home." It was a miracle we weren't shot full of holes when we evac'ed.

"Trefor," Roark stated.

It wasn't a question, but I answered it anyway. "Yeah, it's me."

"I'm not coming to work for AES," he warned.

"Understood." I'd already asked him half a dozen times. His answer was always the same. "But for the record, you're wasting your skills flying seaplanes for tourists in the Keys."

"I don't get shot at."

I couldn't disagree. "Fair point."

"Why are you calling?"

Knowing I was about to ask for the exact kind of shit he was trying to avoid, I selfishly did it anyway. I asked the best Marine pilot I knew for help. "I need a favor." If it had wings, Roark could fly it. Certified or not, the man had a gift for keeping birds in the sky.

"What kind of favor?"

"I can't tell you over the phone, but I'd need you at Teterboro before oh-seven-hundred, geared up and ready to fly with an untraceable ID. I'd also be asking for you to cover your tracks getting up here and back."

Silence.

Fuck. "Roark?" He was my only shot at this, the only pilot I'd trust with this outside of Zane, but I was heeding Ghost's warning.

"Who's this for?" Roark asked with a sixth sense.

I didn't lie. "Me." I also didn't insult him by offering money, but I'd find a way to pay him back. "It's personal."

This time, Roark didn't hesitate. "I'll be there."

I scrubbed a hand over my face in relief. "Thank you."

"Oh-seven-hundred," he confirmed before hanging up.

FIFTEEN

Quinn

MY HEAD POUNDING, I STRUGGLED TO OPEN MY EYES.

My legs feeling like dead weight, my arms not much better, I tried to roll.

"Shit."

The expletive slipped out at the exact moment flashes of memory sank in.

Airplane, dark ocean, red dress, shoes, the… the…

The what?

Unable to remember, I forced my eyes open and had to blink rapidly to adjust to the bright lights. Correction, dimmed light. One overhead lamp, on low. Not too bright, but I blinked again before I could focus.

Then all I saw was white.

White ceiling, white walls, white floor.

Alarm spread, and I turned my head.

White toilet, white sink.

I sat up rapidly.

Simultaneously my head spun, my wrist caught, and nausea overwhelmed me. Swallowing down bile, I glanced at my wrist, but I already knew what the bite of cold metal meant.

Handcuffed.

I lifted my head back up slowly so I didn't puke and took in everything around me a second time.

Then it hit me. Khalaf, the syringe, the car ride. Panic seized my chest. Taking a breath, then another, I told myself to assess—myself, my surroundings, my situation.

I swung my legs off the bed. With my bare feet hitting the cold tile floor and my lethargic body protesting at the movement, I stood.

And turned in a circle.

Or as much of one as I could manage with my left wrist handcuffed to a metal loop welded onto the side of a single-size bed frame with a mattress, fitted sheet and one pillow. All white. The bed shoved into one corner of the six-by-eight cell, I had a small, white-painted wood nightstand with one bottle of water on it, the label in Arabic. Dehydrated and so thirsty, but not trusting the water, I didn't reach for it.

I took in the white sink and toilet across from the bed, the overhead single light fixture, and the delineation of a door in the wall opposite the bed with no handle on the inside. There was exactly nothing else in the room except me in my almost see-through silk slip, but no red dress.

I ran a hand over my hip.

And still no underwear.

My alarm deepening, my breath fast, my heart rate kicking up, I tried to stay calm. Always calm. People who had nothing to lose were calm. Intelligent people were calm. Quinn Michaels was calm.

So I took a deep breath and did what I needed to do.

I lifted my dress to look between my legs.

Then I assessed. Calmly.

No pain between my legs. Fingerprint bruises on my thighs. Nothing sticky coming out of me or on me.

I exhaled and dropped the dress.

Then I glanced around the room and really looked.

Multiple screws in the wooden side table. Exposed pipe under the sink. Ceramic lid on top of the back of the toilet. Working faucet. A fitted sheet.

I glanced up, but this time I looked closer than simply taking in the single light fixture. I traced the outline of the room where the walls met the ceiling. And one, two, three cameras, all small, all white, and all barely visible were mounted eight feet up.

Every move I made was being recorded. Or watched live.

I was hoping for the first when the sound of a lock being unlatched echoed in the small prison cell I was being held in.

The door banged open, and Fahad walked in with a tray in one hand while his other hand rested on the 9mm holstered under his right arm.

Unceremoniously dumping the tray on the foot of the bed, he muttered a single word. "Eat."

Before I could see past him into the hall outside my room, he retreated and yanked the door shut, the same lock-engaging sound echoing through my new space.

I guess that answered the question if someone was actively watching those cameras.

I glanced at the tray. Shawarma wrapped in roti and five dates.

No utensils.

Damn.

SIXTEEN

Adam

Sitting in the cockpit of a new-to-me Gulfstream G650 with a fabricated backlog of flights for a fabricated company Adam Hunt owned, all courtesy of an off-the-books employee I relied on for this exact scenario, I glanced at my watch.

Thirteen minutes before oh-seven-hundred.

Teterboro already busy with morning commuter traffic from the city, I did the last of my preflight checks, then glanced across the apron.

No sign of Ghost.

No sign of Roark.

And no new texts on the old number since the single one I received three days ago.

Exhausted, I scrubbed a hand over my face just as footsteps sounded on the airstairs.

I glanced back toward the open door of the plane.

Roark MacElheran ducked his six-foot-five frame and stepped into the cabin, but he wasn't alone. A golden retriever in a tactical vest followed on his six.

"Missy," Roark clipped. "Retreat."

The dog obediently went to the back of the cabin and lay down without so much as a glance in my direction.

Thrown, I stepped out of the cockpit and stared at the animal. "You brought a dog."

Roark shucked his rucksack onto the nearest seat. "Yeah."

"A dog," I repeated before pointing out the obvious. "We could be in for a fifteen-hour flight." I hadn't seen Roark in years, but we'd kept in touch. I knew he didn't want to give up his business, but he'd occasionally helped a mutual friend, André Luna, who owned a personal security outfit based in Miami. Neither Luna nor Roark had ever mentioned a service animal.

Roark stowed a large duffle on the floor behind the front passenger seats. "She's handled longer."

Roark, like me, was combat wounded. It was the reason neither of us were still active duty. You didn't serve in the Teams or in combat without walking away with scars. PTSD was an issue for anyone who'd seen action, and we all coped in different ways. I didn't judge, but I needed to know if Roark was solid.

I had to ask. "Is she your service animal?"

Roark's glare cut through my insensitivity like a round from an M4.

"She's Missy." He whistled once.

The dog immediately jumped up and trotted to him before sitting right at his feet. Looking up at him expectantly, she wagged her tail.

"Missy, greet Adam," he clipped, issuing the command and nodding at me as if she would know what he was talking about.

Missy stood, turned, nudged my hand with her nuzzle, then turned right back around and sat at Roark's feet again.

"Good girl," he quietly praised, laying his palm on her head once before issuing another command. "Go out." He stepped away from the door. "Hurry up."

The golden retriever rushed down the airstairs, ran across the apron to the nearest patch of grass, did her business, then came running back. Never breaking stride, she flew up the airstairs and took up her previous position in front of Roark, seated and wagging her tail like crazy.

This time, Roark didn't pet her. Reaching into the pocket

of his jeans, he retrieved a small bone and issued another command. "Retreat."

Practically dancing with joy at the proffered bone, she gently took the treat and pranced down the aisle to the back of the cabin, lying down where she'd been before.

"She's well trained." Complete understatement. "Wish some of the AES guys took direction that well."

Roark didn't comment about Missy. "You said on the phone this was personal."

There weren't many people I trusted implicitly, and Roark was one of them, but I hesitated. "You flew here commercial?"

"You asked for no tracks. Flying commercial with a canine isn't under the radar. I hitched a ride, stayed off all passenger manifests, and I'm using a clean alias to pilot today."

I nodded. "Thank you."

He waited.

Rubbing the back of my neck, I glanced at his dog, happily going to town on her bone. "You remember Billy Nilsen?"

"Of course."

"His sister's missing."

Roark frowned and asked the right question. "Missing or taken?"

"The latter, I believe."

"But you don't know."

He didn't ask it as a question, and I didn't answer it. "Which is why you're here. I needed a second pilot." Pausing, I leveled him with a warning look. "And backup."

"Understood. Prechecks?"

"All set." I glanced at my watch. "We're waiting for one more." I hadn't told him Ghost was coming when I'd spoken to him last night because I'd wanted to give as little information as possible over the burner.

Roark didn't ask who we were waiting for as he stepped toward the cockpit. "First chair or second?"

"I'll copilot."

Without comment, Roark got in the pilot seat and started his own preflight checks.

I glanced back at the dog. "She need water or anything?"

"Once we're in the air, I'll take care of her."

"She fly with you a lot?"

"Usually," he answered without any of the previous hostility he had when I'd asked if she was his service dog. "What's our flight plan?"

"I don't know."

Roark paused to glance at me. His look said it all.

Adrenaline wearing thin after the all-nighter I'd pulled setting everything up, I rubbed a hand over the back of my neck. "I'm waiting for more intel. Once the third party arrives, we'll find out." But I had my suspicions because I'd already mapped out where seven thousand miles from New York could take us, and most of it wasn't good.

Roark's stare held. "This isn't like the Trefor I knew."

"I know." Fuck, I knew.

"You got something going with the girl?"

"I got something with the whole damn family." Frustrated Ghost wasn't here, pissed we weren't already in the air, I glanced out the window across the apron.

Roark waited until I looked back at him. "They're all dead except the sister."

Climbing into the copilot's seat, I sighed. "Yeah, well, they were all alive when I was a hungry sixteen-year-old kid with a shit home life. Three of the four of them were anyway. I never had the pleasure of meeting Mrs. Nilsen."

Roark didn't comment. He whistled once.

Missy dropped her bone and immediately trotted toward the

cockpit. Looking up at Roark with her tail wagging, she waited for her next command.

Except Roark didn't give her one, not a verbal one. He merely tipped his chin toward me.

As if she knew what Roark was saying, she looked at me, tail still wagging.

"She's saying hi," Roark explained as he continued his prechecks.

I looked down at her as her mouth opened and her tongue came out like she was smiling. Then she put her head on my leg and just sat there. "Christ."

"Never had a dog?"

"We had a few canine units in the Teams." One, in particular, was exceptional. A Malinois named Husk. His handler worked for me now, but Husk was still in service.

"Not what I asked."

The brown-eyed dog stared at me expectantly. "No." I petted her, and her tail thumped twice.

Roark smirked. "I can tell."

"Is she going to sit here for the entire flight?"

"If I tell her to."

Footsteps sounded on the airstairs, and we both turned as Missy jumped up and moved in front of Roark.

Ghost stepped into the cabin at the same time ground control came over the radio.

"Gulfstream November three eleven Oscar, Teterboro ground, good morning. Taxi whiskey and Delta for runway two right."

Roark stared at Ghost. "I thought you were dead."

Ghost closed the hatch and secured it. "Then I must be doing something right."

"Gulfstream November three eleven Oscar, Teterboro ground, do you copy?"

Ghost lifted his chin at Roark before sinking into a seat. "Answer ground traffic control. I got us cleared for takeoff."

"I don't have a flight plan," Roark warned.

"I just filed it." Ghost buckled in.

"Where are we going?" I demanded.

Ghost met my warning gaze with one of his own. "Dubai."

SEVENTEEN

Quinn

SEVEN MEALS.

I'd been given food seven times by all three of Khalaf's bodyguards at timed intervals I couldn't keep track of because there were no windows, no clocks and the overhead light never turned off. One of the guards would walk in, dump food on the bed, take the previous tray and leave.

I'd been here forty-eight hours... maybe.

I couldn't tell, but I did know two things.

The tracking device in my passport wasn't working, or no one was coming, and I still had the diamond hanging from my bellybutton piercing.

Then there were the guards.

Fahad, always with one hand on this gun, never failed to call me a whore under his breath. Mardon kept a hand on his gun too when he came in, but instead of calling me names, he leered at me, at my slip. But Amir, the one I hadn't seen for four meals, he'd never touched his gun. And the last time I saw him, he'd whispered three words to me.

All is well.

Then he'd paused after setting the food on the bed, and he'd smiled at me.

Amir.

He was the one I was waiting for.

Because I had a plan.

I'd counted how many seconds it took for me to stand, reach for the top of the toilet and, without actually doing it, grasp the ceramic top and throw it with my one uncuffed arm, presumably with enough force to hit him in the head. If he went down, it was all the advantage I'd need.

I hoped.

I'd spent the last day and a half ripping at the hem of my single pillowcase, making a show of tearing it into strips and tying them together. Staring directly into one of the cameras, I wrapped the fabric under my chaffed wrist, around and around, to protect my flesh.

Then I'd waited.

No one came. Not one of the bodyguards, not Khalaf, not one of the other guards whose names I didn't know. At the next mealtime, the door opened, Fahad had walked in, shaken his head when he looked at my wrist, and called me a whore again as he dumped the food. Then he'd stupidly left me with my makeshift bandage.

A bandage that could double as a strangulation device... if I could get Amir to come back and hit him over the head hard enough to stun him. Then I'd strangle him and figure it out from there.

If Amir didn't come back, I was still counting the seconds on how long the other two guards took each time they brought me food. I didn't know how long they planned to keep me here, but I figured each hour that passed I became more of a liability. Or at least lost income potential.

I also hadn't been given any opportunity to bathe. My chained wrist barely allowed me to reach the toilet, and they couldn't keep me here forever if they wanted to sell a relatively undamaged product. Simple fact, the longer someone was kept in captivity with no sunlight, small portions of food and no exercise, their body and mind deteriorated. Make no mistake, Khalaf wasn't stupid. He was going to sell me.

I just needed to make a move before that happened.

If I could get one of the bodyguards down and get to his phone and his gun, I had a shot.

But if I was sold?

I didn't want to think about that. I couldn't. I knew about the potential for forced drug addiction, violence and unthinkable acts.

Compartmentalizing the fear and fighting down memories that were becoming harder to ignore the longer I was kept in this cell, I forced myself to get off the bed and drop to the tiled floor. Tucking my feet under the single-sized frame, I crossed my arms over my chest and started a set of fifty sit-ups.

Having to count, focusing on the bite of uncomfortable cold as each vertebra in my back hit the hard tile, I shoved down an image I didn't want to think about.

An image of piercing blue eyes and thick dark hair.

"Stop it," I bit out, counting the next sit-ups out loud. "Nine... Ten... Eleven..."

But the image, burned in my soul, didn't disappear. It only became stronger.

I forced my body to move faster, but then my mind played a trick on me, and suddenly I smelled a scent I never thought I would experience again.

Losing it, I stilled.

Then I stupidly inhaled.

The scent became stronger.

No. This wasn't real. This couldn't be real.

Forcing my body to keep moving, refusing to acknowledge that I might be crumbling, I heard the lock disengage.

My breathing too fast, my heart racing, adrenaline priming my veins, I shot to my feet. It was too soon for the next meal. Much too soon.

The door swung open and Fahad walked in, but this time, he didn't have a tray with him. Moving with purpose, he came right at me.

"What's happening?" I took a step back, putting myself closer to the toilet.

"Shower," he growled in English before switching to Arabic. "*You stink, whore.*" Switching back to English, he barked an order. "Give me your wrist."

I didn't have time to grab the lid off the back of the toilet. I couldn't undo my makeshift weapon from around my wrist fast enough, and there was no way I was going to overpower him handcuffed. Kneeing him in the balls, shoving my fingers into his eyes, punching the bottom of his nose with the heel of my palm—the self-defense moves ticked through my mind rapid-fire, but I knew none of them would net me results. Not with this bodyguard. His height, his strength, his weight, his aggression—I was no match for him, and apparently, he knew it.

Smirking, he held up a handcuff key. Then he lowered his face close to mine, and his putrid breath washed over me. "Go ahead," he taunted. "Try to escape."

Not giving him the satisfaction of showing any emotion, I held my wrist up.

He let loose with a sinister chuckle and unlocked the handcuff before grabbing my upper arm in a painful grasp. "This way."

I didn't walk.

I was dragged.

Out of the cell, down a short corridor and around three corners where the only open door in the hall was to a bathroom. This one with a shower, a tub, a double vanity, plush towels and toiletries neatly spread out like the hotel Khalaf had first brought me to. But better than all of that, there was a window.

A blessed window.

It was high up and narrow, but it was still a window and sunlight was pouring in, and I could definitely fit through it.

Fahad walked me into the bathroom and let go of my arm only to shove me toward the shower. "Clean," he grunted.

I turned toward him. "You can wait outside."

"No."

Forcing myself not to glance toward the window, I tried again. "I would like privacy, please."

He stared at me.

I feigned embarrassment. "I need to use the toilet."

"Use it." He didn't back up, he didn't take his eyes off me, and he didn't give me an ounce of privacy.

I went for another tactic, even though I knew it'd be useless. "I have to undress to shower, and I don't want you watching."

His hand went to his gun, but he didn't speak.

"Point taken," I muttered, giving him my back and whipping the slip over my head.

After two days, I wasn't going to choose modesty when the promise of a hot shower and shampoo were within arm's reach.

Stepping into the shower and turning the water on, I waited until the temperature was just shy of scalding, then I stood under the spray. For a whole minute, I just let the pressure of the water soothe my body while I tried not to think.

Then I got down to business because I suspected my time was limited. Soaping everything there was to soap and washing my hair with a rose-scented shampoo before using the same brand conditioner that was already in the shower, I didn't want to think about how many women had been exactly where I was now.

Shoving it all down, I rinsed the last of the conditioner out of my hair, and not a second later, a beefy arm was reaching into the shower to shut the water off.

Fahad threw a towel at me and tipped his chin toward the double sink vanity. To his credit, he didn't leer at my breasts like the other guard. He didn't even let his gaze wander down my body. Not knowing if that made me lucky or if I should be more alarmed, I took the towel and dried off quickly before wrapping it around me.

"Fix," he demanded, tipping his chin at the shit laid out on the counter.

If I hadn't been locked up for days, barely given enough food to survive, and hadn't had my arm cuffed so long there was no circulation, I would've turned and kicked him in the balls as I throat punched him. But my feet were wet, the floor was slippery, and the asshole still had his hand on his gun. I wouldn't even get my leg lifted for enough leverage before he'd have the barrel shoved against my forehead.

Glancing mournfully at the window, trying not to think about what was coming next, because in this moment there wasn't a damn thing I could do about it, I instead looked at the stuff on the counter—hair products, makeup, perfumes, all the exact same as the hotel—and something snapped.

Irrational, fucking angry, I spun on Fahad.

Immediately drawing his 9mm, he aimed at my head. "*Fix,*" he demanded again in warning.

"Fix what?" I demanded right back. "My hair? My makeup? *My body?*" I seethed. "So you can sell me to the highest bidder like I'm a piece of meat?" Every word out of my mouth was a mistake, but something deep had been triggered, and I couldn't stop myself. Dropping my towel, raising my voice to a perfect losing-it pitch, I threw my arms up. "Why don't you rape me, finish what you started? Give me more bruises, or are you not man enough?" I kicked out.

My foot made contact with his shin, his gun hit my temple, and he grabbed my arm before slamming me against the wall.

Khalaf calmly walked into the bathroom. "*Habibti,*" he

placated, nodding at his guard, his tone one hundred and eighty degrees different than the last time I saw him.

Fahad dropped my arm and his gun and stepped back, but he didn't leave.

Khalaf spared him a single glance as he issued an order in Arabic. "*Leave*."

Glaring at me, Fahad holstered his gun and walked out, slamming the door shut behind him.

"You should speak with him about his manners. He has a problem with slamming doors."

Khalaf studied me, but he didn't drop his eyes to roam over my nakedness. "It seems you both have a problem with your temper."

I didn't say anything. I silently fumed.

"I have to admit, American Quinn, I did not anticipate this sort of temper and disobedience from you when we were getting to know each other. I had thought you would be much more grateful for the gifts you were, and are, being given." His gaze drifted, and his expression turned rueful. "I must be losing my touch." His hand waved dismissively through the air. "No matter. I have found there are all kinds of men for all kinds of women."

"You're selling me," I accused, even though I already knew this, anticipated it, studied for it and, finally, planned for it. But I'd made mistakes.

"Did you think you were going to become one of my mistresses?" Khalaf chuckled before giving me a look that said I was naïve as hell. "One of my wives?"

Wives. Another piece of intel I'd missed, unless he was lying. Not that it mattered now. I had a choice—play the game or show my hand. I wanted to do the latter, but I had a job to do.

I played the game. "Do you love your wives?"

This time he smiled without reservation or show. "Such idealism."

Elegant in his prominence, his status and wealth evident in his dress and stature, he was a handsome and distinguished man. He was also malicious and evil. He didn't love anyone except himself, but I was stalling because I didn't have a plan.

No idea where I was, no clue how many other women were here—I didn't even know where I'd be transported to if I were sold. I couldn't just jump out that window in a towel and survive the desert. More importantly, I couldn't run, not after seeing a half dozen other cell doors lining the halls as I was dragged to this bathroom. Running wouldn't save any other women being held here, but if I had a gun and a cell phone, I could call in. It probably wouldn't save my life, but it could save the lives of other women.

I had to do something.

Khalaf stepped forward and grasped my chin. "Just so we are clear, no man loves the merchandise, but he especially will not tolerate disobedient merchandise."

Forcing myself to ignore his reprehensible comment, seeing his cell in the inside pocket of his open suit jacket, I aimed to get more time with him. "What if I said I wanted to stay with you?"

Suspicion drew his eyebrows together. "Do you think I need you?"

"No, but you made me promises." All of them purposely said in vague enough terms that they could've been misinterpreted by the receiver. "You said you would give me a good life. That I wouldn't need money or have to work. You said I would be taken care of." Subtly training me to be submissive, he was never offering me any of that.

He was grooming me.

Khalaf laughed before leaning forward and dropping his voice. "You are an orphan, American girl. Growing up with too many parents, but none of them yours," he said with condescension, regurgitating my lies. "What does your country call it? *Foster care.*" He spit the word out with disgust. "No relatives willing to take you in?" With a dismissive, disapproving sound, he dropped his hand and stood to his full height. "Of course anything I give you will be a good life compared to that, but only if you choose to follow the rules. If you don't?" He shook his head and tsked as if watching a misbehaving dog, but then he spoke in a calm, almost serene tone. "I will kill you myself. Slowly and painfully, until you beg to be as submissive as I instructed you to be, but of course, by then it will be much too late."

He dropped the composed pretense and issued a stern order. "Make yourself presentable. You took my hospitality, now it's time for you to pay it back, and you will behave. Guests are waiting, and I will not tolerate any further disobedience." He nodded toward the window. "And in case you're thinking of changing your mind, know that my guards will shoot you dead before the elements have a chance to take you."

Turning, he opened the door, stepped out and pulled it shut with purpose.

EIGHTEEN

Adam

"NO." MY JAW CLENCHED, MY NOSTRILS FLARED. "NO FUCKING way. There're a hundred ways this could go south."

"You want her out?" Ghost asked rhetorically. "Then this is how you're going to do it."

"I'm not doing this to her," I warned.

He gave me a barely perceptible shrug. "Sometimes you do the wrong thing for the right reasons."

Fuck. *Fuck*. "I'll bring my own team in." I could scramble resources I had in Europe, and they could meet us on the ground.

Ghost gave me his own warning. "You call in a team, I'm not making the introduction to the sheikh or telling you the location."

"Why the fuck not?"

"It's a big desert out there." He kept talking as if I hadn't asked the question. "By the time you find her, *if* you find her, she'll be moved." He gave me a pointed look. "Or sold."

"How the hell did this happen?" I asked for the third time.

"Again," Ghost repeated himself, "I can't tell you that."

"Can't or won't?" He was withholding intel, acting like he had a personal stake in this when I was the one who brought him in, and generally being a cagey fuck. It was pissing me off, and no part of this should've been a surprise. I knew what I was getting myself into when I went through the trouble of contacting him.

Drinking from a bottled water, he just stared at me.

"CIA?" I asked again uselessly. "What's their role in this?"

Ghost finished his water and capped the bottle. Then he ignored my question and gave me the same narrative he'd been giving me since we took off hours ago. "Like I said, you're going in as Hunt, wealthy suit with a proclivity for a certain type of woman. Don't pay the first number they give you or the second, and for fuck's sake, don't look at only one woman." His gaze cut into mine in warning. "Shop."

"I'm not fucking shopping sex-trafficked women."

This time his shrug was deliberate. "Heavily secured, multiple cameras in every room of that compound, they'll be watching you. Sample the women or don't, I don't give a shit. But know this." His hands clasped, he leaned forward. "If you don't handle the merchandise, that'll be a dead giveaway. It'll also be the last anyone ever sees or hears of Adam Hunt again."

I was a SEAL. "I've survived a hell of a lot worse than infiltrating some asshole sheikh's guarded compound. I'm not going to be taken down by sex traffickers in the middle of the Arabian Desert." Nor was I going to walk out of there without her, if I got in. Which was a big *if*, and one of the many flaws in Ghost's plan.

Ghost stared at me as if he was looking into my head. "This is bigger than you and one woman."

"If they have American hostages, then why the hell isn't Special Forces on this?" And why didn't I know about this specific sex trafficking ring? My company had taken down others. I had a high-level security clearance. This was the exact type of situation AES handled—getting hostages out of high-profile, nonmilitary situations in countries the United States didn't want to piss off.

Holding my gaze, Ghost didn't answer.

"The CIA must have actionable intel." They had to. The warning had come from them.

Leaning back in his seat, Ghost's expression didn't change, but his eyes narrowed. "You're invested."

It wasn't a critical observation. It was condemnation.

I didn't defend myself. "I'm getting her out." One way or another.

"Are you?" He didn't wait for a response, and he wouldn't have gotten one to that question. "Because no one else on this plane can do it. Not me, not MacElheran, and there's only one way to play it—as Hunt."

I wasn't buying into his bullshit, but I was at his mercy. "How is it that you're making the introduction to the sheikh but you can't step foot on his compound?"

"I didn't say I couldn't. I said I wasn't." A small smile played across his face. "Besides, no one wants to see a ghost." His expression sobered. "Understand that once you're in, you're on your own. No intel, no weapons, no comms, no cell phones. The sheikh'll move fast from meet to greet, and he'll expect you to as well. Any hesitation on your part is a giveaway. You'll need to play it up, be the part," he schooled as if I'd never done covert ops before.

"Tell me again why I'm not bringing a team in?"

"I didn't tell you why in the first place," he corrected. "I only told what would happen if you did."

Choosing my battles, I let that one slide and tried another tactic, even though I knew it was most likely futile. "How do you know she's there? Where exactly did your intel come from?"

"It doesn't matter where. It's concrete." Ghost continued to eye me.

"Goddamn it, Ghost. If you're not going to tell me shit else, then at least tell me how the hell was she taken in the first place. She works at a pharmaceutical company for fuck's sake. She's not on social media, she's not out partying. For three years, all she's done is go to work and company conferences." At least, that's what the intel Vance had gotten on her over the past few years revealed. Before that, all I'd found was once a year, for the first four years after Billy died, she withdrew a large sum from the bank account her father had set up for her. I figured she was in college somewhere, using an alias to avoid me.

Ghost stilled. "You've been keeping tabs on her?"

If I didn't know him, if I hadn't been a SEAL and gotten the same training as him, I wouldn't have picked up on the slight shift of his shoulders then utter stillness as he waited for my answer.

"Indirectly," I admitted, watching him like he was watching me.

"Three years?" he asked.

He'd fucking heard me, and whether this was a guilt trip or something else, I didn't give a shit. Yeah, I'd had Vance checking in on her periodically ever since he'd found her, but I also kept that note in my wallet, and I fucking read it, weekly, as a goddamn reminder. There was a lot of shit I'd done in my career and in the private sector—I wasn't a saint—but I hadn't personally breached her privacy. I'd done what she'd asked.

"You got something to say?" I challenged Ghost.

"You've been watching her three years, and you're asking me how she was taken?"

I glared at him.

"How does any woman get taken?" Ghost continued, saying it so damn casually that I was beginning to wonder if he really had gone off the grid or if he was working covert ops for an unsanctioned branch of the military or CIA that was above my security clearance.

Getting nowhere, I flipped the script. "Who's the sheikh?"

"Does it matter?"

If I wanted to go back and kill him after I got her out it did.

Reading my intent, Ghost sighed. "You're going to need to remain mission-focused. Get in, get out, bury Hunt, then stay away from that corner of the world for awhile."

"Or what?" This whole conversation was fucked. Hell, the entire situation was fucked.

I'd dealt with the need-to-know excuse my entire career. Being a SEAL wasn't about the politics of the situations, it was about the missions at hand. We were given jobs, and we did them. End of. Not asking questions, mainlining the adrenaline, every op was mission-critical and every move was based on tactics, techniques and training. Standard operating procedures were our lifeline, and familiarity with weapons was our mistress. Both were treated with reverence.

But this shit Ghost was spoon-feeding me now?

I wasn't onboard.

At all.

The woman I'd already destroyed once had her life hanging in the balance, and I wasn't fucking around with Ghost's need-to-know intel anymore.

As if reading I was at the end of my rope, Ghost didn't answer my question. He asked one of his own. "Are you willing to risk losing her permanently?"

Not bothering to answer his bullshit, I stood and went back to the cockpit.

Taking the second chair, I put the headset on as we approached for landing.

Roark's gaze hidden behind his aviators, he didn't glance my way as he spoke into the mic so only I could hear him. "Do I want to know?"

"Know what? How he hasn't changed or how fucked we are?"

Roark dished out his own brand of wisdom. "One is a given, the other is a variable."

Calculating all my possible moves, the only constant was that I needed more intel. "If this starts with the CIA and goes all the way to the top, how far do I stick my foot in it?" Because the more I thought about this, the more I became suspicious. About everything.

This time, Roark turned his head to look at me. "You're already neck deep."

NINETEEN

Quinn

MY HAIR WAS DRIED AND CURLED.

My eyes were smoky.

My lips were plumped, and my body was perfumed.

I couldn't stall anymore.

In only my towel, I turned toward Fahad who'd opened the bathroom door after Khalaf had left, stepped inside, closed the door behind him, then stood there. If I didn't hate him, I might've been impressed with his uncanny ability to remain statue still, staring into nothingness.

"Now what?" I demanded. "I *fixed* myself."

Without a word, he opened the door and walked out, going back the way we came.

This time, as we rounded the corners, I got a glimpse of the hallway in all directions.

My stomach bottomed out as I started counting the number of doors.

Six, eight, ten... .

Twelve doors to twelve rooms like mine.

Pressing his thumb to a fingerprint scanner, Fahad unlocked the door to the room he'd taken me from and unnecessarily shoved me in. "Dress," he muttered before slamming the door behind me.

The bright red dress on the bed stood out as much as the black stilettos on the floor next to it. They were the only spot of color in the room, but I wasn't thinking about that. I was looking at the shoes with a newfound hope.

Not even pissed that there wasn't any underwear, I picked the dress up and barely noticed the Valentino label before I slipped it over my head. Long and fitted, it fell to my lower calves and hugged every curve on its way down. The sleeves went to my elbows, and the scooped neckline was enough to have my girls falling out if I bent over, but I didn't care.

I sat on the bed and picked up the shoes.

Pretending to admire the red soles adorned with tiny red rhinestones in case someone was watching on the cameras, I turned them over in my hands several times.

Then I held them by the heel.

One hundred and twenty millimeters of a black, leather-wrapped weapon.

Thank you, Christian Louboutin.

TWENTY

Adam

Roark brought the Gulfstream down with a smooth landing as the sun was setting across the Arabian Desert. While he taxied across the apron of the private airport, I climbed out of the copilot's seat and headed down the aisle.

Ghost looked up from his phone. "Meet is confirmed. He's sending his driver. Remember, he has a strict no-cell-phone policy."

Grabbing one of the freshly pressed shirts I'd brought, I paused. "We'll use our own transport." This asshole's no-phone rule was one thing, but not having our own ride was another.

"Not how the sheikh works," Ghost answered, absently petting Missy as she sat next to him.

Goddamn it. "That's asking for trouble." I wasn't the best security contractor in the business because I took K&R risks.

"Trouble or not, that's how it's going down." Straightening the sleeves of the dress shirt he'd changed into before we'd landed, Ghost stood. "He's extending his hospitality." He grabbed his suit jacket.

Fucking great. Full-service sex traffickers. "You're walking us into a hornet's nest." At best. Having our own vehicle would ensure no explosive devices, our own tracking, and we'd have weapons. Roark could monitor our location from the plane.

"What's wrong, Alpha?" Ghost smiled as he slipped into his suit jacket. "Afraid of a little blind ops? All the high-tech equipment you've got at AES has you going soft?"

"This wasn't the deal," I warned, buttoning my own dress shirt and slipping on my suit jacket.

Grabbing sunglasses despite the setting sun, Ghost didn't back down from my intimidation. "None of this should've been *the deal*, but here we are." He glanced toward the cockpit as Roark parked the G650 in our spot for the night. "If Alpha's not back by oh-five-hundred, leave."

Roark slid his aviators off and glanced between us as he came out of the cockpit. "And you?" he asked, not challenging Ghost's bullshit. We both knew this was a two-pilot plane.

Ghost slapped him on the shoulder. "I'm moving on from here. Good to see you again." Daring to glance at Roark's left leg, his expression sobered. "Keep it real." His cell vibrated, and he looked down at it. "Our ride's here."

I caught Roark's gaze. "Refuel, resupply and get some rest but be at the ready. I don't know when I'll be back or what condition she'll be in."

"Understood," Roark replied as he opened the main passenger door, then stepped back.

Oppressive heat filled the cabin, and Ghost tossed the burner cell he'd been using on a seat before descending the airstairs.

I glanced one more time at Roark. "He's right. If I'm not back in twelve hours, get out of here. Call Vance, and he'll arrange for another pilot."

"Going in without backup or intel is—"

"I know." Fuck, I knew. "Whatever happens, I appreciate the help."

Roark stared at me a moment. Then he reached in his pocket and pulled out a set of keys.

I frowned as I glanced at them.

"The car key is a knife, the house key has a laced needle and the fob doubles as a tracking device." He quickly demonstrated how both keys pulled apart then handed the set over. "Better than nothing."

I pocketed them. "Do I want to know what's on the needle?"

"It's lethal," was all Roark admitted.

Christ. "Thanks."

Roark nodded once. "I'll be waiting."

"Remember what I said," I ordered.

Roark didn't comment as Ghost called for me. "Hunt, you ready?"

With one last glance at Roark and his dog who sat dutifully behind her master, I made my way down the airstairs to Ghost, who stood next to two bodyguards, one of which had a handheld metal detector.

Without introductions, the first guard patted me down while the other used the wand. When it beeped by my pocket, the guard made eye contact and lifted his chin.

I reached in my pocket and extracted the keys, but I didn't offer them over.

With barely a glance at them, the wand guard nodded at the other.

The second guard opened the rear passenger door to a tinted-out Escalade and ushered me inside. The cabin retrofitted to be like a limo, there were two bench seats facing each other. Ghost got in after me, and the guard shut the door.

"Floor," I murmured at Ghost, pointing out where a retractable safety screen was embedded in the space between the two bench seats.

"I see it," he replied under his breath. "Armored."

Which also probably meant this vehicle was equipped with a whole lot of extras like tracking, listening devices, filtration system in case of a bio attack, run-flats and, if I had to bet, firepower stowed throughout.

Both guards got in the front, and minutes later we were

speeding down an almost deserted highway covered with sand drifts. To the left and right, as far as the eye could see, it was sand, but ahead in the distance were the famous skyscrapers Dubai was known for.

No one spoke for the half-hour ride into Dubai proper, where the guard behind the wheel pulled up to the Burj Al Arab hotel. Glancing at us, he spoke in accented English. "Sheikh Khalaf Al Ka'abi is in his suite. Jasur will take you up."

I made a mental note of the sheikh's name as Ghost smiled and said thank you in Arabic. "*Shukran.*"

The driver nodded as the guard named Jasur got out and a valet opened the door on my side.

Jasur led us through an opulent lobby teeming with color to a bank of elevators and swiped a key before pushing the button for the top floor.

Seconds later, the door slid open to a penthouse suite, and two more guards stopped us. We repeated the same silent pat-down treatment, but this time there was no metal detector wand. Before the new guard had stood back up, a bearded man with a welcoming smile came around the corner.

Mother. *Fucker.*

It was the man from the market in Manhattan.

Reaching Ghost first, he grabbed his shoulder and spoke in perfect English. "My American friend with no name." Still holding his shoulder, he shook Ghost's hand. "So good to see you."

I wracked my brain, recounting every fucking second of that night two months ago. Had he looked up? Had he seen me?

Ghost smiled as he shook his hand. "I have a name."

"Yes, yes." The sheikh laughed. "An apparition. Perhaps you are simply hiding a common name you do not wish to divulge. John?" he asked in good humor. "Bob?"

Ghost chuckled. "Khalaf Al Ka'abi, this is my friend, Adam Hunt."

I held my hand out and greeted him in Arabic, praying like fuck my cover wasn't blown. "Mr. Al Ka'abi, *as-salam alaykum*."

He stared at me a beat too long, but then he nodded in approval. "*Wa'alaykum as-salam*." Not releasing my hand, his eyes narrowed. "Have we met? I never forget a face, and yours, Mr. Hunt, seems familiar."

I forced a polite smile. "We have not." If Maila was so much as bruised, this fucking prick was dead.

He released my hand. "I did not realize you speak Arabic. Your background check did not mention you have traveled to my country before. Perhaps you have been in the military?"

Not missing the fact that he admitted to checking out Hunt's identity, I lied. "I'm afraid nothing that exciting. My international businesses have taught me several greetings in different languages, but I would be hard-pressed to converse past a formal hello."

The sheikh laughed, but his dark eyes took in every inch of my face as if looking for a thread to unravel. "Please, remind me, what business are you in?"

"Many that keep me busy." I held the smile that was already wearing thin as I rattled off half a dozen shell corporations that I hoped to God had held up under his scrutiny. "From real estate to software development, I've been fortunate with my success."

"Ah, fortunate with wealth, but not in love?" He glanced at my left hand. "Perhaps you spend too much time with these corporations."

I stilled at his use of corporations and the way he said it but kept up the Hunt persona. "I'm a pragmatic man."

The sheikh eyed me for a full measure.

Ghost broke the tense beat of silence with one of his practiced chuckles. "Aren't we all pragmatic until that one particular woman comes along?"

Khalaf turned to Ghost with a smile. "Says the man who has named himself after an apparition."

This time, Ghost laughed outright, as if he knew this asshole personally and they were old friends. "You know my real name, Khalaf."

The sheikh winked. "I do." He gestured toward me before lowering his voice. "But I was not sure if he did."

Ghost dropped the smile and turned deadly serious. "Would he be here if he didn't?"

"You are vouching for him?" The sheikh's gaze narrowed. "With your life?"

Ghost didn't hesitate. "Always."

The sheikh's smile was wide. "Then let us proceed." Issuing orders in Arabic to his guards that had been standing back but not out of sight, Khalaf Al Ka'abi headed for the elevator.

Instantly the three men took up well-trained positions, and the six of us stepped into the elevator.

The guard Jasur pressed the button for the ground floor.

The doors closed, and Khalaf turned to Ghost. "How is the young wife I gave you?"

If it hadn't been for my military training and the years spent in this business, my expression wouldn't have remained locked as I glanced in shock at a man I thought I knew.

Ghost chuckled. "Not so young anymore."

Khalaf grinned as he gripped Ghost's shoulder. "Well, my friend, you are in luck." His smile turned sinister as the elevator doors opened to the lobby. "I happen to have just what you need. Come, we will discuss on the drive to my home."

"Unfortunately, this is where we part company today." Ghost smiled at Khalaf. "I have other business to attend to."

Khalaf's friendly attitude did a one-eighty. "I insist."

Ghost eyed Khalaf. "I'm not in the market for any merchandise right now."

"No merchandise for you, none for your friend," Khalaf countered.

Two of Khalaf's guards stepped out of the elevator first and scanned before they nodded back at us.

Khalaf eyed Ghost. "Make a decision."

Ghost stonewalled. "Not why I came here today."

"And this is not how I do business. You contact me, you are *in the market.*" Khalaf stood his ground. "All or nothing. Choose now."

Ghost slowly shook his head, but then he half laughed and clapped Khalaf's shoulder. "You better have something I want."

Khalaf smiled wide. "I know my customers. I will always have something you want." He walked off the elevator, and the third guard followed.

Ghost threw me a lethal glare before following Khalaf through the lobby to where there were now two waiting Escalades.

The guard Jasur got in the front passenger seat as the two guards from upstairs ushered Khalaf into the back, then motioned for Ghost to follow.

Ghost glanced at me, and I raised an eyebrow.

Holding my gaze for a split second, but not giving me a single fucking clue as to what the hell just happened, Ghost got in the SUV with Khalaf.

I moved to follow.

One of the guards from upstairs stopped me. "No." He pointed to the second SUV. "Get in."

TWENTY-ONE

Quinn

THE DOOR TO MY CELL OPENED, AND FAHAD BARELY TOOK ME IN before nodding toward the hallway. "Come."

Standing in the too-high heels, I casually glanced at his ever-present hand on his 9mm before walking toward him with a practiced grace that had taken me weeks to perfect. Stopping just short of the door he was holding open, I looked him in the eye. "Where?"

His nostrils flared and his jaw clenched as if in insulted anger. "No eye contact. No speaking. You break either rule, I shoot you. Understand?"

I understood it was the most words he'd ever strung together in my presence, and I understood his eye twitch when he'd said *shoot*. He'd love to shoot me. Not fuck me, not make me perform lewd acts, just shoot me.

He hated me.

He hated what I represented.

He hated this part of his job.

Interesting.

"I understand."

"Move," he growled.

Mentally filing away my observations, I did exactly what he said.

I moved.

Stepping out of the cell, I'd barely crossed the threshold when a burst of chilled air from the hall hit me in the face, and suddenly I smelled it.

Cold wind and sharp angles.

My body's reaction was instant.

My knees buckled, and my legs started to give out.

No.

This couldn't be.

Fahad's hand roughly gripped my upper arm, and he yanked me upright. "I said, *move.*"

Desperate, I inhaled deep, but the scent of my past was already gone, replaced by Fahad's sweat and anger.

Propelling me down the corridor in the opposite direction of the bathroom, Fahad's boots barely made a sound, but my heels clicked on the white marble floors like a time clock rapidly ticking down.

Forcing myself not to think about my past and focus on the present, I catalogued every turn he took and how many steps we'd made before he stopped at an innocuous door and pressed his thumb on a fingerprint scanner on the wall. The door clicked, he pushed it open and suddenly we were in a different world.

Red oriental carpets, tall ceilings, ornate chandeliers, marble floors, walls and columns, priceless paintings and a sweeping, curved staircase—it was a grand entrance for a palace that was built to impress. A palace that could easily host a party of fifty in the foyer alone.

Except there wasn't a single other person in sight.

Before I could study the paintings, let alone catch a glimpse of the setting sun out of the tall but narrow windows on either side of a ten-foot, solid wood front door, Fahad was propelling me across carpets too pretty to walk on.

Aiming us toward the opposite side of the grand entrance, he stopped just short of plowing us into the wall before he utilized another fingerprint scanner.

I quickly glanced around at the six sets of closed double doors as a hidden door popped open with a click.

Fahad ushered me inside, and I almost tripped in shock.

Lined up on a narrow, carpeted platform that was one step up off the ground were eleven other women. All in fitted dresses, all with their gazes downcast, every one of them faced forward.

Mute silence that was so deafening it made my ears ring tunneled through the dimly lit space. I could smell the fear radiating from the platform that was positioned perpendicular to the door we'd just come in.

As Fahad began to walk me down the length of the platform, I forgot his earlier warning and looked up at the first woman we passed.

Before I could blink, Fahad drew his gun, spun me away from the other women and pressed the barrel point-blank between my eyes.

"*What* did I say?" he spit out with barely contained rage.

"No eye contact, no speaking," I answered, breaking his precious fucking rules. "If I disobey either, you shoot me." But the asshole was a liar. My glare cut from him to the middle of the giant one-way mirror behind him.

He wasn't going to shoot me.

He wasn't even going to hurt me.

The second I'd looked down the line of women, I'd known I was the grand prize of this shit show.

Daring to glance from left to right across the entire length of the mirror before I stepped back from the 9mm shoved against my head, I turned.

Then I walked down the line of women, all in white dresses, and I stepped onto the platform.

TWENTY-TWO

Adam

MY HEART FUCKING STOPPED.

Blonde hair, green eyes, red dress, sky-high heels—seven years disappeared, and I was staring at my past as a twelfth woman was escorted into the viewing room.

Before my gaze could cut from the telltale bruising on her left wrist to her right, the guard dragging her by the arm lost his shit. Spinning Maila to face the mirror, his back to us, he pressed his 9mm into her forehead as his voice carried through hidden speakers. "*What* did I say?"

The only woman I'd ever loved straightened her spine and spoke without an ounce of fear. "No eye contact, no speaking. If I disobey either, you shoot me."

I moved to step forward.

Ghost chuckled as he stopped me with a hand on my arm. "You've got a live wire on your hands this go around, Khalaf."

The fucking guard touching her was a dead man.

The sheikh frowned. "I only deliver the highest quality—"

"No one can be one hundred percent, one hundred percent of the time." Ghost pointed at a too-thin girl who looked barely sixteen. One of the first ones brought in. "That one." He turned toward the double doors of the extravagant sitting area we'd been ushered into after a forty-five minute ride through nothing but desert.

Then we'd been told to wait while Khalaf came and went

and his parade of guards took their damn time bringing women, one by one, into a room on the other side of a wall of one-way glass. Each woman, ushered or dragged in, was then made to stand there, head down, without speaking or moving. The whole fucking appalling process took almost two hours, and I was ready to kill every sick fuck in this place. I also wanted to ask Ghost about the comment Khalaf had made in the elevator, but not once had we been left unattended in the *viewing room*, as Khalaf had called it.

Ghost stopped at a table by the door that had a tablet sitting on it. "Have one of your guards bring her to the SUV. He can drive us back to the hotel and pick up your next client." He tapped on the screen. "Wiring the transfer now." Ghost tipped his chin at me before glancing at Khalaf. "Always a pleasure." He walked out of the room.

I was going to fucking throttle Ghost the next time I saw him, if I ever saw him again, but he gave two important pieces of information. Khalaf had more clients lined up to buy these women, and I had an hour and a half, max, to get the fuck out of here with her before anyone else showed. After I got her to the plane and we were wheels up, I was sending in one of my teams to grab the women, then take down every sick fuck in this place.

"Why is only one in a red dress?" I demanded of Khalaf.

Khalaf nodded at one of his guards. The guard touched the comm in his ear and spoke too low for me to hear. The guard who was in the room with the women grabbed the young girl Ghost had pointed at, then using a thumbprint scanner on the wall to unlock the door, he dragged her out of the room.

"Escort our friend and his new purchase," Khalaf ordered the guard he'd nodded at before turning his attention to me with a disingenuous smile. "Since you are unfamiliar with the way I do business, Mr. Hunt, let me explain." Dropping the smile, he surveyed the women, who all looked scared as hell. "I deal with a particular client set, and let's just say my clientele prefer a certain type of commodity." He looked pointedly at me. "One that is both submissive and untouched." Looking back at the one-way glass, he zeroed in on Maila. "However, I occasionally come across something that while perhaps isn't both of those things, it is no less delightful." He waved a hand dismissively through the air. "Thus the red dress to differentiate the difference in product, but you do not need to concern yourself with that. I guarantee all of my products and will provide photographic proof should you request it. However, in the unlikely event you are unsatisfied for any reason, you can return your purchase within a reasonable timeframe." His gaze cut to mine again. "In its original condition, of course."

The guard who'd held a gun to Maila came back into the room.

Khalaf smiled wide again as he clapped his hands once. "Now, please tell me, do you see anything that you like, Mr. Hunt?"

My expression locked, my hand itching for a gun I didn't have, I held Khalaf's gaze for a beat too long as I envisioned a bullet sinking into his skull exactly where his guard had held a gun to Maila's forehead.

Without looking back at the women, I spoke. "The two blondes."

"Two." Khalaf paused a fraction of a second before he laughed. "Wonderful. I will have one of my men give you the account number and amount to transfer the funds too." Subtle enough that anyone else except his guards would have missed it, he tapped two fingers against his leg twice in rapid succession as if it were a nervous tic.

It wasn't.

It was a warning to his guards.

As one of his guards casually reached inside his jacket, I clarified. "I'm not purchasing both. I want to meet each one."

Khalaf raised an eyebrow as he tapped the same two fingers

once. "My apologies, Mr. Hunt, I misunderstood, and of course. We always allow our clients to inspect the product. As previously discussed, the purchase price for any single product is five million US dollars. Please be aware that if you damage the product in any way upon inspection, that you will be purchasing said product."

"Three million for the blonde in the red dress, four million for the one in white. Depending on my preference after I meet them, I'll let you know if I decide to purchase either one."

For five seconds, the asshole Khalaf stared at me. "I think perhaps you misunderstood our earlier discussion. I am not a cartel trafficker plucking disposable women off the streets from drug-infested brothels. My quality products are carefully vetted, culled and trained. The price for each is five million."

"It wasn't a discussion," I corrected. "I heard your inflated price tag, and I'm willing to pay the numbers I offered, nothing more. I can get my own *quality* women for a fraction of the price you're offering, and I don't need to fly halfway around the world to do it."

Anger colored Khalaf's face, but he didn't tap his fingers against his leg. "My product is superior in every way to anything you could acquire on your own. My women are untraceable, come with extensive conditioning, etiquette, submissiveness, and an eagerness to please. Every one of them has a personal guarantee from me that they will outperform your expectations. I do not take the time to train my product to be the best so that I can sell at a value far less than what they are worth."

Remembering Ghost's warning, but more importantly, having dealt with too many criminals over the course of my career, I knew the game and I knew it well. "Then we're done here. You can have your driver take me back to the airport." I turned toward the doors.

I didn't make two paces.

"Wait," Khalaf ordered.

I glanced over my shoulder.

He gestured with his hands. "Fine. If you choose, you may have the product in red for three million, but I will not go lower than four-point-five million for the other."

I turned and looked back at the women who were all still standing with their heads down. All but one. Green eyes firing daggers, Maila Marie Nilsen glared at the one-way glass.

Forcing myself not to stare at her and her alone, I slowly walked the length of the window and took in each woman, but nothing could dispel the draw I had to the only woman I'd ever felt connected to. Since the moment my sixteen-year-old self had laid eyes on her, I'd thought of her as mine. I'd wanted to protect her how no one had ever protected me.

The fucking irony had been that I'd walked into her house underfed, underdressed and about three years past all fucking hope. Then she'd smiled at me like I was the goddamn center of her universe.

I turned toward Khalaf. "Fine. Terms accepted. I'll meet the one in white first." Because the second Maila saw me, this game and my cover were going up in flames. I'd have one fucking shot to get her out of here, but in order to do that, I needed props.

"Excellent," Khalaf replied, nodding at a guard who then spoke into his comm. "I will have them taken to their rooms, and you may have fifteen minutes with each of them to inspect them and do as you please, except any form of vaginal penetration of the merchandise." He smiled. "That will have to wait until after you've purchased the product."

The fucking bastard was as sick as he was rich. "I don't need fifteen minutes." I needed a goddamn miracle. "I want two blindfolds, two forms of restraint, and I'll spend five minutes with each woman." I hated what I was about to do, but I hated Khalaf more, and I was fucking channeling that.

Without missing a beat, as if this was a common request,

Khalaf nodded at the same guard, and he left the room. Then Khalaf turned toward the glass and watched for a moment as the guard inside with the women grabbed both Maila and the other blonde before dragging them toward the exit.

When there were only nine women left standing, Khalaf turned toward me. "I must admit, Mr. Hunt, I had my doubts about you. Our mutual friend never mentioned you in passing before."

I took a calculated risk. "That's because Ghost isn't my friend."

His short, quiet laugh laced with irony, he shook his head. "Mine either." His expression sobered, and he looked almost normal. "But then again, Ghost doesn't have any friends, does he?"

I didn't answer. I waited. For his guard to come back, for whatever bullshit Khalaf was going to say next.

Khalaf rubbed a hand across his beard. "In my culture, women are very different than where you come from. That is why you are here, no?"

This piece of shit needed to be taken down. I didn't answer his fucked-up question. "The woman in red spoke with an American accent."

Khalaf smiled. "That she did, but I can assure you she has been well informed in all of the ways that are customary for how a woman should behave. She may have had a minor outburst today, but that is only because she has been neglected for a few days. I can guarantee that with a strong hand, which you seem to be prepared for, she will submit easily."

Instinct prickled at my consciousness, the same instinct that'd been building since I'd traced that text. Ignoring it for now, I maintained my cover. "I don't need a woman to easily submit. I can train them to my own standards."

His laugh was louder this time as if being a criminally, morally corrupt, sick bastard was the key to happiness. "I have no doubt of that, Mr. Hunt."

Wanting him to let his guard down further, I took another calculated risk. "Adam."

His head dipped once in respect. "Perhaps, unlike our mutual acquaintance, we will be good friends, Adam. Maybe you can regale me with the benefits of a G650." He clapped my shoulder. "And please, call me Khalaf."

I refrained from breaking his arm and nodded once as his guard came back.

"Ah, here we are. Thank you, Amir." Khalaf took the items from him and handed them to me. "*Ma'a as-salam*, Adam. Amir will show you where to go."

"*Ma'a as-salam.*" I shoved two strips of white silk and two zip ties into my pocket and followed his guard out of the room.

TWENTY-THREE

Quinn

The asshole Fahad dragged me and the only other blonde woman out of the room and back across the huge foyer. The other woman, trembling and quietly whimpering, tripped.

I reached for her, but she jerked back from my touch as if in fear.

"Slow down." I glared at Fahad. "You almost made her fall."

Instead of turning on me like I expected him to, Fahad grabbed the other woman by her hair. Yanking her head back, he jammed the barrel of his gun under her chin. "Speak again," he taunted me.

Fuming, I glanced at the woman to try to catch her attention, but her eyes were squeezed shut. She was also shaking so bad, I didn't know how she was keeping upright other than the fact that Fahad had a relentless grip on her hair.

Keeping my mouth shut, I looked back at Fahad.

He held my gaze, and for a second, I honestly wasn't sure if he was going to pull the trigger. I'd long since stopping caring if I lived or died, but I'd seen the look in the other woman's eyes before she'd closed them. Fear wasn't a reaction when you thought you had nothing left to lose. She still cared about her life, a lot, and I didn't want to be responsible for her death.

So I turned and walked toward the small fingerprint scanner

on the wall next to the door we'd used to get into the entryway and waited.

No shots rang out behind me, and a moment later, Fahad reached past me and pressed his thumb to the scanner.

The door clicked open, and he unnecessarily shoved me forward using the barrel of his gun on my back. Still gripping the other woman's hair, he yanked her through the doorway, and she whimpered in pain.

Faster than I could blink, Fahad released her hair and slapped her. "Did I give you permission to make a noise?"

The woman's hands flew to her mouth to stop her gasp of pain as tears sprung and dripped down her made-up face. She violently shook her head.

Fahad's glare cut to me, but he held his gun on the other woman. "Walk," he barked as the door shut behind him, locking us in the halls of our white prison once again.

Vowing that I was going to make him pay for what he'd just done, I walked.

Reversing the route we'd taken before, my heels clicking in a purposeful gait, the other woman's half clicking, half sounding like she was being dragged, I walked in silence all the way back to my cell.

Still holding the other woman hostage, Fahad pressed his thumb to the scanner and opened my door. But then he caught me off guard.

Letting go of the other woman, he rushed me. I barely had a split second to take in her sinking form as she slid to the floor before Fahad slammed his fist into my stomach.

Bile rose a fraction before the pain hit and I doubled over.

Before I could fall to my knees, he gripped my hair how he'd gripped hers and he yanked me up.

The sudden extending of my poor stomach muscles made me cry out in pain.

The asshole jammed his gun against my temple. "You stand. You wait. You do *not* move." His gun left my head only to aim at the crumpled heap in the hall. "You move, she dies."

If anger had a taste, it was bile.

The asshole shook me by my hair. "*Understand?*" he bellowed.

My stomach in such agony I feared internal bleeding, it was still on the tip of my tongue to ask the piece of shit if I could speak to respond. But the woman in the hall chose that exact moment to look at me through tears.

I nodded.

Sweat and a stench I could only describe as evil emanated from Fahad as he kept his grip on me for a moment longer to make his point.

Then, retreating backwards from the room, his aim on the other woman, he tipped his chin toward one of the cameras in the corner of the room as he pulled a cell phone out.

He didn't need to make a show out of what was on the screen he brought up with two swipes of his thumb. But he did. With sick excitement in his eyes, he turned the phone around and showed me my own damn image, red dress, useless heels and all.

With the first smile I'd ever seen him make, he made a final step back. "One move, she's dead."

He slammed my cell door shut.

TWENTY-FOUR

Adam

I FOLLOWED THE GUARD ACROSS THE OVERSIZED FOYER AS HE STOPPED at the opposite wall and used a fingerprint scanner to open a concealed door.

Pushing the door open, he moved aside for me to enter.

Stepping into a bright white, empty hallway that went in three directions, I glanced at rows of doors with fingerprint scanners.

Tamping down rage, I changed my mind. "Take me to the woman in red first." Fuck Ghost's warnings and fuck this.

The guard nodded without comment and walked to the left. After two turns, he stopped at a door that had another fingerprint scanner and pressed his thumb to it.

The door unlocked, and just like before, he pushed it open, but he didn't walk in.

I had two choices.

Show my face and hope the same girl in pigtails who'd grown up with a vice admiral as a father would know not to show surprise at seeing me, or I could send the guard in and let him blindfold her. The latter option was exactly why I'd asked for the blindfolds in the first place.

Adrenaline pumping, my senses on overdrive, I locked my expression. Then I made my decision.

I stepped into the room.

With tears running down her face, the blonde in the white dress gasped and stumbled back.

I fucking pivoted.

Grabbing the guard's holstered weapon and shoving him against the wall, I pressed my arm over his throat and clicked the safety off.

I aimed point-blank at his dick. "Do you speak English?"

The color drained from his face. "Yes."

"What did I instruct you to do?" I calmly asked, pressing the gun harder.

"Take you to the woman in red first," he answered, his English nearly perfect.

"Then why didn't you?" What the fuck kind of game was he playing at?

"I... I thought..." He glanced down as I angled the barrel exactly where a point-blank bullet would do the most damage.

"You thought what?" I pressed my arm harder against his throat. "That I wouldn't notice? That your boss told you to do the opposite of what I asked? That you thought you would take it upon yourself to do as you pleased? Is that how you show your respect to the sheikh?" I wanted to kill every asshole in this place.

Anger flared and he turned indignant. "I never disobey him. I will take you to her now if you please."

Stepping back, I released his neck, but not his gun. Shoving the 9mm in my back waistband, I barked out at an order. "Wait."

"My gun," he countered.

Ignoring him, I strode into the room and took in every fucking sterilized corner and mounted camera without moving my head. My gaze on the woman cowering on the bed with her knees up, I didn't stop until I was hovering over her.

Purposely not softening my tone in case the cameras had audio, I asked what I needed to. "Are you injured?"

Her blue eyes wide and frightened, she shook her head.

"Speak," I demanded.

"No," she whispered.

"Stand up," I ordered, hating that I was playing this goddamn part instead of getting every one of these women out of here.

Hesitant but compliant, she got to her feet, but then she hovered next to the bed.

"Move," I ordered. "Middle of the room."

Glancing at the still open door and the guard standing there, she dropped her gaze and did as she was told.

Like a fucking piranha, I circled her.

When I was behind her, I lowered my voice. "Why are you here?"

Her slight frame shaking with fear, her left wrist bruised, her face red on one side like she'd recently been slapped, she apologized. "S-sorry, sir?"

I glanced toward the door.

The guard, watching me with intent, didn't even blink at her fear as he listened to my every word.

"Why are you here?" I asked again, louder this time.

She looked up. "For you?"

"On your knees," I ordered, playing the fucking part.

She dropped.

I circled her again as if I were inspecting the merchandise.

Then I put myself between her and the guard, grabbed a handful of her hair and leaned down to her ear. I dropped my voice. "Do not speak, do not look at the guard. If you are here willingly, nod once." Releasing her, I straightened.

Her eyes wide, her lips pressed together, she stared straight ahead.

Her stillness all I needed to know, I walked out of the cell.

The guard closed her door behind me.

"Too weak. Take me to the other one." Noting the cameras in the hall, I held his gun out to him.

He reached for the 9mm.

When I didn't let go, he looked up at me with fear and anger.

"If I take your piece again, you won't get it back." I let go.

Shoving his gun in his holster without comment, he turned and walked down the hall.

I followed.

TWENTY-FIVE

Quinn

I HEARD THE LOCK CLICK OPEN.

My heart pounding, my nerves on edge, I stared right at the door and waited.

But when the heavy metal swung open, it wasn't the asshole Fahad or some dick who'd probably been in the room on the other side of the glass who appeared.

It was another guard. One I knew.

"Amir," I stated. "Where's the other girl?"

For a moment he paused, as if I'd taken him by surprise, then he issued an order. "Turn around."

"I was told not to move."

Amir frowned. "By who?"

"Fahad." I refrained from calling him an asshole just in case Fahad was listening. "He told me if I moved, he would kill her."

With an ounce of humanity I didn't know he had, Amir inhaled and shook his head slightly. "She is fine. Turn around. This is not a request."

Fucking great. "Why?"

"Turn," he barked.

I turned, but slowly.

Stepping behind me, Amir slipped a band of silk over my eyes. His voice dropping to a whisper, he tied the material tight. "Please, behave."

"Why?" I whispered back.

"You are about to have company." He raised his voice to a normal pitch and issued another stern order. "Hands. Behind your back."

Seriously? "Afraid I won't behave?"

"Quinn," he chastised.

Damn it. "Fine." I couldn't use my heels if my hands were tied, but I did what Amir said because another strip of silk was nothing. I could get out of that easily.

Except it wasn't silk he secured around my wrists.

The bite of thin plastic cut into my flesh and smarted around my left wrist as the sound of the zip tie being tightened practically echoed off cold, white walls.

Fucking perfect. "Is this really necessary?"

A warm hand covered my shoulder, and Amir whispered again. "You did not used to be this challenging. What happened to the conciliatory beauty we met in London?"

I was never conciliatory. I was just very good at lying. "She got locked up in a cell then paraded like the day's fresh catch on a makeshift stage." But now I was done. Screw Khalaf and his threat. Screw Fahad, screw all of them. Hoping they were listening to every word through the cameras, I raised my voice. "Tell Khalaf he lied." Even though I couldn't see Amir past my blindfold, I looked over my shoulder in his direction anyway. "This is *not* how you treat a mistress."

In my ire, not paying attention to the abrupt change in air molecules or the loss of Amir's cheap cologne scent, I didn't notice the sudden shift in the atmosphere until it was too late.

Deep and resonant, a voice hovered over my right ear. "Mistress?"

All of the air was sucked out of the room with one single word.

A single word spoken by a voice that sounded so familiar, my heart leapt and chill bumps raced across my skin.

Every muscle in my body went fear-induced still.

He spoke again. "Quinn, is it?"

A voice that was so ingrained in my memories, it had to be my mind playing tricks on me ruptured from the past and exploded into the impossible present. This wasn't real. It couldn't be. But then the whisper of the expensive fabric of a fine wool suit flooded my hearing a split second before a scent I couldn't deny floated down around me in a living, breathing nightmare.

Cold wind and sharp angles.

No.

No.

This was impossible.

My head spun, and my equilibrium distorted.

This wasn't possible.

My pulse erratic, my hands suddenly shaking, my breath short, I turned. Then I pushed a demand past my suddenly dry lips. "Speak."

"What shall I say?" he asked smoothly.

I listened. I digested. I analyzed.

Formal but not mocking, inquisitive, deep… Deep like a bottomless lake at the top of an isolated mountain where the water was so cold, you could feel it without touching it.

I knew that deep.

But I didn't. I couldn't. Not here. Not now.

"I…." Swallowing past the disbelief in my throat, I tried again. "I think you should start by telling me why you're here."

Air shifted, his scent swirled and his voice landed on my opposite shoulder. "Maybe I should whisper words of seduction in your ear." My hair was brushed off my shoulder before his intoxicating breath touched my neck. "Watch what happens to the color of your skin… here." A rough finger glanced across my cheek. "And here." The larger pad of a thumb drew down with intention between my breasts.

Every second of the past two months stilled.

Fear dissipated.

Disbelief evaporated.

My flesh heated, and God help me, moisture pooled between my legs.

I was lost.

Lost and alone with a faceless man.

The power emanating off him was as thick as the desire burning through my traitorous body. He moved again, and hard heat covered my back. "Or maybe I should take what I want." A large hand brushed over my shoulder before strong fingers coasted down my back and over my hip. "What do you think?"

I didn't think. I was losing my mind.

It was the only excuse for what I said next. "Do it."

Hot breath that was drowning in dominance and laced with mint landed on the exposed skin of my nape. "Do what, exactly?" he asked, a smile coloring his words.

I shivered.

"Mm." His low moan was all throat and dark desire. "I like this reaction from you, beautiful."

"I...." My throat suddenly dry, I swallowed and tried again. "I didn't react." My voice not my own, the lie coated my tongue in bitterness.

"No," he whispered, his fingers snaking across my nape before tangling in my hair. "You didn't." Wrapping strands around his hand, he gripped. "But your body did. Betraying you, didn't she?"

I didn't answer. I couldn't.

Pulling my head back by his grip in my hair with a calculated slowness intended to drive me to insanity, he dripped words onto my throat like thick honey. "Your skin is flushed, your pulse is racing, and if I had to bet, you feel an emptiness between those luscious legs of yours right now."

Oh God. This wasn't happening.

"Go ahead." Dominance lacing his every word, he pushed. "Tell me I'm right."

"No," I panted like a wanton mess. "You're wrong."

Giving my hair a final sharp tug, my neck arched all the way back until he had me fully exposed. "Am I?" Hot lips touched my heated flesh with a single teasing kiss.

Involuntary, reactionary and completely at his mercy, I groaned.

"Would you like more of me being wrong?" he asked in cruel joke of fate.

Desperate, beyond reason, and out of my mind, there was only one response. "Please."

"Impeccable," he murmured a moment before his mouth pressed an open kiss to the side of my neck just below my jaw. "Manners suit you."

I didn't have time to tell him I had no manners.

His tongue swirled with exquisite skill, and my previous shiver felt like mere child's play. A full body flush rolled through my tight muscles, making my limbs tremble like a magnitude seven shaking the earth.

Telling myself it was the blindfold heightening my senses, justifying his scent as only a reminder of my past, I reasoned the exact current of his voice was only my treacherous imagination. This man would turn any woman into the pliant traitor my body had become.

Forcing myself to focus on why he was here, why *I* was here, I saved my best lie for last. "You can't seduce me."

"Can't I?"

I parted my lips to commit perjury, but his hot mouth covered mine.

TWENTY-SIX

Adam

I DIDN'T GIVE A FUCK ABOUT WHAT GHOST HAD SAID.

I didn't give a damn about the guard in the hall.

I wasn't even thinking about the cameras.

Her cheeks had flushed, and her throat had vibrated with a moan under my mouth, and I was taking what was mine.

What should've been mine seven years ago.

I slanted my mouth over hers and sank my tongue into utter madness.

Before I could claim her with a single stroke, the cold steel of a barrel hit my temple. "Khalaf wants a word."

Releasing her mouth but not her, I ground out a response instead of wiping the fucking floor with the asshole's face. "Tell Mr. Al Ka'abi the next time one of his guards pulls a gun on me, it'll be the last."

"How about you tell him yourself, *Mr. Hunt.*"

Fuck.

Fuck.

I'd been made.

The barrel pressed harder into my temple. "Now."

Tilting her head back up, I reluctantly released all of her.

Then I turned.

Holding a cell phone to his ear with one hand, the guard she'd called Amir made his first mistake. He stepped back to aim at my forehead. Saying something in Arabic, he then held the phone out.

"*Mr. Hunt*, I told you I never forget a face." Khalaf's voice carried through the phone's speaker. "It seems we have much to discuss. Follow Amir and the woman won't be harmed." He hung up.

Meeting a dead man's eyes, I gave fair warning. "What did I tell you?"

"I don't listen to liars." Pocketing his phone, he made his second mistake. He waved his gun toward the exit. "Let's go. Your business here is done."

My body still, my stare intent, muscle memory from years of training putting me squarely where I needed to be, I moved.

Grabbing the wrist of the hand that held the gun, I shoved up at the same time my knee made direct contact with his groin. Before he'd bent fully at the waist from the first blow, my next two hits made solid contact with first his jaw, then the back of his skull.

I grabbed his gun as he dropped to the floor unconscious, his skull bouncing off the marble.

Reaching for Roark's keys in my pocket, I unsheathed the hidden knife on the car key and sliced through the zip tie on her wrists.

She spun toward me as she reached for the cloth over her eyes.

I bit out a warning. "You remove that blindfold, and I will take you over my knee."

Her hands at her face, she froze. "What happened to the asshole guard?"

Filing away her response and the fact that she didn't mention Khalaf's warning or ask who I was, I stuck my head out of the open cell door just enough to glance up and down the still empty corridor. "He's taking a nap." I checked the magazine of the gun. Full. "Cover your ears."

She didn't hesitate.

Four consecutive shots and I took out the video cameras in the cell and the one in the hall. As the distinctive smell of gunpowder filled the room, broken glass and plastic littered the floor.

I took her arm. "Time to move."

"Like this?" she challenged. "You're going to steal me away blindfolded?"

I didn't have time to appreciate the sarcasm and fight still left in her tone. "Yes. Keep it on." My intent was twofold. I didn't want her to be able to identify any more of the asshole guards that would be on us any second, and I didn't want her to see me. Not yet. "Let's go."

She resisted my pull. "Maybe I want to take my chances with the other guards."

Anger I didn't have time for flared. "You want to kiss them too?"

Heat flamed her cheeks under the white silk. "No. But this would be a lot easier if I could see where I was supposed to be walking to."

The distant sound of voices arguing filtered down the corridor. "We're not walking. We're running. On my go."

Her head lifted as if she heard the voices too. "We can't outrun them. They outnumber us, and it's a closed corridor hallway. There's no way out except a ceiling-height window in a bathroom around three turns."

Fuck. "Which direction?" The distinctive sound of a lock releasing sounded down the corridor.

"Left," she answered confidently. "Three left turns."

Exactly toward the sound of the opening lock. "We're going right. On my go, run straight and don't stop. If I give a directive, follow it." Her arm in my grasp, I aimed us out of the cell and pointed her in the right direction. "*Now.*" I let go of her.

Like a bird in flight, she took off.

TWENTY-SEVEN

Quinn

PICKING MY DRESS UP, I RAN.

Blindly.

Following his deep-voiced commands like a bitch in heat because he'd kissed me better than any man I'd ever kissed, I fucking ran for my life.

And thought about that kiss.

Jarring, inflaming, mind-altering… familiar.

Familiar like a ghost.

My thoughts spinning, my legs pumping, I stupidly didn't take the blindfold off because I was a coward.

I didn't want to see the man behind the kiss.

I didn't want to see that there weren't piercing blue eyes and a face I'd known better than my own seven years ago. I didn't even want to think about that face, but this was where my mind was when I should've been focused on the fact that no matter how many guards the mystery man could take down with the remaining bullets in his clip, we were most likely in the middle of the Arabian Desert and no amount of firepower could save us from the midday sun.

My heels rapidly clicking, his steps on my tail, I prayed he had a car if we got past this labyrinth of white halls.

Before I could ask, he issued a command like a military-trained operative who expected his orders to be followed. "Right turn in two paces."

One, two, I turned.

"Stop," he barked.

His huge hand wrapped around my upper arm again, but this time, my back hit a wall and his body pressed into mine.

His masculine scent now laced with heated musk made me want to reach for him as I felt his muscles move and his right arm stretch away from his body.

He was aiming.

"That's a bad idea," I whispered, trying to catch my breath both from running and the pressure of his chest and thighs caging me in like his only purpose was to protect me.

"Which part?" he whispered back, his minty breath touching my lips and reminding me of his kiss. "Running with you or stopping now?"

Either. Neither. Both. "There are too many of them, and you don't have enough bullets."

Arguing voices and running footsteps filled the other end of the corridor. I tried to count the number of distinctive sets but couldn't. Distracted by the man pushed into me who was at least a head taller even while I wore five-inch heels, I kept my hands fisting the hem of my dress to stop myself from grabbing on to him.

"What makes you think I need a bullet for every headcount?" he asked in a calm, hushed tone as if we weren't about to die.

Doors opened and slammed shut as the arguing voices grew louder.

"Let me take the blindfold off." I didn't want to see him, but I needed to know. "I can help you." I didn't even know why I was asking. I could reach up and grab the blindfold before he'd have a chance to stop me, let alone make good on his promise. Or he could kill me the second I removed it. But instinct told me he wouldn't because as much as I was being a coward and not removing it, there was the flip side of the coin.

He didn't want me to see him.

"You're going to help me by doing exactly what I say when I say it." The hand not holding the gun grasped the side of my face. Lowering his voice to the seductive tone he'd used on me in the cell, he stroked my cheek like we were lovers. "Understand, beautiful?"

It hit me.

He wasn't panicking.

He wasn't running.

He wasn't even moving except for the steady rise and fall of his chest with each of his measured breaths.

This man was not here to buy me or steal me.

He was here to rescue me.

But no agency operative would stay and fight. We would've already been in that bathroom and out the window. "Which branch?" He was military. Highly trained military.

The footfalls came faster and grew louder.

But special ops military operatives didn't operate alone.

"Shh," he whispered against my lips as if we were having an illicit affair of words. "Wait." He drew the word out. "*Wait.*"

Without warning, he fired three quick, consecutive shots.

The sound of the gunfire exploded in the echoing corridor, and he spurred into action before I heard the bodies drop.

"Move, move, move," he clipped with the same speed and cadence of the three shots.

Except he didn't give me a single moment to follow his command.

His hand landed on my arm, my body spun, and my back hit his chest. Then we were moving, with me in front.

Before I could panic about not being able to see where we were going or how many more men were after us, his body shifted behind mine.

Shoving me to his side, but still keeping a hold of my arm,

he flexed and I heard and felt the familiar movements of a boot hitting a door.

"Inside, inside," he ordered in the same rapid succession that was both authoritative and commanding but not said in panic or fight-or-flight.

The smell of soap and shampoo and blow-dried hair hit me a split second before he fired two more shots.

The sound of tinkling glass rained down around us as desert heat rushed into the cool space, choking out all the air conditioning. Doors opened and slammed in the corridor.

"Wait," he commanded.

I didn't know a towel being pulled off a metal rack had a distinctive sound until a rush of hot air moved past me while his scent and body heat grew distant.

More glass hit the floor and bottles were knocked over as I suspected he cleared a path on the counter. Then I heard the sound of a towel being shaken out.

"Here." His hand grabbed mine and urged me forward. "Get on the counter on your knees. You remember the position of the window?"

He couldn't be serious. "You're making me do this blindfolded?"

"Only until you're out the window."

"Then what?"

More footsteps echoed in the hallway, but this time they were heavier and there was no arguing.

"Hurry, we're out of time. Reach up, three feet, towel's over the bottom sill. One leg out, then drop. It isn't far, but if you can't land in those heels, take them off."

Practicality won out over reality. "I don't know what I'm dropping into."

"Desert. Go."

Reality landed. "You're not coming."

He dropped his voice to barely a whisper. "Not yet. Go."

The footfalls grew louder and closer as I scrambled onto the counter and blindly reached for the windowsill.

Then Arabic cut through the hall and slid under the bathroom door like poisonous gas. "*Grab him. I'll get the whore.*"

"Go," the man who'd kissed me commanded in an urgent whisper. "*Now.*"

The bathroom door banged open.

TWENTY-EIGHT

Adam

THE FUCKING IDIOTS KICKED THE BATHROOM DOOR IN, BUT IF THEY were smart, they would've fired through it.

They weren't smart, and I was waiting.

Weapons drawn, they burst in as Maila swung one leg over the windowsill.

Their eyes on her, not even looking in my direction, they both rushed her.

I was faster.

Locking the guy who was closer to me in an arm bar, I grabbed the M4 still in his hand and fired at the second asshole. His head exploded, blood spray covering Maila and the bathroom wall. Before his body hit the floor, I broke the neck of the first guy.

Then everything went FUBAR.

Maila shoved her blindfold off.

Three more guards rushed into the bathroom.

And I made the biggest mistake of my entire life.

I hesitated.

Green eyes landed on me for the first time in seven years, and I *fucking hesitated.*

Cold metal hit the back of my head as a guard grabbed her roughly and dragged her back inside over the broken glass of the windowsill.

That was all it took.

Twelve years of SEAL training fucking kicked in, and I focused up.

Another guard moved strategically between me and her, rifle aimed at my head.

Tactics, techniques and procedures flew through my head, and I calculated. Rapid-fire.

"*Mr. Hunt.*" Khalaf walked casually into the crowded bathroom. "Or should I say, Mr. Trefor? Keeping the same first name was a nice touch. Except I have to say," Khalaf glanced between me and Maila. "This was a surprise, even to me, but then I asked myself what motivates a man?" He met my impenetrable gaze. "And it became all too clear. You think she is yours, don't you?" He chuckled. "Of course you do." His hand waved through the air dismissively before his tone turned with disgust. "No man kisses a whore like that."

Sight lines, bullet trajectories, muscle response times.

With blood splatter covering her right arm and leg and a gaze more haunted than I remembered, Maila's eyes stayed locked on me as she remained silent. Even as the guard dragged her off the counter and dug his fingers into the flesh of her arm hard enough to leave marks, she didn't react.

Neither did I.

Focused up.

Three-foot world.

Targets in sight.

I executed.

"Your man better take his hand off her." I palmed Roark's keys. "Consider that my only warning."

Khalaf let loose with his insincere laugh again. "Really, Mr. Trefor, former Navy SEAL, outnumbered four to one, I do not believe you're in a position to make demands, let alone threats." He foolishly leaned toward me and dropped the pretense. "You're a dead man."

"You know what I think?" I asked, calmly holding the now unsheathed knife key in my hand.

"Do tell." Khalaf grinned. "Since this is your last chance. Or rather, last words."

Ignoring the gun shoved against the back of my head, I leaned toward him and waited.

The barrel followed, but then so did Al Ka'abi—leaning right into the sightline of fire between me and the guard at my back aiming at my head.

My three-foot world came into acute focus.

Al Ka'abi's face near mine, I moved.

Precisely.

My head tilted, my right hand swung out, my left swung back.

I slit Al Ka'abi's throat.

The guard behind me fired wild.

Kicking back, my heel connecting with his groin, I grabbed the barrel of his gun a split second before he fired again. His shot hit the asshole holding Maila, my upper body twisted, and my elbow shattered the guard's nose as he bent from the first blow.

Yanking his rifle from him, I spun and double-tapped his chest.

Three down, one left, six seconds, I turned.

The last standing guard made a fatal mistake.

Dismissing Maila, he shoved her back to raise his weapon toward me.

My finger on the trigger, a flash of glinting red catching my eye, I hesitated.

This time on purpose.

Expression locked, mouth set in determination, a blonde-haired, green-eyed firestorm launched forward. Her spiked heel held steady in both hands, she jammed it into the guard's neck, point-blank, hitting his artery.

Blood spray arced everywhere.

The guard twisted and dropped, the heel still embedded in his neck.

Splatter covering her entire face, chest and arms, Maila looked up at me.

Without so much as a single blink, she spoke in a calm, measured tone not even her brother had possessed. "Do you have a car?"

TWENTY-NINE

Maila

ADAM.

Adam Michael Trefor.

In front of me.

With my first kill at his feet.

Adam.

He'd kissed me, come for me, killed for me.

I'd killed too.

Fahad. He was going to kill Adam.

My chest rose with an inhale of metallic copper as death dripped down my face.

The voice that came out wasn't my own. "Do you have a car?"

THIRTY

Adam

TAKING A SECOND WE DIDN'T HAVE TO GAUGE HER MENTAL STATE, and coming up empty, I glanced down the vacant corridor. "Probably not one that isn't being tracked." I bent over and fished in the nearest guard's pockets. Coming away with an old flip cell phone and car keys, I pocketed both and nodded toward the window. "Let's go."

Without comment, she kicked off the remaining shoe she had on and turned toward the counter.

Regretting that I didn't have time to go back and find her a pair of shoes, I grabbed a 9mm from one of the dead guards, shoved it in my back waistband and slung the strap of the M4 over my shoulder. Reaching for her waist, I helped her up.

Not paying attention to the blood coating her skin or the streaks her hands were making on the blood-splattered counter, she reached for the windowsill and looked out. "There's nothing out here but sand," she commented calmly.

Too calmly.

"I know." I'd seen men with years of training lose their shit this way. "We're about a half-hour from the outskirts of Dubai proper."

She swung one leg out the window and glanced at the faucet. "We won't last long without water."

I made her a promise. "I'll make sure you're okay. But we need to get some distance between us and any more guards."

She looked at me but didn't comment or give a single tell. Swinging her other leg out, she pushed off, and a split second later, she was out of sight.

Inhaling, I shook my head. "Flip the switch, Trefor," I muttered under my breath before hopping on the counter and ducking out the window.

Standing in desert sand with her back against the building, she glanced up at me as I dropped down next to her.

Scanning left and right, I reached for the 9mm and held it out to her, handle first. "You still know how to shoot?" Her father, brother and I had all taken her to the indoor/outdoor range when she was younger, and we'd all taught her. By the time she was thirteen, she could hit the middle circle of a target with anything from a twelve-gauge to a semiautomatic AR-15. I could still remember the bruises on her shoulder from the kickback of the shotgun the first time she'd asked to fire it and I'd stupidly let her. For a week after, every time she'd put on her one-piece and jumped in their pool, I saw the mottling and felt guilty as hell.

"Yes." With blood all over her hands, she took the 9mm, dropped the magazine, glanced at it and slammed it back home.

I did a double-take of the blood on her hands. It wasn't drying, it was fresh. "You're injured." *Damn it.* "Let me see your hand."

"I'm fine."

"Maila," I warned.

"I said I'm fine," she countered with no emotion in her tone. "We can keep moving."

Dropping it for now, I scanned the desert around us again. "You still right-handed?"

"Yes."

I should've been thankful for her non-emotive answers, but they were fucking with me. "Keep the safety off. Left hand on my left shoulder. Tap once if you see something, otherwise, stay on my six, stop when I stop, move when I move. Understand?"

She nodded. Then she did something I wasn't expecting. She scanned our surroundings. Not in panic but the way I just had, as if looking for any threats.

Following her glance out of habit, I palmed the cell I'd lifted. "All right, we're moving."

Thankful for once that I wasn't holding a touch screen smartphone with a six-digit lock code, I flipped open the cell and dialed the secure local number AES kept for in-country emergencies. One of thirty-seven similar local numbers we had across the globe for this exact scenario. Numbers I made every single employee memorize before they were allowed in the field. All the numbers routed through a series of untraceable cell tower pings thanks to specialized software before ringing at AES's central command.

"Housekeeping," a nondescript voice answered.

"Seven-seven-two-one-four," I rattled off my AES ID number as I hugged the side of the building. My M4 aimed, I moved toward the front of the compound. "I need service."

"Of course, sir. Just one moment." The line clicked, followed by a beat of silence, then it was ringing.

"Alpha," Vance answered, all business, as substantial background noise came through the line. "Status?"

"Mobile. Two parties. Need immediate exfil. Call Roark for coordinates. Hot LZ." Even though her hand was on my shoulder like I'd instructed, I glanced behind me.

Her gaze locked with mine, her hand unmoving, she didn't speak.

"On it," Vance answered, the background noise on his end growing louder. "You secure?"

I glanced at the cell signal to make sure it wasn't my line losing reception. Full bars. "For as long as I can be with no overwatch and limited ammo." I scanned the sand trap behind us again. Still nothing. Focusing on the landscape in front of us again, I wondered why no one was coming to look for us yet.

"Already have eyes on you," Vance clipped. "Southeast side of the main residence."

I fucking paused. "Where are you?"

"Eyes in the sky, brother."

The background noise clicked. "Wings or a bird?"

"Helo. I'm eight minutes, thirty seconds out. Satellite images are showing heat signatures all over the fucking building you just left, but so far, no squirters. The front of the compound is clear except for the guard shack three hundred yards in front of you, two heat signatures inside. Can you get past them?"

I checked the magazine on the M4. Sixteen rounds left. "Yes."

"Copy. I'll pick you up half a klick down the road to the east. Touch and go. And before you thank me, you're welcome. Zulu's with Roark, they're already wheels up. Dubai is dust, Ghost is in the wind, and you don't get to blame Roark for calling it in because he did exactly as you asked and kept his mouth shut. Be glad I'm curious as fuck and Zulu felt like flying to the fucking Arabian Desert on his day off. That and Roark was smart enough to give you a tracking device. You're doubly welcome. Seven minutes now. Move."

Maila's hand safely on my shoulder, I didn't argue. "Good copy. Get a cleanup crew here STAT. Full sweep, clear the compound. Bodies, vehicles, surveillance footage—" She tapped my shoulder. "Hold." I glanced back.

"I have a passport, wallet and cell phone inside somewhere."

I nodded. "They'll handle it." I spoke to Vance again. "No identifying markers left. Sweep it all, but leave the victims. Ten headcount, all female. They see nothing. We're in and out. Call it in anonymously to local authorities after we're clear."

"On it," Conlon confirmed. "Anything else?"

Fucking hurry. "No."

"Keep your head down. See you in six minutes, thirty." Vance hung up.

I glanced at my watch, then wiped my fingerprints off the cell with the inside of my suit coat that wasn't covered in blood, repeated the process with the dead asshole's keys, then tossed both across the sand. "We need to move fast." I glanced at her bloodied feet, especially the left one she was holding on point like a dancer or an injured dog. "I'm going to carry—"

"No." Her pointed foot went flat, and she dropped her hand from my shoulder, wrapping it around the hand already holding the 9mm. "I'm fine. Go."

No time to argue, I moved us toward the corner of the building and stopped, issuing a quiet command. "Against the building, stay low."

She dropped to a squat, her weapon in front of her, her eyes trained on my target.

Going to one knee, the front gate in my visual, I watched as the door to the guardhouse flew open and one of Khalaf's armed men stepped out, his cell to his ear, his weapon in hand but stupidly pointed down. Scanning the perimeter of the compound, the guard paused when he got to the corner we were concealed behind.

Sighting my stolen rifle, calculating the heat, the trajectory and distance, I aimed.

My breath slow and steady, I pulled the trigger.

The sound of the shot traveled across the two-hundred-yard distance, and the guard had less than a fraction of a second to react.

Instead of ducking, he raised his weapon.

My shot hit him between the eyes before he could pull the trigger.

His body dropped, and the second guard came out of the gatehouse frantically firing his automatic.

Gunfire rained down around us, hitting the sand and the corner of the building, sending chunks of stucco flying.

I was already waiting.

My second shot sailed across the distance and hit the second guard dead-on.

Taking her arm, I stood us both up and scanned the front of the compound before looking back at her as the sound of an approaching chopper grew louder. "Can you run?"

"Yes."

I glanced at my watch. "Fast? Or do you need me to carry you?"

"I can run, Adam."

For a split second, hearing her say my name, I paused as a heaviness weighed down my chest. Mentally shaking it off, I nodded. "We're heading for the guardhouse, then out the gate, half a klick east. A chopper will pick us up. I don't want you to pause, I don't want you to look back. I'll be on your six, but no matter what happens, you do not stop. Run toward that chopper and get the fuck on, understand?"

She blinked.

I gripped her arm tighter. "Damn it, Emmy, tell me you understand?"

THIRTY-ONE

Maila

"RUN TOWARD THAT CHOPPER AND GET THE FUCK ON, understand?"

Seeing Adam Trefor in full Navy SEAL mode made me speechless, but hearing him say *fuck* made every one of my synapses fire until I felt like I was going up in flames.

My equilibrium spinning, my hand throbbing, my stomach hurting, my feet burning, I blinked.

He gripped me tighter. "Damn it, Emmy, tell me you understand?"

Emmy.

His slip to my childhood nickname jarring the fractured pieces of my soul, I stared at him.

Making a sound low in his throat that was part growl and all frustration, he reached for me as the air filled with the deep base of rotating blades.

Afraid of him touching me again, afraid I would never let go, I snapped out of it and stepped back. "I understand."

With a short, clipped nod, he dropped his arm but kept his gun aimed. "Let's go. Double time, aim for the gates. I'm on your six."

I didn't hesitate again.

My feet smarting from the broken glass I'd stepped on and the hot sand, I held the 9mm in my right hand, picked up the hem of my dress again with my left, and I ran.

Halfway to the gate, my feet landed on solid ground. The blistering pavement of the driveway seared like fire as pieces of glass drove into my cuts worse than in the hot sand.

My mind spinning, my body weak, I faltered.

A shot sailed past my head.

Then it was like Armageddon.

Gunfire rained down all around us.

"Keep running!" Adam barked before his footfalls stopped behind me.

Every molecule in my being fighting against his command, not wanting to leave him, I forced my suddenly rubber legs to keep moving.

Swerving left and right like I'd been taught, I heard his semi-automatic return fire as I reached the gatehouse. Stumbling over the first body, then stepping on the second, I fell into the small space, catching myself on the control panel. Frantically searching the board with Arabic lettering, I hit every button that looked like it would open the gate. A panic I hadn't experienced in seven years crawling up my throat, threatening to choke me, I didn't even pause to look if the gate opened. Climbing back over the dead body in the doorway and skirting the second, I rushed the slowly opening gate, silently chanting, *Don't look back.*

Don't look back.

Don't look back.

Bullets flying everywhere, pinging off the gate, hitting the concrete driveway, plunking into the guardhouse, I kept chanting.

Get to the helicopter.

Get to the helicopter.

I ran through the gate.

Don't look back.

I turned east.

Helicopter.

I kept running.

He'll be okay.

My feet burned.

He won't die.

Half a klick.

Keep fucking running.

A large, shiny, black-and-blue bird descended from the Arabian sky like a Greek myth.

Rotors thumping, wind churning, sand flying, grit filled my eyes.

Don't die, Adam.

My hands flew to my ears, my legs pumped, I aimed.

The helicopter touched down, and the pilot's door flew open. With the blades still spinning, a man in aviators and a suit jumped out, an automatic weapon in his hand. Laying down cover fire on the compound behind me, he casually opened the passenger door of the chopper as if he did this every day. Glancing in my direction, he jerked his head toward the waiting bird.

I ran straight for the open door and launched myself inside, scrambling onto the floor on hands and knees. Not bothering with the seat, I turned and pulled my knees up.

Seconds later, the pilot stopped firing and got in.

"No," I uselessly yelled over the noise. "Cover Adam!"

My words drowned out by the engine, I reached for the 9mm I'd been holding only to realize it was no longer in my hands.

A cry of desperation and fear ripped from my lungs and throttled my throat as the pilot increased the speed of the rotors. "No, *no*!" I scrambled to hit the pilot's shoulder.

His headset on, he barely glanced over his shoulder at me.

"Adam!" I yelled, pointing a bloody finger toward the compound.

The pilot no sooner tipped his chin behind me than the helicopter bounced with the weight of Adam as he jumped in and slammed the door shut. Throwing down the gun I'd dropped, a murderous look in his eyes, he plucked me up by the waist and tossed me in a seat. His deft hands flying across my body, he buckled me into a four-point harness as the helicopter lifted into the air.

My head swam from the swift change in altitude, and my hand throbbed. I hugged my left arm to my chest.

Adam grabbed a headset from behind me, put it over my head, and lowered the mic before climbing in the front next to the pilot and buckling himself in.

The helicopter angled forward and took on speed as Adam put his own headset on.

The pilot glanced at him, and a smile spread across his handsome face before his voice carried through the headset. "Love the new look."

"Where's the G650?" Adam demanded.

"Wiped, swept and left at Sharjah International."

"Abandoned?" Adam asked, indignant.

The pilot glanced at Adam. "If you think you would've done a better job under the circumstances and timeframe, get your own ass out of a hot exfil next time. Besides, you have insurance. Let them handle it."

"Not a company plane."

The pilot chuckled. "No shit."

Adam ignored what sounded like a dig from the pilot. "Where're Zulu and Roark?"

"Abu Dhabi," the pilot answered as he banked the helicopter to the left.

Even though I was buckled in, the sudden tilt of the helicopter made me reach for the edge of my seat with both hands out of instinct.

My injured hand made contact with the edge of the leather right where the laceration on my palm was, and pain exploded. My eyes welled. Then I couldn't stop it.

For the first time in seven years, I silently let tears fall.

THIRTY-TWO

Adam

THE GUN SHE'D DROPPED, THE BLOOD ON MY SHOULDER, THE LOOK in her eyes—I was silently losing it.

"Abu Dhabi," I repeated Conlon's bullshit, my nostrils flaring. "You left an untraceable jet in Dubai, and now sitting in Abu Dhabi is one of *my* company jets?" I ground out, emphasizing *my* like an asshole when I knew damn well this company would be nothing without him, Zane, November, and all the other men who worked for me.

"That's what I said." Vance banked the bird too steeply.

"Do you know what you've done?"

"Saved your ass?"

I didn't give a damn about my ass. I gave a damn about hers. And that was the problem because saving my ass was directly linked to the dozens of employees I had working for me, and sex trafficker or not, if I went down for murder, I wasn't going to be signing anyone's paycheck.

I reached over and shut off the comms on the headsets for the passengers, then I glared at Conlon. "You fucked up."

Unapologetic, he didn't hesitate. "You left me no choice."

"I told you to steer clear of this."

"You called in Ghost. Did you really think I was going to let that go?"

"How *the fuck* do you know I called him in?"

Conlon looked at me, really fucking looked at me. "How the fuck do you think he knew where to find her?"

For the first time, I truly realized just how much I had underestimated Conlon over the years and, conversely, how much blind fucking faith I'd ignorantly put in Ghost.

Sitting back in my seat, I glared out the windscreen. "*Fuck.*"

Conlon tipped his chin at the mess on my shirt. "So what really happened?"

"I was made."

"How?"

I looked at Vance. "The asshole in the market in Manhattan was the trafficker."

THIRTY-THREE

Maila

Tossing his headset aside with a stern expression, Adam rose from his seat and ripped my headset off before the helicopter even touched down. His strong, veined hands all over me, he unbuckled the four-point harness.

Cradling my injured hand as the sudden increase in noise became overwhelming, I didn't protest.

Shoving the thin helicopter door open while the blades were still chopping through the air in a repetitive whooshing motion, Adam stepped out and turned.

Without asking permission, he plucked me from my seat as the pilot hastily flipped switches and undid his own harness. The whine of a large motor rapidly slowing took up my headspace for a split second before I could process the impossibly strong arms snaking under my legs and behind my back.

Then I was being held against Adam's blood-soaked shirt as the pilot appeared next to us and the two men rapidly stalked across hot pavement toward a private jet.

As if Adam commanded it, the airplane's door opened and stairs unfurled seconds before his foot hit the first step.

I didn't demand a cell phone, and I didn't tell him I could walk.

I didn't think about having killed a man.

I didn't care that my DNA was in the bloodbath we'd left behind.

I didn't let go of my hand or check the bleeding.

I didn't do anything… except let him carry me onto a private jet and set me on my burned feet in front of a small galley.

Adam glanced at the helicopter pilot as he opened an upper cabinet door in the small kitchen. "Plane secure?"

"Swept twice," the helicopter pilot answered as he brought the stairs up and secured the door.

My knees shook, and I wobbled.

Adam's arm snaked around my waist. "The chopper?"

"It'll be handled."

Riffling through the cabinet, Adam barked out more orders to the helicopter pilot as he grabbed a pile of hand towels. "Get a SITREP from the cleanup crew. I want them gone before we're airborne."

"Copy." The helicopter pilot was already pulling out his cell phone and dialing.

Adam glanced over his shoulder toward the cockpit and issued more orders. "Wheels up, no flight plan, get us out of here, now. New York if we have the fuel, UK if we don't."

"Greece is as far as we'll get without a refuel," came the response from the flight deck.

"Do it." The small towels already in his hand, Adam two-fingered an expensive looking bottle of alcohol around the neck before moving us past the galley and down the aisle.

The distinctive whine of airplane jets coming to life sounded through the cabin, but Adam didn't stop at the first or second grouping of four oversized leather seats. His arm securely around my waist, his strength still supporting me, he moved us past two plush couches facing each other and opened a gleaming wood door.

Angling me inside, stepping in behind me, he closed the door.

Even though it was the largest airplane bathroom I'd ever

seen, his height and wide shoulders ate up the space, but his quick and purposeful movements didn't even pause.

Tossing first the towels then the bottle into the shiny metal sink, he reached past me to rummage through a tall, slim vanity cupboard. Coming away with a flexible metal hose, he barked an order at me like he'd barked orders at the other men. "Undress."

The engine noise grew louder.

My hand throbbing, my stomach muscles hurting, my feet stinging, I didn't move. But my gaze did. It went everywhere large, capable hands with bloodied knuckles went, and I tracked his movements. Hooking one end of the hose to the sink faucet, he secured it with three quick turns. Reaching into a smaller cabinet on the opposite side of the sink like he knew where everything was, he came away with a small bottle of liquid soap.

The plane jerked and started to taxi.

My balance thrown, my back hit the wall, and I glanced at the closed toilet lid. But then I made a mistake.

I looked up and caught my reflection in the mirror.

Blood splatter covered my entire face, chest and arms like mismatched red dots.

Everything suspended.

No airplane noise, nothing else in my vision, no burning on my feet or pain in my hand or stomach.

Just blood.

So much blood.

My body convulsed, and I started to gag.

Without missing a beat, as if his movements were a pre-planned, choreographed event, Adam grabbed my splatter-stained hair with one hand and bent me over as he flipped up the toilet lid with the other.

The engines grew louder, the plane took on speed, and I retched into the metal toilet.

The stench of vomit filled the small space, and my stomach heaved again.

The plane angled sharply, but Adam moved quicker. Still holding my hair with one hand, his legs went to either side of mine and he braced against the wall. Cradling me in the stance of his body, he held us steady as the private jet lifted into the sky like magic.

A second, a minute, an eternity, we stood like that.

My ass against his hips, his legs caging mine, his hand in my hair, his body supporting my weight, his arm braced—could I stay here forever?

The plane leveled out, and my ears popped.

Adam let go of my hair and flushed the toilet. Then he was all quick and precise movements again. His jacket came off, his shirt following in a flurry of ripped buttons and bunched material as hard muscles flexed and shifted, revealing his perfect torso that was marred only by a grouping of scars on one shoulder. A plastic trash bag materialized, and he shoved his clothes in it. Undoing his belt as he toed off his shoes, they followed the shirt and suit jacket into the bag.

He undid his pants next, but then he was reaching for me and grabbing the neckline of my red dress that was littered with even darker red dots all over it. Yanking the silky, stretchy material down over my shoulders and past my bare breasts in a clinical fashion as if he did this every day, his granite expression finally broke and he paused. The left side of his jaw ticked.

"They hit you," he ground out, his eyes on my upper stomach.

He didn't ask it as a question, but I wanted to answer it anyway. I wanted to say I was fine. That I was always fine. Because saying it would make it true. Except when I opened my mouth, nothing came out. Swallowing, forcing muscles to work that felt unused, I tried again. "Punched." My voice scratchy, my throat burned, I forced the lie out. "I'm fine."

His nostrils flared, and suddenly I understood something I

hadn't seven years ago. Something I never wanted to be forced to understand in my life, but should have known instinctually from circumstances.

There was no cure for death.

Not even with the countermeasure of life.

Degrees didn't matter.

Comprehending a realization I didn't grasp at eighteen while in the throes of grief, but one that coated my conscience with resignation now, I was no longer angry with Adam for having kissed me after telling me my brother was dead.

"Did my brother's blood splatter like this?" In a ruthless separation of life?

He shoved my dress down farther. "No."

He lied. "You're lying." I pulled my arms free of the sleeves, and the material slid past my bare hips and hit the floor.

His gaze landed on the three-carat diamond, and every muscle in his body stilled. Then he reached out, and with the gentlest of touch, he fingered the loop where it bit through my flesh.

Reactionary, my wounded stomach muscles flinched.

His jaw moved with tightly controlled anger, but his voice came out with disciplined restraint. "Did they do this?"

They. This.

I suddenly wanted it gone. I wanted it all gone. "Get it out."

With shockingly swift dexterity, his long fingers removed the piercing and tossed it on the counter.

As if he hadn't just removed another man's jewelry from me, he fished his keys that he'd used as a weapon out of his pocket and tossed them next to the diamond. Resuming his macabre striptease, his suit pants that I was sure were custom-made to match his long legs and tapered waist hit the floor, along with his black, fitted boxers. Grabbing both of the ruined articles of clothing, along with my dress, he shoved them into the plastic bag in a quick, efficient manner. Then he stood before me, as naked as

I was, with the same splatter covering his hands and a patch of chest he'd had exposed with the top two buttons of his shirt open.

His piercing blue eyes that were both frightening and beautiful met mine. "Your brother didn't suffer."

Our eyes locked, we stood there.

No ground under our feet, no pretense, no clothes hiding his erection that stood proud, jutting from beneath chiseled abs, a defining V and trimmed hair that said he wasn't celibate.

Death, sex, and blood all mingled in my head, and a flare of jealousy so profound hit me harder than my own mortality.

"How many?" my voice rasped.

His jaw worked the same tic as he grabbed the hose and turned the faucet on. "I'm not going to tell you how many kills I have."

His hot gaze and warm hand hit my shoulder at the same time as the cold water. "Not kills," I corrected, my nipples hardening. "Women."

His rough fingers working with the cold water to wash the blood off my shoulder paused, and he looked at me. His voice turned dangerously quiet. "You were in a red dress."

Not understanding, my heart leapt anyway. A leap that was entirely different than when I plunged the heel of that shoe into a man's neck. "They dressed me."

The water running down my body, his hand stayed still. "What else did they do to you?"

Cold seeped into my bones, and I said the words I needed to say. "No one raped me."

His nostrils flared, and his gaze cut back to my shoulder. Seeming not to care that red-tinted water was staining the fancy airplane bathroom, he swept his hand over my chest and shoulders. Then he issued a command in a tone full of gravel and pain, but worse, a deep quiet I didn't understand. "Close your eyes."

"Women?" I self-destructively tried again before doing as he said and closing my eyes, but not in submission, in cowardice.

Water rained down on my face, but then his hand followed and thick fingers swept over every inch of forehead, nose and cheeks like salvation. I basked in the attention like a baptism, reading into his ministrations as if they were caresses.

Then his thick thumb rubbed hard across my lips, and he broke me like he broke me seven years ago. "You gave up the right to ask me that question seven years ago."

THIRTY-FOUR

Adam

MY WORDS INTENTIONAL, I HURT HER LIKE I DID SEVEN YEARS AGO. "You gave up the right to ask me that question seven years ago."

Her haunted eyes opened as water sluiced down her face. "You were buying a sex slave."

She was a beautiful child, but as a woman, naked and covered in red-stained resilience, she was stunning.

My thumb dragged across her full bottom lip again. "I was buying you."

"You're taller than I remember."

Turning the water off because I didn't know how much reserves the plane had, I picked up the soap. Pumping the liquid into my palm, I met her gaze again. Shamelessly rubbing my hands all over her shoulders, chest and arms, and gently across her face, I then allowed myself to venture lower. Her nipples hard, her breasts perfect, I languidly scrubbed with slow circles as I held her gaze and studied every nuance, but her locked expression didn't falter.

My cock harder than it'd ever been, I increased the pressure and rubbed my thumbs over her nipples.

That time, her breath caught. Her eyes stayed haunted, and her expression remained elusive, but I took the inhale as mine. Sweeping my hands gently down her bruised stomach and over her hips, I brought the tips of my fingers to the top of her shaved cunt, then I stilled.

Holding her gaze, I looked for signs of shock. "I'm the same height now as I was seven years ago. Have you ever killed a man before?"

"Have you ever bought a woman before?"

I didn't hesitate. "No."

She stared at me a beat. "No."

I nodded once. "Put your hands on my waist and tip your head back." We were at cruising altitude, she didn't need to hold on to me for support, but I wanted to see what she would do. How far she would go.

Submissive or in shock, her uninjured hand landed on my hip and her head tipped back.

"Good girl," I quietly praised as I pumped more soap into my hands and ran them through her hair.

"I'm not a girl."

She'd always be my girl. "Turn of phrase." Massaging my fingers through her thick hair, I shamelessly watched her perfect breasts move with every inhale. "You're a beautiful woman."

"You're in a custom suit, and we're on a private plane."

"Company jet," I corrected, wondering what had happened to the girl I knew seven years ago. "And I was in a suit. Now I'm not." Now I was inches away from fucking the fantasy I'd had for too many years to count. Except I didn't want to fuck this woman. I wanted to sink inside the young woman I'd left shattered in Florida all those years ago and claim the fuck out of her. I wanted the girl who used to smile at me. I wanted to go back in time and take that woman. Take her before the piece-of-shit sex trafficker had gotten to her, but I fucking couldn't.

Her eyes opened. "Whose company?"

Guilt ate at me as I stared into the still-haunted look in her eyes. As haunted as when I'd left her seven years ago, but now it was even more pronounced. Except with it had come something else I didn't usually see outside of the military. Specifically in men who'd served in combat.

I turned the water back on and avoided her question for now. "How did you wind up in Dubai?"

"You're soaking the bathroom floor with evidence."

"There's a drain under your left foot. Do you usually worry about evidence?" The more I thought about it, the more I was convinced she wasn't in that compound by accident.

"Only when I kill a man." She looked down and lifted her left foot, then gingerly put it back down.

Goddamn it, her feet. They'd been bare when we'd jumped out the window. "Tip your head back."

Closing her eyes again, she complied.

I ran the cool water over her head. Goose bumps raced across her pale flesh, but she didn't shiver. Brushing my hand over her hair, her shoulders, I remembered summers in Miami.

"You used to have tan lines." I rubbed my thumb over an imaginary line from a memory.

Stark green eyes void of life looked up at me. "You used to kiss my knee."

"You used to smile." Always. Every time she saw me. Even that last time, for a split second, when she'd first opened the door and saw me before she saw the uniform.

Hardness descended over her delicate features. "That was then."

"And this is now?" What the hell had happened to her?

"The Adam I used to know would've checked my hand and feet by now."

"The man I am now is rinsing the blood off you because I already know the bleeding on your hand has slowed, the burns on the bottom of your feet can wait, and the bruises on your stomach and chaffing on your wrist from handcuffs will heal." But the look in her eyes? I didn't have an answer for that. Worse, I feared I was too late.

"How do you know I was cuffed?"

Guilt eating at me, I didn't give her room to reply. I handed her the hose. "Hold this."

Taking it, her eyes on me, she said nothing.

I quickly soaped up my face, hair and chest, then reached for the hose.

When she handed it back, disappointment warred with relief. The last fucking thing I needed to be thinking about was her hands on me.

Quickly rinsing off, then spraying down the keys, that fucking diamond, the cabinets and the floor, I turned the water off and unhooked the hose before stowing it.

"Is this your company's plane?"

"Yes," I admitted, picking up a hand towel and running it over her hair.

She took the towel from me with her good hand and slowly dried her face. "Is that why you knew where the towels and shower attachment were?"

Grabbing my own small-as-shit towel, I dried myself off and gave her too much information. "You're asking the wrong questions."

"Did you know where it was because you specifically stock your planes with equipment you need because you encounter this type of scenario often?"

Better. "Yes." I tossed the towel into the plastic bag and reached for the Lagavulin. Unscrewing the cap on the single malt, I held the bottle out to her. "Drink."

"I'd rather have a toothbrush and toothpaste." As if it were a dance, she gracefully ran the towel over her arms and down her stomach.

Mesmerized, I watched. "You can have that after."

Not drying her legs, same as I hadn't because any sort of bending at the waist would put our bodies in direct contact in the confined space, she dropped the towel into the plastic bag. Seemingly unconcerned about her lack of clothes, she took the bottle, but she didn't take a sip. She took a gulp. Three of them. Without flinching.

She handed the bottle back.

The move was so reminiscent of her brother and father, I spoke before thinking. "You took that drink like Billy or your father would have."

"I should." She almost shrugged. "They taught me to drink."

By the time she was eighteen, they were both dead. How the hell had they *taught* her to drink?

As if reading my thought, she answered the unspoken question. "Dad and Billy made sure by the time I was sixteen that I could hold my liquor without getting alcohol poisoning."

Anger at the thought of them purposely getting her drunk and doing it without my knowledge flared. "I must have missed that."

"They wanted you to miss it."

The bottle almost to my mouth, I paused. "Why?"

"Because they wanted to protect me."

My eyes narrowed. "From?"

"Boys, men…" Her gaze dropped to my dick, then dragged up my stomach and across my shoulders before she looked at me again with the same direct stare she'd been giving me since she'd taken off the blindfold. "You."

Sucker punched, I took a swig of the scotch to hide it. Inhaling through the burn that coated my throat, I capped the bottle and set it down. Closing the lid of the toilet, I threw a hand towel over it. "Sit."

She sat, but she kept her eyes on me. "Why were you in Dubai?"

My hard cock inches from her face, I told her the truth. "For you. Give me your hand."

She held her hand out. "Do you want to fuck me?"

If I hadn't already swallowed the Lagavulin, I would've fucking choked. "No." Not yet. "Are you always this blunt?" She used to be sweet.

"Yes, and your answer contradicts what's right in front of me."

Holding her small wrist in my hand, looking at the laceration across her palm, I ignored my throbbing dick. "I'm a man. You're a naked, beautiful woman." Besides the fact that she was the one woman I'd always wanted, I wasn't fucking blind. She was gorgeous, every closed-off inch of her. I also knew the drill after a combat adrenaline rush where your adrenal glands were pumping more cortisol than your brain knew what to fucking do with. Not to mention, I couldn't remember the last time I'd fucked, let alone who it was.

"You're saying it's biology?"

I glanced from her hand to her eyes. "I'm saying you don't need stitches."

She studied me a moment with those emerald eyes that I could never fucking look away from all those years ago, and still couldn't.

"Were you this calm in the Teams?"

"No." Yes. My cock was the exception here.

"I don't believe you."

On purpose, I didn't hold back. "My dick wasn't this hard."

Unfazed, as if I'd told her something she already knew, like my hair was black, she didn't fucking react. "May I have my hand back now?"

"After I treat it." Still holding on to her, I reached under the sink for the small first aid kit that was kept on all company jets in the lavatories. The full medical kits were kept in the main cabin, but I didn't need it. Riffling through the smaller selection of supplies, I grabbed antiseptic and the liquid bandage shit that would be more comfortable for her than stitches.

She watched my every move with a calm disconnectedness. "I can do this myself."

"I'm sure you can." She'd shoved a five-inch heel into a six-foot, two-hundred-and-twenty-pound man's neck without batting an eye.

"But you're going to do it for me."

"Humor me." Holding her hand over the sink, I poured the antiseptic over the wound.

She flinched marginally but didn't comment.

I patted the area dry. Then I held the wound closed and ran the liquid bandage across it. "Give it a minute." I let go of her.

She pulled her hand back toward her body and blew on it.

"Let me see your feet." If I had enough room, I would've squatted in front of her. "Left foot first." I patted my thigh.

She lifted her leg, but at the same time, she pressed her thighs together.

A better man wouldn't have looked at the juncture of her thighs before checking the bottom of her foot. A better man also would've gotten her clothes by now. And let her clean up by herself.

I wasn't a better man.

Inspecting her foot, noting the small lacerations from the broken glass, I found a small remnant still embedded. "This is going to hurt," I warned.

I pressed on either side of the cut, and she flinched, but the edge of the glass shard popped out enough for me to grab it. I tossed it in the sink and checked the rest of her foot. Not seeing any remaining remnants, I issued an order. "Other foot."

Dropping her left leg, she lifted the right to the same position on my thigh.

The bottoms of both of her feet were cut up and red but not blistered, and I thankfully didn't have to dig any more glass out. "They burning?"

"A little."

"Wait here."

Opening the lavatory door, I walked the few paces to the door that separated the sleeping area from the main cabin and started to close it.

Talking on his cell and looking pissed as hell as he paced the aisle, Vance glanced up at me and mouthed *problem*.

"Five minutes." I secured the door and grabbed my bag. Quickly dressing in jeans and a button-down, I pulled out some clothes for her and went back.

Still holding her hand, still sitting but now with her legs crossed, she looked up at me. "Where do you live?"

Giving her the entire truth felt like a dirty admission I wasn't ready to make. "Wherever I need to."

"Meaning?"

The girl I knew was always inquisitive. She'd never had a problem asking any question under the sun. But this woman throwing non sequiturs at me since I'd gotten her on the plane was disconcerting. I hadn't expected her to break down after the scene in the compound, but I hadn't expected this detachment either.

I handed her the clothes. "Meaning I work all over, and I have several residences."

"*Work*," she repeated, taking the clothes.

Pissed that she still wasn't asking what I did or questioning the fact that I'd specifically come for her, but equally unwilling to admit I knew where she worked and I'd kept tabs on her, I stood at the open lavatory door at an impasse.

Either unconcerned about my presence or resigned, she simply pulled my T-shirt over her head and gingerly threaded her feet through a pair of my gray sweats.

"Need help?"

"Do I look like I need help?" With no intonation, she asked the question as she'd asked all the others—without emotion.

Reaching over her, I opened one of the smaller cabinets I knew had toiletries and fished out a clean toothbrush and toothpaste for her and deodorant for me. "Here you go." I placed the items for her on the counter. "Cabinet's stocked. Help yourself to whatever else you need."

"Stocked with everything except women's clothing?" Standing, she rolled the waistband over two times, then pulled the T-shirt down over it.

Using the deodorant, then capping it and putting it back, I watched her in the mirror as I buttoned my shirt. "Should I have women's clothes on board?"

She opened the new toothbrush. "If you do this often."

I did. "Often enough." AES handled more shit than the average citizen ever wanted to think about.

Nodding, she squirted toothpaste onto the toothbrush. "You must lose a lot of your T-shirts."

I gave her the truth. "You're the first. If you keep it," I added, tipping half my mouth up.

She didn't return the smile, she didn't even bite on it. Watching me in the mirror, her expression unchanged, she brushed her teeth.

Reaching around her, I grabbed the antiseptic spray for burns and antibiotic cream from the small med kit. Then I pocketed Roark's weaponized keys and the fucking diamond. "Meet me in the cabin when you're done." I stepped out of the lavatory.

She immediately shut the door behind me.

THIRTY-FIVE

Maila

ADAM TREFOR.

Naked.

With more sculpted muscles than I'd ever seen on a human being. Also with more bullet wound scars. A grouping of six round telltale scars covered his left shoulder, along with the thin lines of two incisions near them that said he'd been cut into. Probably to be put back together so he could go back out and do the same thing that'd given him the wounds in the first place.

I needed to find a cell phone.

I needed to think about what would happen when I got off this plane.

I needed to do anything except think about his large, rough hands caressing my breasts and his hard, naked body.

But I wasn't.

I wasn't even upset Fahad was dead.

The bourbon had settled into my empty stomach and spread its temporary tendrils outwards, reaching to the farthest corners of my battered body, and I no longer cared about pain or details or protocol or anyone who'd seen me covered in blood.

I cared about one thing.

The one thing I couldn't care about.

Not now.

Not ever.

THIRTY-SIX

Adam

GRABBING A PAIR OF BERLUTI BOOTS THAT WEREN'T STAINED WITH blood, I stepped into them and slipped on a fresh suit jacket. Fishing my work cell out of my bag and pocketing it, but not powering it up yet because I knew it could be tracked, I made my way to the galley.

Still on the phone, Vance stopped me and held up a finger.

Shaking my head, I bypassed him and made two ice packs with hand towels.

Zane stepped out of the cockpit before I could get back to her. "How is she?"

Anger I was barely keeping under control bled out. "That's all you have to say to me?"

Hands on his hips, he stared at me a beat. "Is this how you want to play it?"

I glared at him.

He glared back. "Vance tracked you. By the time you got your ass in hot water and called it in, we were already in-country."

Fucking great. "Who can track that chopper?"

He shook his head. "I know you're not seriously asking about my or Victor's capabilities right now, so I'm going to let that slide. And for the record, you didn't have to call MacElheran. I would've fucking flown you."

"You also would've been recognized." I may own AES, but Zane was my front man. He met with the clients. He flew the hard missions. He handled operations from the ground. He put the layer between me and the rest of the shit that allowed me to do my job. He'd also been to Dubai more times than I could count. The second Ghost told us where we were going, I knew I'd made the right call bringing Roark in.

Zane didn't drop it. "I would've had your six. We all would have."

"This wasn't a client mission."

"No fucking shit," he said, slow and angry like he was talking to an idiot. *"It's Emmy."*

At his last two words, Missy came out of the cockpit and leaned into Zane's leg, whining twice.

His glare still on me, Zane petted her head. "It's okay, girl. I'm not going to pound his face in. Yet. Go lie down."

The dog retreated after a nudge of her muzzle against his leg.

Zane crossed his arms. "I'm going to say it because your closed-off bullshit-self won't. We're good, but don't do this shit again. I wouldn't do it to you, and you sure as hell wouldn't allow me to do it to you. We're more than this, man." He tipped his chin toward the rear cabin. "And her? Of all people? She deserved better from you than a sloppy one-man hot extraction. That blood covering her face better not have been hers or you're answering to me." He turned and went back into the cockpit.

I kicked the fucking ice compartment shut.

"Alpha." Vance held his phone out to me. "You need to take this."

Zane's words fucking with me, I needed to get back to her. "In a minute." I pushed past him.

"Adam," he quietly stated.

I threw him a warning look. "She needs me. It can wait."

Vance glanced over my shoulder.

I followed his glance.

Swamped in my T-shirt and sweats, the only woman who'd

ever fucking owned me stood in the open pocket door of the full bulkhead to the aft stateroom looking lost as fuck.

"Have a seat."

She glanced from where she was standing to the single seats in the conference area of the cabin.

"On the divan," I instructed, closing the physical distance between us.

"Divan," she repeated.

"Couch," I explained, wishing there was a single damn thing I could do about the emotional distance between us.

"I knew what you meant." Retreating, she sat in the middle seat.

"End seat," I ordered. "Put your legs up."

A flash of weariness crossed her features, but using her good hand, she pushed herself back and repositioned to the end of the couch before putting her legs up.

I sat at the opposite end and lifted her feet onto my thigh.

"You're making a habit of that," she commented casually.

In better light, I inspected the bottom of her feet again. "Of what?" The bleeding stopped, they weren't too bad, but it still pissed me off that she was injured at all. Every scratch on her was my fault.

"Putting my feet on your thigh."

I used the antibiotic cream on the cuts and spoke without filtering. "Maybe I enjoy it." I sprayed the antiseptic over the bottom of both her feet.

"Maybe I don't."

I pressed the makeshift ice packs against her feet, then searched her face for tells.

Watching my movements, she didn't look up.

I waited.

After a long moment, she met my gaze.

I aimed for an apology for something I couldn't apologize for. "That's my fault."

"What is?"

"Your distrust of me."

"I didn't say I didn't trust you."

She didn't have to. "I'm sorry for what I did seven years ago."

Her chest rose with a sharp inhale, and she turned her head.

Switching to holding both ice packs with one hand, I grabbed her ankle with the other. "Hey."

"What is it that you think you did?" she asked without meeting my eyes.

"Look at me," I quietly commanded.

Her gaze cut to mine, and her voice turned lethally quiet. "Is that an order?"

Vance stepped through the door I'd forgotten to close. "Take this."

My eyes on her, I took his cell and held it to my ear.

"Adam Trefor?" a woman asked.

"Yes."

"Please hold."

The line went silent for a moment, then a deep male voice came on. "Trefor?"

"Yes."

"Mike Cohen, Associate Deputy Director of the CIA."

I fucking stilled. "How can I help you, sir?"

"We've not met, but I know both your history of service as a Navy SEAL and your reputation and track record with AES. All stellar. I also know your security clearance level, and what I'm about to tell you is above your clearance."

She looked away from me.

Alarm bells going off in my head like a fucking casino, I saw it coming, but I was still in denial. "Understood, sir."

"I'm not sure you do, but you're about to. You have one of my operatives."

My expression locked, I stared at her, but she wouldn't look at me. "Come again?"

"Quinn Michaels. You know her as Maila Nilsen."

Mother.

Fucking.

Shit.

CIA.

She was goddamn CIA.

Using my middle name as the last name of her alias. "Sir, I—"

"We're beyond pretense, Trefor. You left a mess in Dubai, and one of your company jets just took off from Abu Dhabi. A three-year-long operation has gone to hell, and one of my agents has been compromised thanks to you."

Three fucking years and they hadn't neutralized that asshole Al Ka'abi? *Jesus Christ.*

Standing up and signaling at Vance for a pen as I moved to the conference area of the plane, I tried to wrap my fucking head around something I should've figured out the second I knew that goddamn text came from Langley.

Not sure what was going on with her, or why, I knew one thing. There was a reason she'd kept everything tight, even after we'd gotten on the plane. More, there was a reason behind the look in her eyes, and I wasn't fucking giving her up if she hadn't so much as asked for a damn cell to call her handler.

Aiming to stall and buy some time, I lied to the ADD. "With all due respect, sir, I'm not sure I know what you're talking about."

Vance grabbed a pad of paper and pen from the conference area and handed them to me.

"Your footprint is all over this, Trefor," Cohen warned.

I wrote two words down for Vance. *Cleanup crew?*

Nodding, Vance grabbed the pen and wrote his response. *Come and gone.*

Fuck, well that was at least one thing. Probably the only thing I had going for me at the moment. "Sir, as you can imagine, if I either confirmed or denied any activities related to the dealings of any of my clients, I would not have my reputation, let alone my company. Out of respect, I will tell you that I was recently in Dubai, but now I am not."

The man let out an aggravated sigh. "Do you know how I rose to this position, Trefor?"

"No, sir, I do not." Why the hell hadn't she said something to me? She could've told me without giving specifics. She knew what it meant to be a SEAL. At a minimum, she knew I had security clearances. Our history aside, she should've known she could trust me.

"By smelling bullshit a mile away," Cohen answered. "Do your refuel in Greece, then bring her in. She has a lot to answer for." The associate deputy director of the CIA hung up on me.

I handed Vance his cell back. "Give us a minute."

Without comment, Vance took his cell, and I retreated to the stateroom, closing the door behind me.

Taking a seat opposite her, I looked at a woman I didn't know at all. "You're CIA."

THIRTY-SEVEN

Maila

His jaw set, his eyes hard, he stared at me with a look I'd never seen on the sharp angles of his face. "You're CIA."

My stomach bottomed out even though I'd known this moment was coming.

Since he didn't ask, he'd stated the two words as if he already knew, I didn't bother answering him.

His muscular biceps stretching the sleeves of his expensive-looking suit jacket, he continued to stare at me with his unflappable expression like I was a stranger. "Why didn't you tell me?"

"You didn't tell me why you came for me." Or how he'd even known where I was or who I was with.

We stared at each other.

His expression impenetrable, mine locked.

I fought for control of something I never had control over around him. "Nice boots."

The tic was so small, anyone else would have missed it, but I didn't. The lower left side of his jaw always moved when he clenched his teeth. When he was younger, it was his tell that he was about to lose his temper. I'd seen him lose it a lot in those first two years I knew him, lashing out at my brother or some kid at school. Sometimes at an innocent door he'd slam or a wall he'd punch.

Then one day he'd shoved away from the dinner table in

anger and knocked over his glass in the process because Billy had told my dad that some kids at school had made fun of his clothes. Before he could storm out, my dad had caught his arm and told him in a calm but authoritative tone to sit back down. Adam had sat, but he'd hung his head, and the whole time my dad grilled him about what the kids had said, Adam's jaw made that tic. The next day, he'd shown up at school in new jeans, and when he came for dinner that night, my dad told him he could be mad his whole life or he could make something of himself and enlist when he turned eighteen.

And that's exactly what he'd done. Both he and Billy had.

The day they shipped out for boot camp, I felt like I lost two brothers.

But the man staring at me now wasn't my brother. Not even close.

The boy I'd grown up with was gone, and in his place was a ruthless, cold-blooded killer who'd stripped me naked and massaged my breasts like he not only had a right to touch me but like he was the only man who knew how to arouse me.

Except he wasn't trying to arouse me now.

His jaw set, his shoulders tensed, he called me on my evasive, erratic questions and comments. "Why don't you cut the bullshit and say what you mean?"

"You dress differently." But his clothes still smelled like cold wind and sharp angles, and I wanted to be buried in them.

He didn't hold back with his rebuttal. "You act differently."

You left. The accusation on the tip of my tongue, I wanted to lash out with it, but I didn't. Not that it would've mattered or changed one thing if I had. I was never his priority, just like I'd never been my father's or my brother's. The Navy had that from all three of them, and now apparently this private jet and the company behind it was Adam's new priority.

"Say it," he demanded.

Feeling the tendrils of sanity slowly slip from my control, I held on to my evasiveness like my life depended on it. "Say what?"

"The thought you're holding back."

"What does it matter?" Would he have done anything differently if I'd stayed seven years ago and waited for him to return, either breathing or in a box? Would it have made a difference back then if I'd told him I was in love with him?

Would it have mattered to him now that I'd fought the urge to drop to my knees the moment he'd undressed in front of me? Would he have cared that with death all over me, a fresh kill on my conscience, and my own blood seeping out of my body, that I'd wanted to put him in my mouth and taste a life I ran away from because I couldn't take the pain back then? Still couldn't take it now? Did he even understand what it meant to lose everything?

"It matters to me." Sitting there in his perfect clothes, his tone not giving away an ounce of emotion, he didn't even say the words with anything close to as much conviction as he used when he barked orders at the other men on this plane.

If I laughed anymore about anything, I would've laughed at the blatant irony of his own bullshit. But I didn't. I didn't even smile.

"Does it?" I didn't want to be a part of this conversation anymore. Nothing had changed. He had his priorities, I had my walls. There was no give.

With a subtle shift of his coiled muscles and slight rise of his chest that was more emotion than he'd shown since he'd walked into my cell, he leaned forward. Resting his arms on his thighs, he steepled his fingers, but he didn't answer my question.

He took me completely off guard. "Five days ago, at eleven-oh-three Eastern Standard Time, I received a text. A text that was sent to a cell phone only you still have the number for because everyone else who knew it is dead."

Alarm stiffened every one of my muscles, and I fought to

keep my voice even as I filed away the fact that he still had his old cell phone number. "What did it say?"

"Three words." His penetrating gaze cut through me like he could see every dead dream I still held on to like an albatross, weighing down my psyche like a terminal diagnosis weighs down the time you have left breathing, but he said nothing more.

Neither did I.

I did what I had been trained to do.

I waited and listened.

I listened to the plane's jet engines. I listened to the space between our bodies. I felt the hum, and I heard my own heart rate and pulse, yet still I waited. I waited for him to tell me why he'd come for me. I waited for him to answer my question. I waited for him to give me answers I was never going to get because I hadn't and wouldn't ask the questions, but I still waited.

With bated breath.

And a locked expression that said I wouldn't be broken.

I couldn't.

I was already so damaged, I was beyond breaking, and nothing this man could say to me would ever repair what couldn't be fixed. Mine was the kind of ruin you couldn't fracture further from.

"Three words," he repeated as if I hadn't heard him the first time. Then he dropped his voice just enough to change his tone to one of lethal warning. "*They took her.*"

They took her.

They took her.

My throat moved with a swallow. The pins and needles of newly surging adrenaline shot through my system, and I didn't break. But I fell from the sky this plane had us in without so much as a blink.

"Who sent it?" I'd been burned.

My cover had been blown.

On purpose.

Watching me, studying me like I was studying him, he leaned back on the couch he called a divan and crossed his ankle over his knee. The leg of his dark jeans coming up just enough to show off his expensive Italian leather boot that he never would've been able to afford as a SEAL, he put his overly muscled arm on the back of the couch. "When I traced the text, it pinged four times before we found the number it came from."

"We?" I knew who *we* was.

I knew all about his company and what they did. But he hadn't told me, and I wasn't going to let on I knew because just as I had resources to track him all these years, he had the same. Maybe he had tracked me, or maybe he hadn't. I didn't want to know either way, because both were bad sides of the coin.

A coin I couldn't control, change or affect.

His unwavering gaze locked on mine, he gave me the truth. "*We* meaning me, using the resources of my company."

My heart pounded a rhythm it only ever played when I thought of him, let alone sat across from him and smelled him and was close enough to touch him. And now I knew what he looked like without those expensive clothes.

Adam Trefor naked was beyond measure.

My brain still processing the vision of him, I faltered.

Replaying his body naked before me, his hard length, his girth, his sheer size, defined muscles that only a man who'd survived becoming a SEAL could possess, and then his gentle but dominant touch—I couldn't stop the flush of raw heat.

It swept through my blood and landed so low in my belly, I wanted to bear down on his damn divan and ride it like I knew how to fuck.

But I didn't.

I knew how to shoot, kill, evade, pretend, and entice a sex

trafficker into kidnapping and training me, but I didn't know how to fuck because I never had.

I'd been waiting.

For a man who'd had to walk away from me when I'd needed him most.

Life was cruel.

But the ugly truth was even worse than that day because I didn't hold any self-preservation of self-worth. I didn't only tell myself he had to walk away and carry on with his duty. I believed it. No, I didn't simply believe it, I breathed it.

Every day.

From the time I was old enough to say Navy, I knew the value of sacrifice.

I'd been bred into it.

I knew what my father, brother and Adam did.

It was selfless and honorable, and they and all the service members before and after them gave me every free breath I ever took.

I didn't begrudge Adam walking away when he was all I had left in this world.

I hated myself for hating him for doing it.

So I did the only thing I knew how to do.

I reached for that sacrifice.

With carefully orchestrated plans laid out, four years later I was a CIA agent living undercover, building an alternate life, waiting to be called into action so I could do my duty.

Do my part.

Contribute.

But I wasn't assigned anything of importance. Not even the four years of college completed in three and acing every aspect of my training, both mental and physical, got me a position of any importance. Because every step of the way I was fighting an invisible enemy I never saw coming.

I was Vice Admiral Erikson Nilsen's daughter.

I was the sister of a decorated SEAL killed in action.

I was untouchable.

And to my horror, that made my life indispensable.

No department wanted me.

Not one single acronym in the intelligence community wanted my blood on their hands.

So I was assigned to sex crimes and told to wait. Live the alias. Build the background. Make it real.

I didn't know who was more surprised when Khalaf Al Ka'abi walked into a hotel lobby in London as I was leaving a bullshit conference for my fake-slash-real job and we almost collided in the vestibule. Before I lost the opportunity, I'd made eye contact and suggested he watch where he was going next time unless he wanted to pick a woman up off the floor. His calculated laugh told me I'd put just enough indignation into my tone. He'd then smiled and asked me to dinner, as an apology of course.

Before I could say yes, my cell was pinging with encrypted messages, my handler was fired, and a new handler I'd never met with a name I was never given told me to *play it safe and walk away.*

I didn't play it safe.

I did everything I'd been trained to do.

I said all the right words, made all the right gestures, and performed the perfect dance between demure and vulnerable. One dinner turned into three, and I'd delayed my flight home. Then I made my move and said I needed to get back to New York. He said he had business there, and I'd given him my phone number. Told him to look me up.

Not even an hour after my commercial flight landed at JFK, he was tracking me to a market, pretending it was coincidence.

Focusing back on Adam, I asked what I needed to, but I already knew what he would say. "Where did the text come from?"

Piercing blue eyes I dreamt about bore into me. "A Langley area code."

The breath that came next was years in the making.

I knew, without a doubt, my career was over.

I was purposely burned.

THIRTY-EIGHT

Adam

SHE DIDN'T COMMENT.

She didn't even blink.

But I saw it in her eyes. She knew she'd been burned. Whether it was in the name of her own safety or not was irrelevant to her career.

I gave her the rest. "That call was ADD Cohen."

Her façade broke for a fraction of a second as disgust twisted her delicate features. "No surprise."

"I didn't tell him I had you." I wasn't looking for appreciation of my loyalty. I expected her to know she had it. I was merely stating fact.

"It doesn't matter. He knows."

"Do you know how?" I'd told Zane not to file a flight plan, but we were flying over international borders, and if we wanted to land, let alone refuel, there was only so long we could go under the radar.

"Do you?" she countered.

"No." Not yet, not the specifics, but this was the CIA. They had feelers everywhere.

"Whoever sent the text," she stated as if it were obvious. "That's how."

I wanted clarification. "Someone on the inside burned you to keep you safe or purposely get rid of you?"

With the first shift of what seemed like uncalculated

movement, she leaned back and looked up at the ceiling. "Both, either, does it matter?"

Fuck yes, it mattered. "It's one thing to burn you, but if your safety is in jeopardy because someone wants you eliminated, then—"

"It's not that."

"Then tell me what's going on, Maila."

"Isn't it obvious?"

Performance wise, no. She'd handled herself like an agent with years more experience than she had. So much so, that I should've guessed exactly what was going on, but the fact that she'd even be CIA in the first place wasn't something I'd ever considered. Not because of her unquestionable talent under pressure, but because no matter how good she was, there was one thing she could never outperform.

Not answering her question because I already knew the answer, I waited.

Her gaze cut back to mine. "We both know it's my last name. I'm tainted goods," she added before looking back up at the ceiling.

"You're not tainted goods." But she was the liability of all liabilities in the field. "You're Navy royalty."

A knock sounded on the door to the aft stateroom a second before it slid open.

His eyes only on her, Zane walked in. "*Jesus fucking Christ*, Em." Sitting beside her hip, he pulled her into his arms. "Fuck, girl. You gave me a heart attack."

Anger, deep and thick and coated in something I refused to name, surged. I was on my feet before her stiff arms hugged him back.

"*Zulu*," I snapped. "She's injured."

"Fuck you, Alpha," he threw over his shoulder without taking his hands off her but pulling back just enough to inspect every inch of her. "Where you hurt, sweetheart?"

"I'm fine." Withdrawing from him, she pulled her arm in front of her and cradled her injured hand.

Zane's knowing gaze cut from her hand to her feet then back to her face. "I told this guy"—he threw a nod in my direction—"that if that spray on you was yours, I was going to rearrange his pretty-boy face."

"Not what you said," I corrected, wanting to choke him out.

"You're right." Zulu looked up at me, and his tone turned hostile. "I said it better not be her blood, the rest was implied." Turning back to her, he ran his hand down her arm. "You good?"

"Fine."

When that was all she said, Zane cocked his head and waited.

She didn't elaborate.

"That's it?" Zane leaned back, but he didn't budge from the fucking divan. *"Fine?"*

I looked at her, she looked at me, and Zane looked between us.

Vance appeared at the doorway. "Right." He walked into the already crowded space. "Fine," he mimicked both of them with a chuckle, but it wasn't his usual dismissive laugh. This one was laced with tension. "I just fielded not one but three calls from the associate deputy director of the CIA while Alpha was too busy lapping around you like a lovesick pup to answer his phone. Now we all have our asses in a line of fire none of us want to be in if we want to keep doing what we do, but you're just *fine*, darling. Is that it?"

"Conlon's got a point." Zane jumped on Vance's sneak attack. "We've got an hour before I have to land this bird and we refuel. Maybe you should tell us what's going on."

"Yes." Vance sank to the divan opposite her. "Start talking, love."

That was it. I'd had enough. "Both of you, out."

For a beat, neither of them moved.

Then Vance slowly stood. "As you wish, *boss*."

Zane didn't follow Conlon's cue. Instead, he leaned closer to her. "You okay, sweetheart? For real?"

For the first time in over seven years, I saw her face soften, but it only lasted a fraction of a second. "I'm good."

"Out, Zulu. Now."

Finally standing, but taking her hand as he did, Zane gave her an exaggerated squeeze. "I made a promise to your brother." He briefly glanced at me before looking back at her. "Both me and Alpha did. You need anything, anything at all, we're here." Leaning over, he kissed the top of her head. "I know it's been a while, but we're still family, honey. Don't forget that."

Barely containing misplaced rage, I glared at Zane.

Emmy, Maila, Quinn, whatever the hell I was supposed to call her now, she simply nodded at Zane, but she didn't acknowledge his family comment. I knew it had to hit her. It hit me. Neither of us had any living blood family. Zane's comment wasn't a fucking comfort. It was a reminder.

Waiting till Zulu cleared the room and closed the door before I sat opposite her, I leaned forward.

Then I made the only play I had toward a woman who'd lost so much and was so closed off she didn't see the difference between trust and detriment.

I brought up the past.

THIRTY-NINE

Maila

I COULDN'T TAKE MY EYES OFF THE SHEER SIZE OF HIS BICEPS STRAINING the dark navy suit jacket he'd put on over his crisp white shirt. Leaning toward me and resting his elbows on his knees, his long, thick fingers laced together.

He focused his Mediterranean blue eyes on me.

In his low, resonant voice that transcended the jet's engine noise but didn't invade the sudden quiet around us, he spoke. "Why did you really run from me seven years ago?"

The question not unexpected, I was still taken off guard by his directness.

Then sudden anger, hot and rash, rushed past my defenses and stormed what was left of my composure.

Except I wasn't angry because he'd kissed me all those years ago, or that he'd had a job to do and his actions weren't his alone. I didn't even blame him anymore for my selfishness that led to me missing my own brother's funeral. I wasn't even upset Adam had put duty before me.

I was pissed he was asking why.

Nodding once as if he'd heard every word of my internal dialogue, he visibly inhaled, like it was an act meant to put me at ease with his uneasiness. "I understand."

He understood nothing.

"I wouldn't have answered the question either," he continued before leaning closer to me. "Here's what you didn't know. That kiss? It was selfish, ill-timed, and completely inappropriate."

I bristled.

"But it wasn't meant to placate. It wasn't a balm. It wasn't anything other than my own impotence because it should've been your brother standing there with Zane, not me."

Pain lanced across a part of my chest I thought was already dead. "Don't."

"Don't what? Tell you that I relive the moment I told you Billy was gone every day of my life? That I wish I'd taken that hit instead of him? That I miss my best friend, but I miss you more? What shouldn't I say, Maila? That I meant for that kiss to be a beginning, not an ending, but I fucked up?"

Startled, I couldn't stop the flinch before my arms drew in closer.

Taking in my reaction and reading it like he knew every inch of my body better than I knew it myself, he soldiered on with his tactical warfare aimed right at my weakness.

"You didn't give me a chance," he accused.

My stoic exterior crumbling, I said nothing.

"You didn't give me the opportunity to prove myself to you. To show you I came back." His aim precise, his hits continuous and relentless, he lowered his voice and fired the final blow. "To tell you I was out." His penetrating stare held mine. "For you."

Finding my voice, I showed my hand. "You didn't get out."

"You didn't wait for me," he countered, calling me on my own demons.

My hand burning, my feet stinging, my career over, my head swam with words and regret and a truth I didn't want to stare down from fifty thousand feet.

Not sure what to say because nothing would change a damn thing about any of it. Not my anger, not my actions, not this moment. Everything just… was.

And I hated it.

Slow, as if making an internal decision, the boy I knew, who'd grown into a man I didn't deserve, nodded. "Okay." He stood and turned toward the thin pocket door keeping us cocooned in this state we couldn't live in.

I panicked. "Wait."

His wide shoulders moved with an inhale, and he looked back at me.

Dark, thick hair still wet, clothes covering a body I'd imagined a million times, sharp angular jawline, blue eyes so intense they could strip me bare with a single look—the man I was closer to than anyone in this entire world was a complete stranger to me.

And it hurt.

Hurt in a way I'd refused to allow myself to think about, let alone feel, for seven years.

Everything left to lose, I gave an inch I didn't have to give. "I couldn't lose you too."

His body still, his gaze unwavering, he didn't take that inch for granted. "I realize that now."

Emotion I didn't allow myself filled my eyes. "Do you?"

He turned, but he didn't sit. Closing the single pace between us, he squatted in front of me so he was at my eye level. Then he cracked harder at the crumbling wall I was frantically trying to hold up around me.

His severe blue-eyed gaze cut into my very essence as his words cut into my heart. "When I brought your brother home, I thought I knew what it meant to have one life to live. I thought I knew the greatest sacrifice and honor a man could make."

Desperate to hide my fall, I turned my head.

Rough fingers grasped my chin and forced me back, but I kept my gaze averted.

"Look at me," he demanded.

Soul deep, where a crushing connection existed that I would

never be able to break no matter how badly it destroyed me, I didn't deny him.

My eyes met his.

"I was wrong." His thumb stroked my bottom lip with the same dominance as when he'd washed another man's blood off me. "When I saw your devastation, I knew. That one life never should've been solely dedicated to my Trident."

No longer holding my broken pieces together, I sucked in a sharp breath and begged. "Don't do this." Not now. Not ever.

"I'm not your father, and I'm not your brother." Leaning close, he brought his full lips a breath away from mine. "I'm doing this, Maila."

Cold wind and sharp angles and musk overwhelmed me. I could no more stop this man than I could the fatal trajectory my life had taken, but I tried anyway. "No."

"Yes." His strained whisper rasped against my heated skin. "I'm fucking doing this." His mouth crashed over mine.

Adam Trefor the ruthless, calculating man, not the Navy SEAL war hero, kissed me.

Unlike every remembered second of seven years ago, he didn't shatter the line between us, forcing my lips to part in the total destruction around us.

With sheer dominance, his hand slid into my damp hair and he angled my head for his and my pleasure. Stroking his tongue across my bottom lip, he wasn't asking permission. He was carefully, reverently showing me what seven years of life had taught him about control.

No willpower, no desire to resist, just like in that cell, I parted my lips and let him in.

He didn't hesitate.

With a feral groan that rumbled from his chest, his second hand grasped my face, and he thrust his tongue inside me.

Taking what was his, what had always been his, he drove

deep and tangled our bodies in an exquisite dance of seduction and need that feathered across my skin like a thousand tiny pin-pricks of fire and ice.

I didn't have a choice.

My body not my own, my fingers drove into his soft, thick hair and my hands gripped hard as my arms tried to cage him into my stratosphere.

I didn't kiss him back.

I gave him everything I'd ever lost.

FORTY

Adam

SHE FUCKING DESTROYED ME.

As if starved for oxygen and I was her air, her hands, her arms, her body—they wrapped around me like I was her own personal life preserver.

My head fucked, my thoughts reeling, possession telling me she'd only ever belonged to me, I devoured her. Then the girl I'd known who'd turned into a woman I couldn't read, she kissed me back.

No, not kiss.

She gave me fucking fire. Life-sustaining, mind-bending *fire*.

Every complicated emotion she'd been holding back, keeping locked tight under her impenetrable façade, she let loose.

She didn't obliterate my self-control, she fucking annihilated it.

Shoving her down, crawling over her, pushing her thigh wide with my knee, I didn't want to fuck her.

I wanted to consume her.

I wanted my clothes ripped off her body and my cock pounding so deep that she cried my name like I was the only man who'd ever touched her. I wanted to dominate her, body and soul. I wanted to show her exactly what would happen when she unraveled my restraint.

I wanted to taste her loss of control.

Endlessly.

Shoving my jean-clad cock against the heat between her legs, I ground my hips and swallowed both of our moans. This wasn't the need to fuck after an adrenaline rush. This wasn't like any other woman I'd ever bedded. This wasn't even close to the shit I'd conjured in my head of how she'd feel under me.

This was explosive.

Biting her bottom lip, sucking her tongue into my mouth, I didn't want to stop. I wanted to fuck her on this damn plane for everyone to hear. But I wouldn't do that to her.

Yet.

Gripping her hair, forcing myself to pull her back, I took in every inch of her wet, parted lips, flushed cheeks and sex-dazed eyes.

I was going to have this woman. No matter what it took. "I'm not making the same mistakes again," I warned.

Her chest heaving, her breath short, her eyes wild, she was so damn gorgeous. But then she opened her mouth and the detachment in her voice I wasn't expecting to come back bled out. "Are you married?"

What? "No." *Fuck no.*

"Attached?" she pushed, in the same emotionless tone.

Not hiding my frown, I threw her line of questioning back on her. "Would I touch you if there was someone else?" Was she that far gone she'd forgotten who the hell I was?

"I don't know."

"You do know because you know me." She'd always known me. Better than her brother sometimes.

"I used to know you," she countered.

Masking frustration and trying not to be irrationally pissed, I leaned up and brought her with me. Pushing her hair from her face before tangling my fingers in the soft strands, I focused on what I couldn't see. "Seven years hasn't changed who I am." I gripped her tighter. "You know I would never touch you if I belonged to another woman."

Something flashed in her eyes, but it was gone so quick, I couldn't decipher it. "You didn't ask if I belong to someone else."

Ten rounds to the gut would've been preferable to the shit that hit my chest. I forced myself to ask. "Do you?"

"You tried to buy me from a sex trafficker."

Fuck this. "I'm going to assume that means you're not seeing anyone. Next time I ask a pointed question, answer it." Not giving her time to rebuff, I cut to what I wanted to know. "How did you wind up with Al Ka'abi?"

"Right place, right time."

I waited for more, but she didn't elaborate. "Did Langley know you were in?"

She nodded.

First the text, then the call from the ADD. None of this was sitting well with me. "Cohen told me to bring you in."

She shrugged. "Not surprising."

"I didn't tell him I have you."

She looked out the window. "He knows."

"All he knows is that we're landing in Greece to refuel." I grasped her chin again and brought her eyes back to mine. "We can reroute."

"What does it matter?" She pulled out of my hold.

I couldn't tell if she was resigned, scared, or indifferent, and I suspected asking wouldn't get me anywhere. Her evasion tactics rivaling those of the men I'd served with on the Teams, I would've been impressed if I wasn't pissed off.

Instead of trying to get information out of her, I switched gears and went for full disclosure. "Four years ago, I was wounded in an op that went south. After I was patched up and had two surgeries and almost a year of rehabilitation, I still wasn't one hundred percent. I'd lost partial range of motion with my shooting arm. If I was anyone else wearing the uniform, I would've been sent back to active duty, but because I wore a Trident, that fifteen percent loss of range of motion became a liability. Not for me, but for the brothers next to me. Facing a future from a bird's eye view behind comms instead of my scope, I made the decision to get out."

"You started a security company."

So she had kept tabs on me. I nodded. "Alpha Elite Security. Three years ago. I had government contracts before I had enough employees to execute the missions. I've been fortunate with a hundred percent success rate on all our contracts. Word spread, the private sector caught on, and it's grown from there."

"Good for you." She looked out the window again.

I couldn't tell if her tone was dismissive or if she actually meant it as a compliment. With anyone else, I wouldn't have given a damn. "The reason I'm telling you all of this is because I'm in a unique situation to help you."

"With what?"

I didn't answer. I waited until her eyes met mine again. When they did, I said what she already had to know. "Whoever sent me that text wanted you out, and they went through a hell of a lot of effort to do it." I took her uninjured hand. "What aren't you telling me?"

FORTY-ONE

Maila

"What aren't you telling me?" His tone was soft, muted, but make no mistake, even posed as a question, it was a demand.

There wasn't a single inch of Adam Trefor that wasn't alpha, dominant and exacting. He wasn't ostentatious about his dominance, but I could feel it surrounding me as sure as I could smell the cold wind and sharp angles that were always uniquely him, even after an improvised shower in an airplane lavatory.

As his large hand grasped mine, firm and still, and our bodies connected, frenetic nerves pinged across my flesh as if I were a live wire. His eyes locked resolutely on mine with a stare I'd known since I was five years old, it felt like home at the same time everything felt different.

Every second of his demanding kiss still lingering, it suddenly occurred to me.

The Navy didn't make Adam dominant.

Even though he'd earned the call sign Alpha as Team leader when he was a SEAL, Adam Trefor had always had a larger-than-life presence.

A memory flashed from when I was six years old, and I'd fallen off my bike and skinned my knee. I'd cried out when I fell, but sitting on the sidewalk, holding my wounded limb, I'd held the indignity of tears at bay because of the tall, dark-haired boy in the yard tossing a football with my brother. Billy had gone into the house for a Band-Aid, but not Adam.

His stark eyes had met mine and held as he'd walked across the lawn.

Dropping to a squat, Adam put his hand over mine, just below the skinned flesh, then he issued an order. "You're not going to cry."

"Okay," I sniveled.

"Know why?"

Biting my lip, I shook my head.

"Because I'm here, and you're okay."

"Okay," I whisper-cried.

Lines grew between his eyebrows as he frowned. "Does it hurt?"

I didn't want to nod. I wanted to shake my head and be brave for him. For Daddy and for Billy too, but mostly for him. Except my cut stung and my knee hurt and I wanted Adam to pick me up and take me inside.

I nodded.

His voice got quieter. "I know." Lowering his head, but keeping his eyes on me, his dark, unruly hair fell over his forehead, and he brought his lips to my knee and kissed right on the cut. "But you're going to be all right, and I'm going to take care of you." He held his hand out.

I pushed away the memory, but my gaze drifted up his arm. The same arm he'd held out to me all those years ago that was attached to the shoulder that now had bullet wound and surgery scars. Fifteen percent loss of range of motion, and his career was over.

Mine was over for a lot less.

A single text.

One well-planned, strategically sent text to a number he swore no one else knew except me, but how could I know if he was telling me the truth? The number he'd gotten in high school his senior year when he'd finally saved enough money to get a cell phone was years ago. A dozen women could've had that old number for all I knew.

And I knew about AES. I'd looked him up. I'd found plenty on the CIA database I had access to. Or used to before two months ago. I was sure his old number was traceable. He didn't have the CIA hiding his identity behind layers of encrypted software and handlers you couldn't break with an ice pick through their eye.

Not that I knew firsthand, but I'd heard the rumors.

We'd all heard them.

Handlers were unbreakable. They were your most valuable asset in the field. Except I'd never met mine in person, and now I was on a plane somewhere over the Middle East or the Mediterranean with a man who'd come to rescue me because he'd been able to get past all the encrypted intel that was supposedly unhackable.

Fucked didn't begin to cut it.

What wasn't I telling him?

Everything.

I took in his expensive suit jacket and the veins on his hands I wanted to trace with my finger to see if they were as impenetrable as him. "What did you find out about me? Before the text," I clarified, reluctantly pulling my hand away.

If I thought he would evade my question, or show any sign of emotion at me pulling away, I was wrong.

"I respected your request, but you're right in assuming I kept tabs on you."

"Such as?" I needed to know how deep this went.

Leaning back, he crossed his ankle over his knee. "You fell off the grid after Billy's funeral except for a large annual withdrawal for four years, which I assumed was for college."

"You assumed?" He didn't look?

"I didn't dive deeper than that. I was still downrange, and the fact that the withdrawals were being made told me you were still alive."

Stark, honest. I couldn't fault his thinking. "And then?"

His hand resting on his leather boot-covered ankle, he tapped one finger. "Then I dove deeper."

"What did you find?"

"Nothing." He studied me a moment. "Vance did."

"Vance?"

He nodded toward the front of the plane. "Vance Conlon."

"The British helicopter pilot?"

"He's not British, and he's not a pilot." He glanced toward the front of the plane, and his eyes narrowed. "Not unless he has to be." He looked back at me. "He was in London for a while."

"You had him follow me?" I'd been going back and forth between New York and London for three years as part of my cover. If someone was following me, I should've noticed.

"Not exactly." He rubbed a hand over his jaw. "I had him look for you. At first, he found nothing. Then he found you in Manhattan, found the co-op you live in, and figured out you worked for a pharmaceutical company."

The co-op lease was under the pharmaceutical company's name. "He found me? Specifically?"

Adam didn't hesitate. "Yes."

"How?"

He frowned. "Facial recognition software."

"You're sure?"

The lines between his eyebrows deepened. "Positive. And there's a lot to question about Conlon, but his loyalty to me isn't one of them."

"That's not what I was implying." It's exactly one of the avenues I was implying, but not the main question.

"Conlon didn't send that text. He didn't blow your cover, Maila."

It'd been so long since someone called me by my real name that it didn't sound right. Except when Adam said it, the two syllables rolling off his tongue with a dip in quietness in his voice, I wanted to be the woman called by that name. "You're misunderstanding what I'm asking."

"Explain," he demanded.

"Did he find me or did he find Quinn Michaels?"

Adam abruptly stood and threw open the door separating us from the rest of the plane. "Conlon, get back here."

The dark-haired man who was too pretty to be some sort of mercenary who worked for an elite security government contractor swaggered into the back of the plane and sat opposite me. "Alpha." He tipped his chin at Adam before looking at me like he could see through my shirt. "Love." He looked back at Adam. "What can I do for you?"

Standing over both of us, Adam's hands went to his hips. "How did you find her?"

Vance Conlon grinned like he was thoroughly enjoying himself. "Which time?"

"Every time," Adam ordered. "But start with the first one."

"Three years ago?"

Adam gave him a clipped nod.

Casually draping a muscular arm that almost rivaled Adam's over the back of the couch, Vance's gaze cut to me and he smiled, but he spoke to Adam. "November had a demo of the first-gen facial recognition software you had him working on back then. I hacked into his server and downloaded it." He shrugged. "I'd been playing with it for a week and got lucky."

"Where?" Adam demanded before I could ask.

"Manhattan." He looked up at Adam. "You'd be surprised at the number of beautiful women walking around the Upper East Side." His gaze cut back to me. "You were one of them."

"Then what?" Adam prompted.

"Then I was in New York the following week and took a stroll." Vance winked at me. "Love the skirts you wear to work, darling."

"So you followed me?"

The dark-haired, hazel-eyed man nodded at me as the corner of his mouth tipped up. "I did. Found you on the same street from the week before, followed you to the co-op—you really should be more aware of your surroundings, love. Then the next day I followed you to work, hacked the co-op's financials, and found a unit leased to the pharmaceutical company you'd walked into. Figured it was a work perk or hiring bonus."

"You did all this without actually pulling background on her name?" Adam asked.

Vance glanced at Adam. "You didn't ask me to find her name, you asked me to find her."

Adam leveled Vance with a warning glare. "Conlon."

"What?" Vance challenged. "She was a ghost. You said so yourself. She'd dropped off the grid seven years ago. Why would I look for her name when we have perfectly good facial rec—"

"Out," Adam clipped.

So my CIA cover had held, and still someone had managed to get that text to the one person in the world who would come looking for me if he thought I was in trouble.

Standing, Vance gave me a screen-worthy smile. "I promise, love, he isn't always this surly. Must be something in the air." He winked. "And for the record, you're prettier in person." He slapped Adam on the shoulder. "Alpha." Then he walked out, closing the door behind him.

I stared at the man I used to be in love with. A man who'd never stopped looking for me even after I'd told him not to. "I asked you not to come after me." Now, just like Vance had said, he was in the ADD's line of fire.

"That was seven years ago. This is now." Leveling me with a look that made a tremor race up my spine, he showed me the SEAL side of him. "Nothing was going to stop me after I got that text."

FORTY-TWO

Adam

"THAT WAS SEVEN YEARS AGO. THIS IS NOW." I HELD HER GAZE, letting her know I was dead fucking serious about not making the same mistakes twice. "Nothing was going to stop me after I got that text."

"The Associate Deputy Director—"

"I don't give a damn about Cohen."

"You should."

"That's not a word in my vocabulary, Maila," I warned. "Know this. I do, or I don't. And right now there's a whole stack of actionable do's piling up. I told you I was in a position to help you, but I need to know two things."

Her green eyes wary, she took the bait. "What?"

Taking the seat across from her because I couldn't sit next to her anymore and not touch her, I asked the first question. Which would be the only question depending on her response. "Do you want your job back?" I was a selfish bastard. No part of me wanted her in the field, let alone in harm's way, but I had to give her the choice.

"Is this a pointed question?"

If my arms weren't resting on my knees with my fingers clasped, my hands would've fisted. "Answer the question, Maila."

"Are you going to kiss me again if I say no?"

The shitstorm of adrenaline, anger and desire coursing

through my veins hit a fucking wall, and I stilled. "Do you know why I'm sitting here and not next to you?"

"Because you're six and a half feet of muscle and tension and there's more room over there for your tightly controlled, barely contained dominance."

Jesus Christ. And this woman said she didn't know me. "I'm sitting here because I'm giving you the space to answer the question."

"You didn't answer my question."

"I'm going to do a hell of a lot more than kiss you no matter what you come back with." It took a fucking Herculean effort not to stare at her hard nipples pressing against my T-shirt as she drew her knees up.

"And if I say no?"

"To me or the CIA?" Her hair drying naturally in waves, no makeup, she was fucking stunning.

"You."

"I'll change your mind." Flip the switch, tip the scales, whatever I had to do to convince her, I'd fucking do it.

"And the CIA?"

"I commend you for making the right choice." The safe choice.

"I didn't say I didn't want my job back."

My jaw ticked. "Answer the fucking question, Maila."

She didn't hesitate. "I want my job back."

Fuck.

I didn't respond. I leaned back.

"I knew it," she stated with the same emotionless tone. "You don't want me working for the CIA."

"I don't want you in harm's way." I didn't want her in the field. I didn't want her identity being leaked, and I didn't want her away from me.

"There's more to it than that."

"Do you know what the largest growing sector of AES's business is?" I didn't wait for her to guess. I told her. "Kidnap and ransom."

"What does that have to do with me?"

"Everything if your identity is leaked." She had to know what the fuck I was talking about. "If it becomes public knowledge that Vice Admiral Nilsen's daughter and Navy SEAL Nilsen's sister is a CIA asset, you'll top every terrorist organization's K and R wish list."

"They're both dead."

"They both had illustrious careers that garnered a lot of enemies."

"That was them, not me."

No one in their right mind would want her as an asset, unless... It suddenly fucking hit me. The part she was leaving out. The missing fucking link in this whole mess. "You didn't seek out the CIA, did you? You were recruited." From the beginning it hadn't made sense that someone with her background would be an asset in the field.

Not saying anything, she stared at me.

"Who was it?" This reeked of her father, but he died when she was only seventeen.

Her gaze dropped, her chest rose with an inhale then she looked back up at me. "My mom was an asset before she died. My father made introductions before his aneurysm. It was all set up before I went to college."

Jesus fucking Christ. "Did Billy know this?"

She shook her head once.

Of course he didn't, he would've lost his shit. "Did he know about your mother?"

"No."

"Who was the introduction with?"

"The then Assistant Director of Counterterrorism, Mike Cohen."

I didn't know if I was more shocked at how her life had been orchestrated or the depth of this whole fucking mess. "That's why you didn't give a shit when I told you Cohen wanted me to bring you in." She knew him. Personally.

"I didn't give a shit because as much as I want my job back, I know I'm not getting it. There's nothing you can do to help me, but I appreciate the sentiment." Standing gracefully as if she hadn't just been through what she'd been through, she tucked her arms across herself. "Do you have something to eat on this plane?"

FORTY-THREE

Maila

EVERYTHING WAS CRUMBLING.

The very reason I got up every day and breathed through another sunset was the cause.

The mission.

The sacrifice.

The greater good.

Everything my father had drilled into me, set up for me, expected of me.

I wasn't emotion or wants or joy or sunshine. I was purpose.

I was CIA.

But the second I'd pulled that blindfold off, I'd known I was in trouble.

I'd walked away seven years ago because I knew I wouldn't survive losing the last person I loved. I also knew I would never be Adam's priority. It hadn't mattered that he'd said he'd walk away from the Teams for me or that he wasn't active duty anymore, or even that he'd come for me halfway around the world. I was on a sixty-million-dollar company jet that I knew was only one of many. AES may not be the military, but it was as much Adam's priority. Maybe more.

I didn't want to fit myself into his world.

I wanted to be his world.

I'd always wanted to be his world.

But that wish, that thought, it was poison, and I couldn't

entertain it any more than I could deny that I was a hypocrite. I'd felt honor-bound to my father's plans for me back then the same as Adam was honor-bound to his commitment to service. Yes, I'd walked away because I couldn't lose Adam. Pretending he wasn't in my life was the only emotional safety harness I'd had, but walking into my prearranged future had been the vehicle that safety harness was attached to.

Now that vehicle had gone so far off the tracks that I no longer remembered why any of this mattered. Khalaf was dead, but there were hundreds more like him. The CIA had more files than I could count, except I would no longer be a part of any of it. The ADD could cover my tracks on all of this, but he wouldn't. I knew what I was. Mike Cohen had been looking for a way to retire me from the field since the moment I stepped into it, and Adam's actions today were the excuse Cohen had been looking for.

Maybe he'd even been the one to send Adam the text.

It didn't matter.

Same as it didn't matter if Adam rerouted this plane a hundred times. My career was already over. Which only made sitting next to Adam right now that much more dangerous. I was freefalling, and pretending like my battered body wasn't humming for every ounce of attention Adam poured on me was independence suicide.

Standing, I crossed my arms over my braless self. "Do you have something to eat on this plane?"

His stark eyes taking in every inch of my body language, he nodded and stood. "Of course, my apologies. I should've offered."

The tight grasp of control I was desperately trying to keep on my emotions slipped. "Don't do that."

Reaching for the sliding pocket door, he paused. "Do what?"

"Flip like that. Kiss me one moment, be formal the next." Calling what he'd done merely a kiss was equivalent to saying he'd simply picked me up today, but I had to minimize it, for my own sanity.

He turned and our pronounced height difference was only muted by the fact that the cabin of his plane didn't accommodate his height without him tipping his head slightly.

Looking down at me, his body inches from mine, his heat, his scent, his presence, all of it made my knees weak. But when he spoke, quiet and reserved like his voice was meant only for my ears, it broke me.

"What would you like me to do, Maila?"

He wasn't asking. "That's not a real question." Adam Trefor would do what he wanted. He'd said it himself, he was an action man.

"What would be a real question?"

Real would be asking how many women he had been with. Real would be knowing if he'd thought of me like I'd thought of him for seven years. Was it my face, my body, my voice he'd thought of when he was fucking? Because he knew how to fuck. No man kissed a woman how he'd kissed me without having years and years of experience. So maybe I didn't want real. Maybe I was only talking myself into a corner.

Trying to change the course of this conversation to something within the bounds I'd imposed on myself for so long, I didn't answer him. I asked a different, equally dangerous question. "What do you want?"

"Is that the question or an actual inquiry, because I already told you what I want."

Had he? "You said you weren't making the same mistakes again."

As easily as if our souls were made for each other, his hand slid up my nape and he captured a fistful of my hair. Using his grip, his arm, he brought my body flush against his and lowered his head. "Tell me exactly what you're afraid of, Maila."

Maybe I was taken aback by his question. Maybe I was alarmed by his insight when I was trying so desperately to shove too many emotions down into a collapsing well. I didn't know because I couldn't think straight. I was staring into his eyes and getting lost.

Maybe I'd been lost in him since I was five years old.

"Pointed question," he added, his thumb glancing dominantly down my neck and over my pulse point as if he knew my heart was attempting to beat its way out of my chest. "Answer me."

What was I afraid of?

His hold on me, his closeness, his touch? The air he breathed? How when he left a room, it was like the barometric pressure dropped?

I was afraid of all of it.

"You," I answered simply.

"I'm not going to hurt you," he solemnly, resolutely replied. "Not this time."

"You didn't hurt me before." Life had. Couldn't he understand that?

Cupping my face, his voice dropped. "Let me love you, Maila."

One single word and the world fell out from under me.

Love.

Let Adam love me.

The slider door opened, and Vance held his phone out. "Alpha, you need to take this."

FORTY-FOUR

Adam

HER PULSE RACING, HER THROAT MOVED WITH A SWALLOW.

Fucking Vance. "Not now, Conlon."

"Now," he insisted.

Fuck. I couldn't leave it like this. I'd felt her muscles stiffen. I knew what I'd done. Laying every damn thing out was a risk, but a calculated one.

She needed to know I wasn't going to back down. Not now.

"Alpha," Conlon clipped.

Lowering my head, speaking so only she could hear me, I gave her what I could in that moment. "I'm only taking this call to give you a minute to think about what I said, because I know you, just like you know me. But understand this, Maila Marie Nilsen—I'm coming for you." Covering her mouth with mine, I sealed my promise with intent.

As I stroked through her heat, she didn't retreat. Kissing me back like I knew she would because this thing between us wasn't a question of if, but when, and I was done waiting. Gripping her face, her hair, I deepened the kiss and fucking groaned as my cock hardened to the point of pain. I didn't give a damn if Conlon or anyone else was watching. This woman was mine.

Reluctantly releasing her, I pulled back. "Coming for you," I repeated in a hoarse whisper before mouthing two words. *You're mine.*

"Time sensitive," Conlon warned.

My eyes on her, I took the phone from Vance. "Trefor."

"It's me," November said tiredly. "You've got a potential problem on the ground in Greece."

"Hold," I told November before glancing at Conlon. "Get her something to eat." Leaning down to her one more time, I touched my lips to her forehead. "Be right back." I walked out and took a seat in the conference area. "Go," I ordered November.

"I'm hearing chatter," November hedged.

Conlon walked her past me to the galley. "You don't call me with chatter." November didn't deal in rumor.

"CIA chatter," he clarified.

Fuck. "And?" Swamped in my clothes, she looked even smaller than I remembered.

"You've got company on the ground waiting for you when you refuel."

Shit. "Hold." Standing, I moved down the aisle.

Conlon looked up, saw my trajectory and ushered Emmy to a seat. "Take a load off, love."

I moved past them to the cockpit. "Zulu, how long to touchdown?"

"Twenty minutes," he answered as Missy looked up at me from her spot between first and second chair. "And before you ask, no, I don't have enough fuel to reroute at this point. We're landing."

"Copy." Damn it. "What kind of company?" I asked November as I moved back to the conference area of the cabin.

"What I know, or what I think?"

"Both. Then we'll talk about you hacking the goddamn CIA." I couldn't talk my way out of that no matter how well he covered his tracks. My connections ran military deep, not CIA deep.

"What I know officially is nothing. What I know unofficially is that our friends in Langley diverted a private flight midair that was aiming for Dubai. It landed twenty minutes ago in Greece where you're due to refuel. The passenger manifest is as bogus as the tail number, so I don't know who's on that plane, but I know the pilot's alias, and it's one of theirs."

It was her handler, it had to be.

Lowering my voice, my gaze trained on her as Conlon handed her a sandwich with a fucking smile, I watched her reserved movements with both fascination and awe. "Who's her handler?" Maila Marie Nilsen had grown into the strongest woman I knew, and I was fucking proud of her. But I also knew the grief she'd endured to become who she was.

"Who was her handler, or who is her handler?" November asked rhetorically. "Because the moment she made contact with Al Ka'abi two months ago, the cell phone number she'd been in contact with once a week for three years was disconnected. Then a new number blew her phone up with several calls in a row before going radio silent, and all activity on her line and the other went dead."

"Can you trace either number?" It was pointless, but I asked anyway.

"I'm good but not that good. I'd have to hack backlogs of data, and you've got seventeen minutes before you land. The best I can do is satellite images of the bogus tail number."

"Anyone get on or off the plane?"

"No, but they're refueling."

I rubbed a hand over my face. "Can we get to the ground crew?"

"I can probably hack a cell number for one of them and call, but it won't do any good. The pilot is Company, and he won't risk the passengers being seen if they don't want to be seen. Ground crew won't know who's on the plane."

"They didn't resupply?"

"No, only refuel."

Conlon walked over and handed me a sandwich.

"Keep me posted," I told November before hanging up and handing Vance his cell.

"Friendlies?" he asked cryptically.

"Depends on your perspective." Missy walked out of the cockpit and sat in front of Maila.

Conlon took the seat across from me. "Her handler?"

"That's my guess."

"It's been two months. Now they fucking come for her?" He shook his head. "Bastards are a little late."

"Too late."

"What do they want?"

Good fucking question. "Grill her, fire her, arrest her, read her the riot act, escort her back stateside." She gave the dog a piece of her sandwich. "Fuck if I know."

"Is it wrong I hope it's the latter?"

My gaze cut from her to Conlon's fucking grin.

He smiled wider. "I'd pay good money to see you go head-to-head with a spook."

"Handler," I corrected.

"Whatever. Spooks, handlers, the Company. I don't give a shit what you call it. This'll be fun."

Christ. Picking up my sandwich, I stood. "Your idea of fun is disturbing."

He winked. "You don't know the half of it." His smile disappeared. "For the record, I got your back."

"That's what I'm afraid of."

"I promise not to shoot anyone." His smile returned. "Unless they shoot you first."

"You're not discharging your weapon at Athens airport." Making my way up the aisle to the forward cabin, I took the seat next to her.

Missy wagged her tail and nudged my knee.

"She wants a bite of your sandwich." Maila gave her another bite of hers, then petted her as she slowly chewed.

"You never had a dog." I opened my sandwich and practically ate half in one bite.

She finished her bite and took a sip of a Coke before speaking. "Neither did you."

I nodded at the soda. "You used to like Sprite."

"I used to like a lot of things." She took another sip, then fed the dog another bite.

I finished my sandwich and helped myself to a swallow of her Coke.

She watched me drink, then tracked my hand as I set the can down. "There are plenty more sodas in the galley."

"I know." I drank from hers on purpose. It was an asshole sign of dominance, but it was also meant to show my intent. Me, her, us. Together. I turned toward her. "It looks like we're going to have company on the ground."

Not seeming surprised, she nodded. "My handler."

"For what purpose?"

She gave her last bite to the dog, then brushed off her hands. "I guess we'll find out."

"Debrief?"

"Probably." She petted the dog and softly spoke to her. "That's all I have."

After Cohen's call, I knew we'd have to face this sooner rather than later, but fuck. "What are you going to say?"

The dog lay down at her feet, and her clear green eyes met mine. "What would you like me to say?"

One question and I knew.

She was in.

Me and her.

Taking her face, I stroked my thumb over her cheek. "You're thinking about what I said. Good."

Ever so slightly, she leaned into my touch. "You deduced that from a single question?"

"Yes." I wanted to fucking kiss her again. I wanted to do a hell of a lot more than kiss her. "Also from your body language, the way you lean into me and the fact that you kissed me back."

Heat colored her cheeks. "This isn't anything other than me asking what you would like me to say to the CIA. What we should say," she added.

We. I smiled. "I know." I was still taking it as a win. Twenty years ago, she'd pushed us together like family, and now she was doing it again. The victory was almost unexpected, but her word choice, her delivery, it was one hundred percent the woman I used to know. Hell, the girl I'd helped raise and grown up alongside of. That girl, this woman, she'd had my six then, and she had it now. I wasn't taking it for granted.

I also wasn't going to let her go down for me.

Stroking her cheek again, I made sure she understood. "You tell the truth. You were taken, held captive, there was a hot exfil, and I took down Al Ka'abi and his guards. You don't know what happened after that."

"You didn't take down all his guards," she corrected. "I killed Fahad."

I brushed my thumb over her full bottom lip. "You're not going to tell them that."

"I'm not lying, Adam," she quietly reprimanded. "I'm not going to do that."

"Final approach," Zulu called from the cockpit.

"It's not a lie, it's an omission, and that's exactly what you're going to do." I reached across her and buckled her seatbelt. "Nonnegotiable." I grabbed the wrappers from our sandwiches and her soda can and tossed them in the galley's trash.

"You have nonnegotiables?" she asked once I sat back down.

"You don't?" The plane banked left, and I buckled in.

She glanced out the window. "You don't need to take a fall for me."

"What fall? My actions were in self-defense, and Al Ka'abi had American hostages. I did the CIA and the US Military a favor."

She looked back at me. "It isn't that simple."

Descending over Athens, the plane lined up for landing.

"I pay a team of lawyers to make it that simple." If I needed them, which I wouldn't in this case because I knew how the game was played. If the CIA believed I was responsible, they'd accept it and leave me alone. My background and experience bought me that luxury. But if they knew her part, they'd put her through hours, if not days of debriefing, questioning every single one of her actions. She'd been through enough. I wasn't going to let her go through that, not if I could stop it.

His phone to his ear, Vance came to the forward cabin and took a seat across the aisle. "Right." He glanced at me. "Understood, sir." Hanging up, he addressed me. "I'm not sure what I dislike more. The ADD knowing my first name or him having my number on speed dial."

"What did he want this time?" I demanded.

"Not what." Vance buckled his seatbelt and tipped his chin at Maila. "Who."

FORTY-FIVE

Maila

THE PLANE TOUCHED DOWN, TAXIED AND HAD BARELY COME TO A stop when Adam was out of his seat.

His jaw ticking, he glanced at me. "Stay here."

"I wasn't planning on going anywhere." I had no shoes and no bra. The no underwear didn't bother me, but the no bra thing was definitely bothering me. More so than no shoes. Which was ridiculous given the circumstances, but nothing made me feel more naked than being around alpha, dominant SEALs in a borrowed T-shirt with no bra.

Adam frowned at me but didn't comment as he went to the passenger door of the plane and opened it before going down the airstairs.

Vance looked down at me and winked. "I think I'm going to enjoy this."

I think he had a screw loose. "Dare I ask?"

He smiled. "Alpha versus Spooks. Should be a good show."

Suddenly exhausted, I exhaled. "You do realize no one calls the CIA that anymore."

"I call them that." He moved toward the open door. "I'll let you know who wins." With a wink, he disappeared down the stairs.

His eyes on me, Zane stepped out of the cockpit. "You doing okay, sweetheart?"

"You can stop asking me that. I'm fine."

His head cocked, and he gave me a look that said I was full of it. "Babe, fine is meeting in a dive bar for drinks after a nine to five. Or in your case, a swank restaurant with white tablecloths and wine I can't pronounce. Either way, fine isn't a hot extraction in the middle of a sand trap with pissed-off traffickers shooting at our helo."

I didn't have time to respond.

A scowling Adam came back on the plane followed by a grinning Vance and a man I had not seen in years.

Crossing my arms over my chest, I stood. "Malik?"

I no sooner got the word out than Zane was rounding on the former SEAL. "You fucking piece of shit, Malik."

Vance stepped out of the way, Adam's hands went to his hips and before Malik had stepped fully into the Gulfstream's cabin, Zane's fist was connecting with Malik's face.

"Zulu," Adam snapped as Missy came out of the cockpit barking, followed by the other pilot, Roark.

Roark, who'd barely said a quiet hello to me when Vance had introduced me before getting me a sandwich, grabbed Zane before he could throw another punch. Pinning Zane's arms behind his back for a moment, Roark issued a calm but stern command to his dog. "Missy, quiet."

Chuckling like the punch hadn't been more than a glance, Malik rubbed his jaw and smiled at me as he set down a small rolling suitcase I recognized. "Maila, good to see you again."

Adam, Vance, and Zane all whipped their heads to look at me.

"Handling the refuel," Roark announced before giving Missy a command to follow him and heading down the airstairs.

"What are you doing here?" I asked Malik.

Vance grinned. "The plot thickens."

Adam threw a warning glare at Vance before looking at me. "Let's take this to the conference area."

"How about we take this fucking dickless shithead outside and I finish him off," Zane spat.

"Bosnia wasn't his fault," Adam stated, but he didn't say it like he meant it.

"The fuck it wasn't," Zane countered.

Malik held a hand up. "Appreciate the vote of confidence, Alpha, but I can handle my own battles."

"If you'd handled them in the first place, we wouldn't have lost Maverick, you asshole," Zane bit out.

Vance looked at me and winked. "My money's on Zulu, unless your new friend takes a step closer to you, then I'm solidly in camp Alpha."

"Conlon," Adam barked. "*Outside.*" His glare cut to Zane. "Do your prechecks, Zulu, *now.*" Taking my arm, Adam led me to the middle of the plane and sat me down in one of four seats that all faced a small built-in table. Taking the seat next to me, he nodded across the table. "Malik, sit the fuck down. You have ten minutes."

Zane glared at Malik as he walked past him, then he retreated into the cockpit.

Vance glanced at Adam. "Sure you don't need a witness?"

"Out," Adam ordered.

Smoothing his hand down the front of his pressed dress shirt before undoing the single button on his suit jacket, Malik sat and aimed his gaze at me. "Thinking you might need them, I grabbed some clothes from your place." He glanced at my T-shirt, my wrist and my hand I was holding close. "Glad I did." He smiled then his handsome face turned serious. "Are you okay?"

"What's going on? I haven't seen you since you were on the Teams." Then Billy had told me he'd gotten kicked, but never said why.

Still built like a SEAL, his presence still one hundred percent alpha, Malik gave me a winning smile. "I'm Company now. I was assigned as your new handler." His expression sobered. "Which, unfortunately, turned out to be a short-lived assignment."

My handler? A former Navy SEAL? He was the one who'd sent me those encrypted texts telling me to back down when I'd agreed to dinner with Khalaf that night in the hotel?

"Cut the fucking bullshit, Malik," Adam interrupted. "Did you send me the text?"

Malik looked at Adam with honest confusion. "What text?"

If they were hiring Navy SEALs as handlers, then I guessed it was true about what they said with handlers and ice picks. Malik may look civil in a suit, but make no mistake, he was lethal under that façade. "Why were you assigned as my handler?" I'd had the same female handler for years.

Malik's gaze cut to me. "Long story short, Al Ka'abi was one of the cases I'd been working, which is why I told you to stand down in those texts you ignored." He gave me a wry smile. "Incidentally, you're very much like your brother in the field. He and your father would be proud." His expression sobered. "Unfortunately, the CIA doesn't take the same perspective, and I regret to inform you that you are no longer in our employ. I'm here to download any intel you may have and officially give you your notice of termination. Within the next week you're to vacate the co-op. The doorman will let you in if you no longer have your keys. "

A feeling I couldn't describe washed over me. Anger, relief, regret, embarrassment—some of it, all of it. "I understand." I didn't. Or rather, I didn't agree with any of it.

Adam's hand landed on my thigh under the table. "Cohen said he wanted her brought in."

"I spoke with him and let him know that wasn't necessary," Malik answered before leaning back in his seat and looking at me. "Can you tell me what you learned?"

I told Malik everything from the first encounter in the hotel in London to the part where Adam rescued me from the cell. I left out the blindfold, and God help me, the part where I killed Fahad. But I gave him everything else, like Adam had told me to do. Names, dates, locations, I told Malik everything I knew, and he intently listened the whole time but didn't comment or ask any questions.

When I'd finished, he merely nodded at me. "Thank you, that's very helpful. I'm glad you're safe." He looked at Adam. "I'm assuming the cleanup was your handiwork?"

Adam didn't say anything, he just stared at Malik.

Malik half smiled as he rose out of his seat and buttoned his suit jacket. "Miss Nilsen, it was an honor and privilege to serve with your brother and work with you. I wish you all the best." He glanced at Adam. "Trefor." He turned and walked off the plane.

Adam watched him leave with a stern expression but then he turned to me, and his face softened. "You okay?"

I stared after Malik even though he was gone. "I have to vacate the apartment in Manhattan."

"I heard." He brushed my hair off my shoulder. "You can stay with me."

"You said you don't have a home."

"I said I have several. We can start at the penthouse in Manhattan and go from there."

Go from there.

Suddenly exhausted beyond words, I fought a yawn.

Stepping back onto the plane, Vance grabbed my rolling suitcase and brought it down the aisle toward us. Leaning on a seat, he crossed his arms and glanced between us before addressing Adam. "All good?"

Adam nodded. "Situation handled, but let Roark and Zulu know we're staying the night. She needs sleep. Is the villa vacant?"

"I'm fine," I protested. "I can sleep on the plane tonight." I needed to get back to New York and pack the few belongings I had.

"Already ahead of you," Vance answered Adam, ignoring my protest. "Vacant and secure. A driver can be here in ten minutes. I'll let everyone know." Vance walked back down the aisle.

I looked at Adam, and suddenly, he looked different. Different in a way that made me feel more vulnerable than I ever had in my life. "I don't need to stay the night in Greece." A lifetime ago, I'd dreamed of seeing the Mediterranean in person.

"I know," Adam answered simply as his huge hand curled possessively around the back of my neck. "See if there're any shoes in that suitcase, and I'll check on our ride." His lips touched my forehead and he stood, walking down the aisle toward the front of the plane.

Gingerly getting out of my seat, I grabbed the handle of my small carry-on suitcase and wheeled it into the bathroom.

FORTY-SIX

Adam

SHE GRACEFULLY WALKED TO THE WINDOWS OVERLOOKING THE CITY lights and the Aegean Sea.

Out of habit, I swept the villa, checking each room. When I walked back into the main living area, I turned a light on.

"Please don't."

I turned the light off and went to stand next to her. She had to be dead on her feet. "Come get some sleep."

"What's it like?"

I searched my memory for the last words we'd spoken before the ride over here, but I came up blank. "What's what like?"

"Sex."

Thrown, I stilled.

Then the fucking pieces fell into place, and every muscle in my body tensed as I remembered that sick bastard Khalaf's words. *Photographic proof.* My jaw clenched, I asked what I didn't want to fucking know because I couldn't kill Khalaf and his men a second time. "Did he take pictures of you?"

Staring straight ahead, not looking at me, she didn't answer.

"*Motherfucker,*" I swore under my breath, pulling my phone out and dialing.

Vance answered on the first ring. "You know, if I were you, the last thing I would be doing right now would be making phone calls. Unless you're surrounded and outgunned, which I doubt because I had the place swept again while you were in transit."

"Was every piece of evidence destroyed?" He'd know what I was talking about.

"Did you not say clean sweep?"

"Did you confirm?"

Conlon sighed. "Yes, boss, I checked and doubled checked. Anything else?"

"No." I hung up and shoved my phone in my pocket. Then I stepped in front of her and took her face in my hands. "There're no pictures of you. The evidence was destroyed. Tell me what else they did to you."

Her eyes avoiding mine, she stared over my shoulder.

"Look at me, Maila."

Slow, with the ambient light from the nightscape highlighting her features, her eyes met mine. "I don't want to talk about Dubai."

If she was asking me what sex was like, I had to assume she hadn't been raped, but that didn't mean there weren't a thousand different things they could've forced her to do. "Are you going to tell me if you ever need to talk about it?"

"No, because I'm not going to." She looked over my shoulder again. "I'm not weak."

"Hey." I grasped her chin and brought her gaze back to mine. "This has nothing to do with being weak, no matter what happened. You're the strongest woman I know."

She made a derisive sound that was almost like the Emmy I used to know. "Is this when I ask how many women you know?" She emphasized the last word.

"I'm older than you," I reminded her, picking up on exactly what she was getting at. "I have a past." Truth was though, from the second I got that text, I couldn't remember it. All I was focused on was her. Then. Now. Our past, our present, this night, tomorrow. The faceless women I'd fucked over the years meant nothing to me compared to her. I'd suppressed my feelings for her. I'd tried to bury them. Hell, I'd spent years denying they even existed because it wasn't fucking right. But I was done with all of that bullshit now.

"Same as your wishes concerning Dubai, I don't want to talk about my past, but if you need me to, I will. There's nothing of significance though. I've never been in a serious relationship, Maila. I've never wanted to be in one." I stroked her cheek. "Until now."

Her emotionless tone came back. "I've never done a lot of things."

Fuck, I got that. "If I was a better man, I wouldn't tell you that I'm fucking glad." So goddamn glad, my cock was hard with a possessiveness I was choking on.

"You didn't use to swear in front of me."

Because she was seven when I'd enlisted. "Now I do." I threaded my hand into her hair. "You have a problem with that?" I wanted her to say yes to me. I wanted to strip her bare and taste every inch of her until that expressionless mask was wiped from her face. I wanted this woman to smile at me like she used to.

Maybe I was asking too much.

"I want to do more things," she whispered, ignoring my question and pulling away from me. "But I can't, Adam." She turned her back on me, and her voice broke. "I just can't."

FORTY-SEVEN

Maila

My breath hitched, and I held in so much, I thought I would explode into a million pieces of insignificance.

Deep and resonant, as if his voice belonged here as much as on a private jet or in the Arabian Desert or the humid flatlands of Southern Florida, he spoke a single, commanding directive. "Tell me why."

I didn't want to tell him why.

I wanted him to know.

I wanted him to understand.

I wanted him to see my pain and share it and realize that standing here with him was harder than anything I'd faced in the last eight years because this was it. This was really it.

I *could* lose it all.

Forever.

Everyone I'd loved left.

"Maila." Not giving me room to burrow into myself and hide, just like he never did when I was little, he turned me to face him and grasped my chin.

I didn't know if it was the color of the sea behind him that matched his eyes, both in daylight and nighttime, or the way he waited for me to speak like I was the one who needed to fill the silence, or maybe it was his grip. Because even though he was being as dominant as he always was, in this moment, he wasn't pushing me with it.

He was waiting.

The words, the real words, the ones I never said inside my head, let alone out loud, they came pouring out like they'd been waiting my whole life for this moment.

"I can't say hello to you and risk another goodbye. I don't have the strength to survive the floor falling out from under me again. Because that's all it has ever done, over and over, my whole life. And I can barely say those words to you without drowning in guilt because I know exactly what you came from. I know you never knew your father. I know your mother passed, but I don't even feel like I can grieve in front of you, or selfishly say I lost everything, because that would be cruel to say to you of all people. You were as close to Billy as blood brothers. My father was a father figure to you. You lost your family too. I honestly don't know who's had it worse between us. And I get this living with loss thing isn't a competition, but if it was, you would win. You act like you're whole and together. As if this is normal, and you're willing to take even more risks." Tears streaming down my face now, I barely paused to inhale. "A risk you want me to take too. You told me to let you love me, but that means I have to give you more, and I don't have more. Everything, *everything*, is broken inside me. I literally don't have anything to give. I can't love, Adam." My voice broke apart with the weight of years of loneliness. "I don't know how."

With his sleeves rolled up and his ropey veins casting shadows on his strong arms, his thumb glanced across my tear-stained cheek, but then he didn't move. He didn't even speak. He simply stood there without a single hint of an expression I could grasp onto.

And that's when it struck me.

This wasn't the man version of the boy I used to know, or the impossibly brave, decorated Navy SEAL. This wasn't the owner of the high-profile security contractor who risked his life to save others.

I wasn't looking at that Adam.

I was looking at the past.

This was the sixteen-year-old boy who'd kissed my skinned knees and picked me up in the rain and bought me ice creams. This was the lost, hungry kid my brother had brought home almost two decades ago, and he was paying it back.

Emotionally sobered, I gave him an out. "Forget it. You're off the hook."

A frown deepened the hard-earned fine lines between his eyes.

Before he could question me, I elaborated so there would be no mistake. "You're not responsible for me anymore." I couldn't do this. I couldn't pretend I was that girl with fairy-tale hopes and impossible dreams anymore. She was gone and wasn't ever coming back. I didn't want to be alone. I'd never wanted this life. I wouldn't wish it on my worst enemy, but I didn't want to be anyone's charity case. The truth was, people near me, they died. Maybe Adam thought he wouldn't, or he thought he could protect me from that. I didn't know, but he couldn't.

No more than I could protect him.

The lines between his eyes smoothed, and his thumb caressed my cheek. Then his voice turned impossibly quiet. "Are you done?"

No. "I—"

"Because I'm done with the excuses." His voice lost its soft edge and took on the commanding tone he carried and delivered so well, you never wanted to question it. "I'm standing right here. I'm not deployed. You're no longer with the CIA, and this has nothing to do with obligation, restitution or whatever other bullshit you can feed your fears with." Gently stroking the side of my face in a heated caress, he kept going. "I know fear. I know grief. I know every shade of scared you're feeling, but this is what we have, Maila. You and me, right now, this one life to live." His voice lowered to a deep dominance that was cut only by the hunger laced through his next words. "I want to live it with you."

I sucked in a sharp breath, but he wasn't finished.

"I can't make myself any clearer. I'm also done trying to convince you. You want me, you go all in. That's the only way this is going to work. Hope over pain. The present over the past." His lips touched my forehead with an impossibly soft kiss. "I love you. I always have. I always will." Releasing me, he stepped back.

"Adam—"

"We're done talking, Maila." He took another step back, and shadows fell over his face. "If you want me, I'll be in the master bedroom. If not, I'll fly you home tomorrow and we'll go our separate ways."

Turning, he walked down the hallway.

FORTY-EIGHT

Adam

Like a fucking prick, I gave her an ultimatum and walked the hell out.

I knew what I'd done.

Ultimatums were for losers and assholes. If you had to give one, you'd already lost, but I was that desperate.

Striding into the master, another dick move, I tossed my cell on the nightstand and stepped out of my boots. My back to the door I'd intentionally left open, I heard her before she spoke.

"Did you just tell me I had to sleep with you tonight or you were walking away from me?"

Fuck me, I fought a damn smile.

That tone, that voice—that was the woman I used to know.

Schooling my expression, I turned. "No." Yes.

Her arms crossed, she leveled me with a look. "Yes, you did."

The smile became harder to fight. "I told you if you want me, you knew where to find me."

"In the bedroom," she added, indignant.

This time I didn't fight it. Half my mouth tipped up. "I knew you were in there somewhere."

"What's that supposed to mean?"

Unbuttoning my shirt, I stepped toward her but stopped inches short. "It means I missed you." Leaning down, I kissed her temple, then stepped back. She had to cross that threshold if she wanted me.

She let out a short, derisive sound. "You can't blackmail me into sleeping with you."

Can and will. If I needed to. "I'm not. I never said anything about sex tonight." Stripping my shirt off, I tossed it over a chair. "But know this." Walking back to the door, I grabbed the top of the frame so I didn't fucking grab her. "If you walk into this room, that's it. There's no turning back, and you are sleeping with me. All damn night, every fucking night."

Slight and short because she tried to hide it, I still saw it.

Her breath hitched.

I leaned closer, but I didn't touch her. "Tell me you don't want me." She couldn't. She was standing right fucking here.

"You know I can't."

"Then what's the problem?"

"Sex isn't a solution," she blurted.

I smiled.

Then I brought my mouth to her neck and inhaled the sweet scent of her that no amount of lost years or distance between us could erase. "It is when I do it."

She shivered. "Adam."

"Maila."

"I'm scared," she whispered.

"Head back," I commanded quietly.

She tipped her head back, and her neck arched beautifully.

I kissed the underside of her jaw. "Does that feel like fear?"

"Yes."

I kissed her throat and swirled my tongue. "What else?"

She didn't hesitate. "Desire."

"Good girl," I murmured, kissing the dip where her neck met her collarbone. "And this?" I nipped her flesh then dragged my tongue across the sensitive spot. "What does that feel like?"

"Like I want more."

I smiled against her flesh. "I want to give a lifetime of more."

My cock fucking hard, my hands still on the doorframe, I leaned back. "Make a choice, Maila."

Her eyes on me, her hands at her sides, wearing a fucking dress Malik had brought her, she stared at me.

Then the girl who was always supposed to be mine stepped over the threshold.

No more holding back, I took her face in my hands and I slammed my mouth over hers. Rough, hard, intentional, I gave her a kiss that said I wasn't going to be a fucking gentleman in the bedroom.

Claiming her mouth with thrusts of my tongue like I wanted to claim her sweet body, I stroked hard and demanded more. Tangling her tongue with mine, pressing my body into hers, gripping her tight so she knew where she belonged, I kissed her like she was oxygen and I was free diving.

Because I was.

Diving so goddamn deep I barely remembered the promise I made her.

Before I ripped her fucking dress off, I pulled back. "Sex or sleep," I demanded, my voice rough.

Her arms around my neck, she tangled her hands in my hair. "Yes."

I gave her fair warning. "I'm going to be demanding, controlling and dominant in the bedroom."

"You're those things outside the bedroom."

Fuck, she was perfect. "Last chance to red light me tonight. You're coming either way though."

Her eyes on me, her breasts flush with my chest, her breathing already heavy, she gave me the full weight of her emerald gaze. "Make me yours, Adam Trefor."

FORTY-NINE

Maila

He surged like a lion capturing its prey.

I'd heard the rumors.

I'd grown up around Navy SEALs.

I knew their reputation.

They fought without fear, and they fucked without mercy.

This was everything I'd ever wanted, but nothing I could have ever prepared myself for.

My dress whipped over my head, my bra unhooked and dropped to the floor, my underwear was torn in shreds, and his hands were everywhere as his tongue held my mouth prisoner.

Then I was airborne.

His hands under my ass, he growled into my mouth as he lifted me, then he pivoted.

Instinctually, I wrapped my legs around his waist even though the position opened me, making me wide and vulnerable.

I thought I would be afraid. I thought I would hesitate, crack under pressure. I thought what had happened in the back of Khalaf's SUV would haunt me, but I should've known better.

His lips had landed on my neck in the doorway and my world became all his.

I wasn't thinking about anything except the man holding me like I weighed nothing as he massaged my ass and began a slow lifting and lowering motion, rocking me against his hard length as he walked me to the bed.

My pussy dragging over every inch of his covered length, I wasn't afraid.

I was desperate.

Wet and needy and breathless and so damn desperate for more, I leveraged my legs and rocked with him as I pulled his hair and growled right back.

Our lips mashing, teeth colliding, I felt his smile against my mouth before it traveled all the way to the center of my core and settled deep in my bones.

This wasn't cold wind and sharp angles. This was masculine dominance that was burning my body everywhere we touched.

Before I could think, before I could question how and where, before I could even form the questions in my own mind, his jeans were unbuttoned and his hard length was pressing at my entrance.

Holding me up with one arm, his other hand gripped the side of my face. Deep blue like a bottomless ocean, his eyes met mine. "I'm entering you just like this, baby." Slow, so slow, he both held me tight and pushed me down on the swollen head of his cock.

My mouth opened, my breath left, and I gasped.

Pain.

Fullness.

"Easy," he breathed, lowering me another inch. *"Easy."*

Sharp pain.

Oh God. "You're too big." He wouldn't fit. I looked down.

"Hey," he almost barked, tightening his grip on my hair. "Eyes on me."

"Stop," I cried.

"Look at me. Right now," he ordered, his tone sharp, his cock sliding in deeper.

Panicked, I looked up at him. "You won't fit." I wouldn't fit him. We wouldn't fit. He would leave me.

His palm moving to my throat, his thick fingers grasped my jaw. "I'm already inside you, baby. You're taking me beautifully. I'm not going to let you hurt for long. You're going to feel every inch of me, but before I lay you down and go deep, before you could get lost in your own head, you needed to feel me." He pulsed so deep inside me, I felt it everywhere. "You feel that?"

Oh God, oh God, oh God. "Yes." A tear slid down my cheek.

He pulsed again and slid in another impossible inch. "You're so fucking beautiful right now." His thumb caught my tear, and he spread it across my lips. "Do you know how beautiful you are, Maila?"

"No." It hurt. It really hurt. *"I can't this hurts you hurt,"* I cried, slurring my fears as one.

No panic, no alarm in his features, his eyes locked on mine, he calmly laid his dominant truth on me. "You need to feel the pain for me." He brought his mouth to mine and spilled truth on my lips. "You need to know you're alive."

The sob ripped from my chest and exploded around the sex-scented deliverance of truth. But before I could get the cry from my lungs and give it life, his mouth slammed over mine and he was grabbing my ass with both hands.

His cock jarringly rocked into my body, his fingers stroked against my forbidden entrance and he ate my pain.

I cried, he kissed me, his finger sunk deep, and suddenly I was coming.

Deep, soul-crushing waves crashed over my body in a relentless pounding, and that was it.

Everything changed.

I wasn't pushing him out. I wasn't holding back. My body wasn't trying to close in on itself and my mind wasn't drowning in fear.

I was soaring.

Like an eagle through ocean mist as my very own deep blue waves surged and surged and surged, battering and caressing my body in equal measure.

I cried, I flew, I shattered apart into a million pieces of tranquility.

FIFTY

Adam

SHE FUCKING FELL APART IN MY ARMS.

Tragic and beautiful and so goddamn sexy, I didn't have a point of reference to compare it to.

Because there was no comparison.

Not for this.

Not for her.

Her cunt constricting around me, her body vibrating with release, she shook and I thrust. Fucking hard.

But then I wanted more.

So goddamn much more.

Easing my finger out of her ass as the last of her shockwaves gripped my cock, I laid her down on the bed and caged her in while I was still buried inside her.

Kissing her, stroking deep and controlled, I brushed her hair from her tear-slicked face. She wasn't just beautiful. "You're stunning."

Her thighs trembling, she brought her legs up like she knew I wanted in deeper. "Give me yours."

I fucking smiled. "You think I'm going to come that quick, beautiful?"

Something close to alarm flashed across her features. "There's more?"

"Every day. Every night," I promised.

The tremor racked up her body as her hands fisted in my hair. "I don't know how much more I can take tonight."

Slipping a hand between us, I winked. "You can give me one more tonight." I stroked her clit.

She jerked under me, and her cunt constricted hard.

I groaned, wanting to fill every inch of her tight heat with my seed. "Are you on anything?" *Please fucking say no.* I wanted to claim her, brand her and make her mine in every goddamn way a man could dominate a woman.

"Do you want children?" she asked, her back arching as I stroked her.

I didn't fucking hesitate. "Yes. I want you swollen with my child, and I want to see you smile again." Kissing her once, I dropped my voice. "I want to make you happy." I wanted everything with this woman who'd given me the one thing I'd needed most when I'd had nothing. "I want you to feel hope."

A blush spread across her cheeks, and her voice went submissively quiet. "I feel you."

Fuck, this woman. "I'm glad." So damn glad. "But that doesn't answer my question." I bit the side of her neck, then soothed it with my tongue. "I want to come inside you, Maila. Are you on anything?"

She moaned, low and sexy. "You call me Maila now."

"I do." She was too much of a woman to call her Emmy. "Answer me." I stroked deep.

"No," she whispered.

A flash of rage I wasn't expecting broadsided me and I was back on that fucking compound for a split second. Not only had she been in a sex trafficker's den without backup, but she hadn't been personally protected either. Inhaling, then letting it out in a low growl as I rocked slow and hard into her, I kissed her deeply. But then I reluctantly pulled out.

Grasping my arms, she inhaled sharply. "What are you doing?"

"Bringing up what I should have before I sank inside you." Cupping her face, I caged her in. "I don't want barriers between us. I wanted to feel you bareback and now that I have, *fuck*. Nothing has ever felt better." My cock pulsed at the mere thought and I kissed her because I couldn't fucking stop touching her. "But I'm not going to rush you into anything. So we're clear, I want you. I want us. I want this." Every damn second of it. "If you were to get pregnant tonight, I would be ecstatic, but this is your choice. It will always be your choice."

Her face softened, and she reached for my cheek. "I thought you said you were dominant in the bedroom."

"I am." But I was trying not to be a complete bastard and ruthlessly rut into her until she was knocked up.

"Yet you're giving me a choice."

"Whether or not I come inside you right now, yes, I am." Beyond that, I wasn't making any promises.

She watched me as intently as I watched her.

Then, just a fraction, she smiled.

She fucking smiled.

My heart rate exploded and for the first time in seven years, I felt a weight lift. "Fuck, beautiful." I surged back inside her.

Her head fell back, and her small hands gripped my arms again. "*Adam.*"

"Right here, beautiful." I ran my tongue down her throat and over one hard nipple before sucking it into my mouth.

Bringing her legs up, she locked her thighs around my hips. "You didn't tell me it would both hurt and feel like this." She clenched around my cock.

I released her sweet nipple and stilled inside her when all I wanted to do was thrust until I made us both come. "When you felt the pain of me taking your virginity, when you feel it now, were you thinking about losing me?"

Heat colored her cheeks, and she shifted under me. "No."

"You needed to feel that pain, Maila." I touched my lips to her forehead. "You needed to feel life." I kissed her. "You needed to feel me." I held her beautiful emerald eyes as they welled with unshed tears. "I'm here and I'm staying."

"Promise?" she asked in barely a whisper.

"Always."

A tear slid down her cheek. "I want to feel all of you inside me."

Slow and controlled, never taking my eyes off hers, I drove in and out of her until she was coming again.

Then I fucking let go.

FIFTY-ONE

Maila

HE WAS RIGHT.

Life was painful, but in that pain, there was sometimes beauty, and I'd forgotten that.

Stretched beyond anything I ever could've imagined, a pulsing discomfort between my legs I'd never felt, I was sore. So sore. But I also felt alive. And I felt his release dripping out of me, and that was a phenomenon I never, ever, could have imagined would affect me so profoundly.

It didn't feel like he was leaving me.

I wasn't afraid.

I was sated, and I felt sexy and cherished, especially the latter, because I knew this stoic, dominant, alpha Navy SEAL at my back, holding me in his arms, kissing my shoulder—he wasn't impulsive.

He calculated everything. He thought things out. He maneuvered.

And he'd come inside me.

On purpose.

In a darkened bedroom overlooking the Mediterranean, a smile formed, and I felt it.

I felt life.

A new life he'd given me.

But not just that.

New hope.

A new beginning.

He'd said the words too. Ones I'd never given him.

His hand ran down my arm, and his voice, husky and rough like I'd never heard it, spilled around me like a warm blanket of safety. "You aren't sleeping."

I gave him what I never thought I had to give. "I love you, Adam Trefor."

His arms, his shoulders, his chest behind me, they all stilled. For a fraction of a second. Then he inhaled deep, and his lips touched my neck. "Good. Because I'm not letting you walk away again." He threaded his thick fingers through mine. "And I have a proposition for you."

Proposition.

Not proposal.

It was my turn to stiffen.

He squeezed my hand. "I'm not talking about us. You know what I want. As far as I'm concerned, we're a done deal. I'm talking about work."

I looked over my shoulder at him.

"Do you want to work?" he asked without any hint in his tone as to how he wanted me to answer.

"As opposed to what?"

Part of his mouth tilted up in a sexy half-smile, and this time he didn't hold back. "Staying home and giving me babies."

A swirling storm of butterflies fluttered in my stomach, and dreams I'd suppressed for so long I thought I'd forgotten them came back like they'd never left. "Where is home?"

His half-smile dropped. "Where would you like it to be?"

My first reaction was to think this was too much all at once. But then I felt his stickiness between my thighs and realized the time for being hesitant or afraid had long passed. I could already be pregnant, and while that should have scared me beyond words, it didn't. "Your company's headquarters is in New York?"

It was a rhetorical question, I knew it was, but he answered it anyway.

"Yes."

"Okay." I hated the winters and all the people in such close proximity, but I didn't want to be far away from him.

"So, New York?"

"Yes." For now.

He nodded once. "And working?"

"This is going to be your proposition, isn't it?"

"Yes." He rolled me to my back and looked down at me. "Come work for me."

"As?"

"As whatever you want. But I could use someone with your training, especially for some of our more sensitive cases."

"You want a woman in the field?" I knew AES didn't have any female operatives, not for the work and clients they took on.

"Is that what you want?" he hedged.

Was it? I no longer knew, but I did know I didn't want to not have the opportunity. "Yes."

He searched my face for a long moment. "I'm not in the field anymore."

Translation, he didn't want me in it either. "Are you happy behind a desk?" I'd hated my fake job behind a desk at the pharmaceutical company.

"I'm happy AES is successful," he stated, evading the question.

I gave up hedging and told him the truth. "I don't know if I can sit behind a desk all day."

"Would you be willing to give it a shot? I promise the work is... varied."

"And if I give it a try and don't find it *varied* enough?"

"Then we reassess."

I didn't have any other job offers, but I also didn't want to be his subordinate by day and lover by night.

Sensing my hesitation, or downright reading me, he took my face. "I'm not asking you to work under me, Maila. I'm asking you to help me build the company." His soft, full lips met mine, and he stroked his tongue once through my mouth before pulling back with a low moan. "I want this for us."

And I wanted him. "Okay."

"Yes?" he asked, the sharp angles of his face beautifully accentuated in the shadows of the darkened bedroom.

I smiled. "Yes."

He shook his head, but he didn't smile back. "You don't how long I've waited to see that." His thumb dragged across my lips. "I was responsible for its disappearance."

I wrapped my hand around his wrist. "No, you weren't. I was." And I was just beginning to understand how much. Deciding to live life was a choice as much as I'd chosen to shut down. I didn't want to be shut down anymore. I wanted to be deserving of this man who'd chosen a different path. A braver path that led him to be successful, a path that brought him back to me. As much as he said he wasn't going to let me go again, I didn't want to let go of him.

His handsome face creased into a frown. "No, you weren't, Maila. No one should've had as much loss as you did at such a young age."

"Your life was any different?"

"I didn't grow up with a family," he countered as if we were talking about some simple, inconsequential truth.

Letting go of his wrist, I feathered my fingers across his strong jaw. "You were my family."

His frown deepened and his chest rose and fell twice.

When he didn't reply, I knew what he was thinking, and I wanted to absolve him of his guilt, but I couldn't do that for him any more than he could take away my survivor's guilt.

"You have to stop blaming yourself for the past," I whispered before leaning up to kiss him. "Please." I pressed my lips to his again. "I can't do it for you."

He grasped a fistful of my hair like he had in that cell, and my body tingled all over. Rough and heady, his voice whispered across my lips. "I know."

I didn't drop it. "Then you'll try?"

His hands tightened in my hair. "Do you know how I know you're mine? How you've always been mine?"

A shyness I'd only ever felt around him fluttered low in my belly. "No." Yes. Maybe. The same way I felt like he'd always been mine?

"I didn't tell you what I was thinking, but you knew." He closed the whisper of space between our lips and spoke against my mouth. "You always know." Deep and soulful, he stroked his tongue into my mouth and groaned through his heady dance of dominance as he entwined our bodies.

FIFTY-TWO

Adam

NAKED, BEAUTIFUL, AND FULL OF MY SEED, SHE FELL ASLEEP IN MY arms.

Not wanting to close my eyes, I watched her until the sun began to rise.

She was so damn beautiful, more beautiful than every fantasy I'd ever had of her over the years. I wanted to take her again and again, but her body needed rest and healing, and I'd already been rough enough with her.

Inhaling her natural scent and the mingling of our bodies, I slowly pulled my arm out from under her.

Stirring, she turned away and curled.

I lay still until her breathing evened out again then I slid from the bed.

Pulling my boxers on, I grabbed my phone and walked into the living room. Scrolling through my contacts, I dialed a number I hadn't in years, not even sure if it was still in service.

After four rings, Malik answered the cell phone he'd had while he was in the Teams. "Let me guess, this isn't a social call."

"You didn't tell me you were with the CIA." Seeing him waiting on the apron yesterday had surprised the hell out of me. I still wasn't sure if he'd been behind the text, and at this point I was trying to figure out how much I gave a damn about it. I had her back, and that was my priority one.

The distinctive in-flight noise of a jet sounded in the background. "You didn't ask."

"You still have your old number." Most of us didn't, unless we had family.

The bullshit polite tone he'd given Maila yesterday wearing thin, Malik sighed. "And you called it. Is there something I can help you with?"

"Why'd you go CIA?" It'd been bothering me since yesterday. Malik didn't play by the rules. The Teams was the exception for him, and despite what Zulu thought, even though I was pissed as hell about Bosnia too, the shitstorm that op had turned into wasn't Malik's fault. "I didn't peg you as a Company man."

"What do you want, Trefor?"

"Two things. I'm having someone clear her place out. This is a courtesy call on that front, and I'm assuming since the co-op in Manhattan is a Company apartment that the furniture stays."

"Correct, and copy. I'll alert the doorman that you're coming. What's the second thing?"

"Did you send the text?"

"Same question you asked last night, and I'm giving you the same response. What text?"

I listened to not his words, but his tone, inflection and the lack of hesitation in his response. He wasn't fucking with me. He had no idea what I was talking about. Fucking CIA. "Come work for me."

Malik laughed. "Got a job, thanks."

"I'll give you a better one." Better pay, at a minimum.

"One where I take a punch every time I see Zulu?"

"You deserved that." He'd been a dick to Zulu in Bosnia, not to mention he'd broken the cardinal rule of every SEAL everywhere.

He smirked. "But you're still offering me a job."

I was. "I am." If he was the handler they sent in to clean up the Al Ka'abi mess, then he had connections. Ones that would thread high.

His tone sobered. "Appreciate the offer."

"But?"

"Not interested at the moment."

At the moment. "Fair enough."

"I'll let you know if anything changes. Just to reiterate, as I already told you on the ground at Athens, once she came on my radar, I did tell her to get out. She didn't listen. Have to hand it to her though, she lived up to her last name."

"You better hope you're not insulting her."

He chuckled. "I'm not. Nothing but respect. And for the record, I'm glad you got her out."

I was done with this conversation. "Keep this channel open." He'd know what I meant.

"Copy that. Later, Alpha." He hung up.

I dialed again.

November picked up on the first ring. "Morning."

It was only morning for me. In New York, it was the middle of the night. "I need Maila's place cleared of all personal belongings. Furniture stays."

"Copy. Where do you want them?"

"My place."

November didn't comment on the location or implication, which was one of the many reasons why I'd hired him and let him name his salary, which he'd insisted be paid in cryptocurrency. "I'll send someone in the morning."

"Who's in town?"

"Echo and Blade."

Christ. I didn't want either one of them touching her clothes. "Go yourself."

"I'm not local at the moment." He paused and I heard him typing. "I could be though, in six hours. How critical is it?"

As critical as it got. I was moving her in with me. "Critical."

"Consider it done. Anything else?"

"No."

"Good copy." November hung up.

"What's critical?"

I turned at the sound of her voice, and my heart fucking stopped. Every time I saw her, she was more beautiful. Wrapped in the sheet, hair mussed, the early morning sun caught her skin. Stalking over to her, I leaned down and kissed her. "Morning. You look beautiful." I wanted to wake up to her every damn day.

Heat flushed her cheeks. "Good morning, and thank you, but you didn't answer my question."

I sifted my fingers through her hair before settling them on the back of her neck in a hold that was one hundred percent possessive. "It's critical that your belongings be moved into my place before we get back to New York."

For a beat, she didn't react, didn't comment.

Then she nodded. "Okay."

I studied the crease between her eyes. "Problem?"

"No." She drew the word out. Maila Marie Nilsen never drew words out.

"Maila," I warned. "We talked about this."

"Did we?"

I reined in a temper only she could elicit. "I thought we had, but let me be more specific. You crossed the threshold. That was figurative and literal. I said I wanted to spend every day with you, and I meant it. That means we live together. I have a place in Manhattan, you don't. Easy solution is we move your belongings into my place. Am I missing something?"

"No."

Another drawn-out word.

Fuck me. I took a stab. "I'm not romantic. Never have been.

You know who I am." I was a problem solver. "I'm cutting to the chase here."

The corner of her mouth twitched. "Yes, this is all true. Although, it would have been very odd to discover you were romantic when I was only a teenager."

Christ. I grabbed the sheet and yanked it off, then picked her up and threw her over my shoulder.

She fucking squealed. "*What are you doing?*"

Fucking her into submission. "Taking us to the shower." Getting her wet as hell. "We have a plane to catch."

"*Oh my God.* Adam Trefor, you put me down this instant!"

"No." I walked into the bathroom and right into the shower, turning the water on.

"Gah! You're a beast," she yelled, sounding almost exactly like the Emmy I used to know.

"I know." Sliding her down my body and over my hard cock, I caught her mouth. "A total fucking beast who's making you move in with me." I kissed her, then pulled back to shed my boxers.

Standing under the not-yet-warm water like she didn't even notice it, she smiled at me, shy and sweet. "I think I like the beast."

"You love the beast," I corrected, stepping into her and cupping her. "How sore are you?"

Her hands landed on my biceps, and her expression turned serious like the woman she'd become. "Sore like I belong to you."

My chest constricted, and my head swam. For a moment, all I could do was stare at her. "So the two drawn-out words in the living room?"

She didn't pretend to not know what I meant. "Me processing."

"You good?"

She nodded.

"We good?" I held my fucking breath.

With her featherlight touch that both made my cock hard

and filled the emptiness in my chest, she drew her fingers across my flesh. "We are."

I exhaled. "Good." Still cupping her, I stroked through her desire. "Do you know what you're going to do before we get on the plane?"

Biting her lip, she shook her head.

"You're going to come twice. First time…" I leaned down and dragged my tongue across her bottom lip before thrusting inside once to taste her sweetness. "You're going to come on my tongue."

She shivered.

I eased a finger inside her tightness. "Second time on my cock."

With a low moan, her eyes closed, and she leaned her head back as her hips naturally swayed into my touch.

I gripped her wet hair and brought her head up. "But you're going to keep your eyes on me, beautiful. Understand?"

"Okay," she whispered.

Taking her mouth again before leaning over and teasing each of her nipples, I dropped to one knee.

Her breath hitched, and her hands went to my hair, but she did as I said. She kept her gorgeous eyes on me.

My hands gliding over her hips and around to her sweet ass, I stared at her as I drew my tongue across her clit.

She gasped, and her hands fisted.

Fuck yes. "You like that?" I tongued her again.

Her whole core shook, and she nodded.

"Words, beautiful." I licked the length of her sweet cunt.

"Yes," she hissed, her head tipping back.

"Eyes on me," I demanded, nipping her thigh.

The sound that came out of her mouth was half squeak, half moan, and she brought her head back up. Her green eyes met mine, and I was done. My cock throbbing, her sweet pussy driving me to the brink, I latched on to her clit, sank two fingers inside her and sucked.

Three strokes of my tongue, and she was fucking falling apart.

No hesitation, I picked her up by the back of her legs as I stood and pinned her against the wall. Then I drove into her in one thrust.

She gasped, and her tight cunt constricted hard around my cock.

Like an IED blast wave, I fucking saw stars.

"Christ, you're so damn tight, beautiful." Forcing myself not to come yet, I eased back, then thrust hard and short, giving her clit friction until I felt it.

Her second orgasm built, and she began to shake.

"That's it." *Fuck yeah.* "That's it, baby. You're going to come for me again, and I'm going over the edge with you. You ready?"

My name spilled out of her mouth like a fucking veneration. "*Adam.*"

"Now," I demanded. "Let it go." I thrust hard and deep.

She fucking detonated, and I exploded inside her.

FIFTY-THREE

Adam

SHE STRODE INTO MY OFFICE IN SKY-HIGH HEELS AND A TIGHT SKIRT and dumped a file on my desk. "Is this a joke?"

My phone to my ear, I stood there and fucking stared at her, because even after a few weeks, hell, every time she walked into a room, I got sucker-punched all over again.

Zulu chuckled. "I heard that."

I refrained from telling him to fuck off. "Call you back." I hung up. "Is what a joke?"

She stabbed a finger with a red-painted nail that I knew matched the color on her toes because I'd obsessively watched her paint them last night. "This," she said with disgust.

I glanced down.

Fuck.

The bullshit Carver case.

"You said I wasn't an obligation," she accused before dropping her voice to a lethal finality. "I deserve better than to be someone's burden."

"You were never my burden," I warned. "Don't go there with me." She knew damn well I worshiped the ground she walked on, but it didn't stop her from glaring at me.

Then she did the last thing I was expecting but the one thing I should've fucking seen coming.

She pulled her access key card out of her pocket and dumped it on my desk. "I'm done."

Fuck. *Fuck.* "Maila."

Without a second glance, she turned and reached for the glass door of my office.

God-fucking-*damn it.* "Emmy, *wait.*"

Spinning around with fury in her eyes, she spit well-deserved anger at me. "You don't get to call me that. Not now. I did what you asked. I gave you everything you wanted." As if they were dirty words, she ticked off my reasons, throwing them in my face. "Come work with me. Help me build the company. Use your skill-set. I need your expertise. You would be a great asset." In a complete departure from her usually unflappable demeanor, she made a derisive sound of disgust. "All lies. I haven't been out of this office once. Not one single time, and why?" She didn't wait for me to answer. "Because you're doing what every other asshole with a dick who knows my last name does—*you coddle me.*"

"That's not true." It was exactly true.

And it was fucking eating at me.

After weeks of thinking about it, I was convinced Ghost had pulled shit behind the scenes and sent me the text. It was the only answer that made sense, and I wanted to confront his ass about it, but I hadn't been able to get in touch with him again. He'd ignored the protocol the second time I'd followed it last week. Which only made me more convinced it was him who'd tipped me off. He had the back channels to do it, and just like me, just like Zulu, we'd all made that same promise to Billy. That we'd protect her.

Except me and Zulu hadn't.

In the end it was Ghost who'd stepped up, and that ate at me every fucking day she'd been walking into this office for the past four weeks, hell, since I'd first seen her in that room with the one-way mirror in Al Ka'abi's compound. I also wanted to beat the fuck out of Ghost for not immediately getting her out. I'd wanted to find him, pound his face in, then tell him to leave her the hell alone, because I was a possessive asshole, and she was mine now.

But Ghost was doing exactly what he'd been trained to do and staying so goddamn well-hidden that not even I, Conlon, or November could get a beat on him.

So here I was, for the past four fucking weeks, watching her walk through doors that held my company's name and doing a bullshit dance of protecting her by giving her assignments so beneath her they were insulting.

Because over my dead body was she ever going out in the field again.

"Yes, it is true," she seethed, enunciating each word. "You think I'm stupid? You think my last name and who I'm related to doesn't make me an eternal target for every terrorist with a vendetta against one of the most lethal SEAL snipers in history? You think my father being a vice admiral doesn't up the ante? *Of course it does,*" she spat in a Maila Marie Nilsen pint-sized fury. "But not you or the CIA or the alpha assholes working for you need to keep stepping around me like I'm made of glass." She jabbed a finger against her own chest. *"I can take care of myself."*

Fucking Christ. "This isn't about you not being able to take care of yourself." She was right, she was a goddamn eternal target. "You can't change who you are or what you come from. You're Navy royalty, and that legacy is going to follow you everywhere. You can't just walk around unprotected, Maila." I knew the second the last words left my mouth, it was a mistake.

It was instant. Her face, her demeanor, every inch of her gorgeous body shut down. Her back went straight, her voice turned to a deadly calm and she quietly gave me three words I deserved.

"Fuck you, Adam."

This time, when she pivoted, I didn't stop her.

She pulled my office door open with a preternatural calm just as Conlon came around the corner and stopped in front of her.

"Hello, love. Mind if I grab Alpha for a moment?"

"He's all yours. I'm not staying."

"Oh, an assignment." He smiled like he smiled when you put new weapons in front of him. "Where you off to?"

"Miami." She stepped past him. "And it's not an assignment."

"Wait." Vance looked from me to her, but she was already halfway down the hall. He looked back at me as my office door closed. "What'd you do?"

"Nothing," I ground out, staring after her.

"Right," Conlon said sarcastically as he glanced behind him through the glass wall of my office to where her office was. "She's throwing shit in her bag and going to Miami because you did nothing."

Fuck. "She's from there."

"No shit. So are we."

Forcing my gaze off her, I glanced at Conlon. "What did you need?" I wanted him the hell out of my office and my calendar cleared so I could do exactly what she'd told me not to do seven years ago.

"I think what I need can take a back seat to what you need, brother." He sat.

"Say what you came to say and get the fuck out." I pocketed my cell. "I've got work to do."

Casually glancing over his shoulder, Conlon smiled. "Does said work involve a petite blonde with a famous last name?"

"Conlon," I warned as she put her bag over her shoulder.

"Right, right." He smiled. "So… Miami?"

I grabbed my keys. "Not discussing this."

"Why not? Miami has perfect weather and gorgeous women." He turned in his chair. "And apparently it's about to have another gorgeous woman."

Maila pushed her chair in as November approached her and asked her something. "What the fuck do you want, Conlon?"

Vance stood and stepped in front of me, blocking my view of her. "It's time."

For fuck's sake. "Time for what?" I grabbed my cell and shot off a quick text to November.

Me: *Stall her.*

"Open a Miami office."

"No." Hell no. "That's André Luna's turf. I'm not encroaching." Impatient, I held my cell, waiting for a reply.

"We're two different entities with different clienteles," Conlon justified. "He could use the help when we have time to spare, and Miami is a perfect jumping-off point for all the South American shit that's been coming up."

I knew he was right, but fuck. "Still no. I'm not doing that to Luna." My cell pinged with a new text.

November: *Copy*

Vance leaned past me and hit the speaker on the landline on my desk before punching in a number.

The phone rang once, and Luna's voice filled my office. "What's up, Trefor?"

"It's both Alpha and me," Vance replied.

"Conlon," Luna clipped. "What can I do for you two?"

"It's what we can do for you." Vance chuckled. "How would you feel about AES setting up a branch in Miami?" He glanced at me. "I think Alpha could use some sun."

"Seriously?" Luna asked in disbelief.

I leveled Conlon with a warning look. "This is all hypothetical, André. I'm not aiming to encroach on your business or clientele, I—"

"Hell yes," Luna interrupted. "A resounding fucking yes. I've got more business than I can handle, and I would love the backup, and of course I would reciprocate."

Vance slapped me on the shoulder. "Excellent. Done deal. I'm already looking at real estate."

I glared at Conlon but kept my tone in check. "Since when?"

"Since I called Christensen three weeks ago." Vance grinned

as he tipped his chin over his shoulder. "And saw that coming a mile away."

"André, hang on a second." I hit the mute button. "What the fuck are you doing? You didn't pass this by me and you're already talking to Neil Christensen about real estate in Miami?"

"Who else would I call? Your unit saved his ass a time or two downrange, and now he builds high-rises overlooking the ocean." He arrogantly crossed his arms. "Who'd give us a better deal on a satellite office in Miami?" He shrugged. "Or maybe a new global headquarters. Hell, put her in charge of the new office. Leave November here and come back into the field. She runs circles around you admin-wise anyway. Besides, you hate New York, and her departure was only a matter of time with the bullshit assignments you were spoon-feeding her. All of this makes great business sense."

I didn't know if I wanted to kill Conlon or shake his hand. "I'm not leaving November anywhere, and I'm not going back out in the field." But one thing he had said made perfect sense. She did run circles around me when it came to certain shit. If I opened a Miami office, I was doing it with her. Hitting the mute button again, I had to resolve any obstacles with Luna first. "You sure, André? Either way, this doesn't affect our friendship."

"One hundred percent," André answered. "How soon can you set up shop?"

Conlon chuckled. "I knew this would work out."

"I'll let you know, André, and thank you. I appreciate the consideration."

"Rising tide, mi hermano. This will be good for all of us. Let me know if you need help with anything."

"Thanks again, will do."

"De nada. Conlon," André clipped.

"Luna," Vance answered before ending the call and giving me a self-satisfied smile. "My work here is done." He stepped aside. "Go get the woman. I'll get the real estate."

"You were planning this."

His expression turned serious, but then he shrugged as if he were being casual, which he wasn't. "Just looking at our options."

"Your brother's in Miami." His twin brother who happened to work for Luna.

"He is."

"You want to be close to family."

"Is that a crime?"

With their history, who knew? "You're right, it's smart strategically."

"I have my moments." His phone vibrated, and he glanced at it. "Go. Get your woman."

"We'll discuss logistics later." I walked toward the door. "Send me links to any property you think will be a good fit."

"Right," he answered absently. "By the way, the Falcon's fueled and ready to go."

I glanced over my shoulder as I opened the door. "Hey."

He looked up from his phone and raised one eyebrow.

"Thanks."

His expression locked, he gave me a warning. "Don't treat her like glass."

Something close to possessiveness and a whole lot like jealously hit, and I frowned. "Did she say something to you?" Those were the exact words she gave me.

"No."

I studied him a beat to see if he was telling the truth.

Goddamn it.

The fucking bastard. I gave him fair warning. "Quit fucking bugging my office."

Throwing his hands up, he chuckled. "I swear, I didn't." His grin amped up. "At least not today."

Shaking my head, I walked out and rushed toward her desk.

FIFTY-FOUR

Maila

"WHERE THE HELL IS SHE?" ADAM'S VOICE CARRIED ALL the way to the elevators. "Goddamn it, I told you to stall her."

"I did," Nathan, November, whatever I was supposed to call him, answered Adam in his quiet tone that was barely loud enough to hear down the hall.

Willing the elevator to open, I frantically pushed the call button five times in a row.

"Stall her doesn't mean let her walk out. *Fuck.*"

The elevator doors opened.

"She surrendered her security card for network login access. What did you expect me to do?"

Rushing inside and jabbing the lobby button, then the close door button, I didn't hear Adam's response as the door thankfully slid closed.

My heart pounding, my blood rushing through my veins like I'd run a marathon, I held down the lobby button in a panic. The elevator started its descent, and air whooshed out of my lungs, but the sick feeling in the pit of my stomach that'd been growing steadily for a week didn't relent.

It didn't matter.

It was too late. I'd already made my decision. There was nothing to do now except follow through.

I couldn't stay here in New York.

Not like this.

Not sitting mere feet from him, day in, day out, and watching him do everything in his power to protect me.

And he was. He'd even gone to look for Ghost just to get confirmation that it was him who'd tipped him off and not someone else because he said it'd make him rest easier knowing. Because that's what Adam Trefor did. That's who he was. He followed through, he did his job. He made people safe because he was an honorable man—in every sense of the word.

I'd been a fool to think I would ever be a contributing part of his company, let alone help build it. It didn't need building. There was already more business than he had men working for him, and I knew my last name was a hindrance, not a help, but I couldn't sell myself short.

I wasn't going to be any man's obligation. I wasn't going to be anyone's burden, period. Just because I was alone and didn't form attachments didn't mean I needed a former Navy SEAL to protect me. I knew I had no one to blame but myself for all those years of loneliness, but I'd had a purpose, and that was work.

More than work, it was my career, one I'd worked hard for. It was a way to make a difference, except now I didn't have that, and the ridiculous assignments Adam had been giving me weren't cutting it.

I wasn't making a difference.

I was being shelved, first by my government and now by Adam. I knew the reason, and only a fool would say it didn't matter, but it still stung to be relegated to being a disadvantage instead of an asset.

Which was why I needed to do exactly what I was doing.

Retreat and regroup, no matter how much it hurt.

Mentally shaking away the image of Adam right before I'd walked out of his office, I shoved it all down as the elevator doors opened. Inhaling, telling myself this was the right move, I forced myself to take that step over another threshold.

I walked off the elevator.

And made it exactly three strides.

Cold wind and sharp angles slammed into my senses a second before a large hand wrapped around my upper arm.

"Come with me." Adam's deep voice, hard and unrelenting, issued the order the same as he would to one of the men who worked for him.

A tingling low in my belly I desperately wanted to ignore flared, and I didn't protest. In a lobby filled with people, my training ingrained, I didn't make a scene. I didn't even question him.

Unable to match his long strides, I did however quicken my pace. To an outsider, it would appear as if an expensively dressed man was merely leading his compliant woman out of the building.

Taking me across the lobby and out the front to a waiting car, Adam held the door for me, then stepped off the curb and got in, street side.

An older gentleman I had never seen at AES greeted Adam. "Mr. Trefor." He smiled and glanced at me before looking back at Adam. "Where to?"

Adam rattled off his address.

Knowing what he would see when we walked into the penthouse, anxiety suddenly gnawed at my stomach. Barely refraining from crossing my arms like a wounded child, I looked out the window and said nothing.

Pulling his cell out and busying himself with texts as his huge, muscular thigh brushed against mine, Adam didn't look up once.

He didn't even speak as the driver pulled up to the building. He opened the door for me, led me to the elevator, and swiped his card for the top floor.

But as we walked off the elevator and I reached for the front door with a shaking hand, he stopped me with a firm grip on my shoulder. "Maila."

I turned and was struck all over again by his stark handsomeness. Adam Michael Trefor wasn't only honorable, he was the most striking man I'd ever met. His piercing eyes that always gave me all of his attention when he looked at me, the hard angles of his jaw, his proud nose and his thick, black hair grown out just enough that it was almost unruly, like it'd been when he was sixteen years old, but on the grown version of him only looked sexy and begged for my fingers.

Adam Trefor wasn't handsome.

He was beautiful.

His Mediterranean-blue-eyed gaze gripping me, holding me hostage, he did what he'd done since he'd come back from BUD/S.

He studied me with intent.

Gone was the boy who would kiss my skinned knee. In his place was a powerful, dominant, unyielding man who thought before he spoke, calculated his moves, and I was sure was ten steps ahead of me despite whatever question I could feel he was about to ask.

His hand on my shoulder skimmed slowly down my arm as if he didn't want to let me go, but then it fell to his side. Casually sliding it into his pants pocket as if he hadn't just set my skin on fire and kick-started my pulse, he spoke. "If I give you field assignments, do you still want to go back to Miami?"

My heart irrationally crushed in on itself. Yes. No. I didn't know. What did it matter how I answered? I couldn't change who I was. "What do you want me to say?" I didn't have any answers anymore. All I knew was that I couldn't keep working next to him, feeling useless and trapped.

His gaze holding me captive, seconds of silence ticking by that were mocked by floating dust particles in the ray of muted sunlight coming from the window at the end of the hall, he stood perfectly still.

Then his broad chest rose with a deep breath, and he tipped his chin toward the front door.

Crushing hurt lodged in my throat, and to my horror, my eyes welled. Before he saw, and without comment, I turned toward the door, but it was too late.

A trigger I kept at bay by constantly moving, relentlessly redirecting my thoughts and doing anything in my power to avoid came crashing down around me, and suddenly I was there. In that place.

The place I avoided at all costs.

My mother's death, my father's death, and my brother's death all tangled into a storm of impossible grief and slammed into me like a thousand-foot wave I had no way of surviving.

My hands shaking, my lips trembling with barely contained sobs, I tried and failed to contain it.

No.

No.

Not now, *not now*.

Don't do this. Don't do this to yourself. *Do not let him see*, I silently, frantically chanted. *Do not let him see.*

But just as fast as it'd happened, the man behind me who knew me better than any living soul, he spoke as if he sensed every molecule of my pain that I couldn't contain. "It's okay."

His large hand reached past me and unlocked the door at the same time his impossibly muscled arm snaked around my waist and pulled me into solid strength.

The door opened, and a deep, quiet voice I didn't know how to live without spoke in my ear. "You're going to be okay. I'm here. Take a breath. Just one breath for me and hold it in, Emmy."

Emmy.

Emmy.

It was the final straw.

The sob ripped from my chest and exploded around us in ugly shattered fragments, and I couldn't hold myself up.

My bag dropped, my hands flew to my face and if it weren't for the arm around my waist, I would have crumpled to the floor.

Seven years of grief shook my body like magnitudes of shifting earth, and I was there. In that place where there was no ground under my feet and no air to breathe and nothing to hold me up.

I wanted to die.

I wanted to crawl into the ground with my grief and leave this painful life behind, and I wanted to do it before the man at my back knew my darkest thoughts, because there was only one thing I feared more than losing him.

Him seeing me like this.

Him knowing.

Him feeling like I was his burden.

"Please," I begged between choking sobs I prayed would drown me. "Go. Just *go*."

The SEAL-hardened arm around my waist tightened as another swept under my legs. For one breathless fraction of a second, I was airborne before my body was crushed against a solid chest.

"No." His commanding voice rumbled with an unbending will as he kicked my purse over the threshold, strode into the penthouse, then kicked the door shut behind us. "I'm never fucking walking away from you again."

FIFTY-FIVE

Adam

I KICKED THE DOOR SHUT BEHIND ME. "I'M NEVER FUCKING WALKING away from you again." No goddamn way.

But one step into the penthouse, and I froze.

Suitcases, five of them, all stacked in the foyer.

Suitcases that hadn't been there when I'd left for work that morning.

Tears staining her face, a grief I hadn't seen in seven years wracking her body, she stilled in my arms when she saw me looking at them.

"You planned this." I didn't intend for the words to come out as an accusation, but that's exactly how they sounded when they left my mouth. Regretting my timing but not the sentiment, I set her down.

Exhaustion I should have noticed weighed down her small frame, but she stood proud and swiped at her face.

My hands on my hips, trying to control my fucking temper when all I wanted to do was dominate her, I looked from her bags to her. "The house, it's livable?"

Staring at me like I was at her, she measured her response. "My father's house?"

"Yes." I knew she hadn't sold it.

"Why?"

"That's where you were planning on landing?" As far as I knew, she hadn't purchased any other property in Florida, but I had. Three years ago, when I'd gone civilian. After landing AES's first major contract, I'd sunk everything back into the company except for two million. I'd taken that cash and made an impulsive decision.

Sinking all of it into a deposit on an oceanfront property.

Eight months later, I had the place paid off.

I'd been there exactly once, when I'd closed on it, because I'd been waiting for a goddamn impossible dream.

A dream that stood in front of me, harboring a grief so deep she was closed off to everything except the notion that she had an obligation to serve that'd been bred into her since before she could spell her own name. A notion so damn strong, she wanted to work in the field and was willing to leave me to do it.

I didn't fault her father for that sense of civic duty. Not for that.

I'd have nothing if it weren't for Vice Admiral Erikson Nilsen and his influence.

But he was gone, and the woman standing in front of me was lost, and *that* I faulted her father for—as well as myself.

Turning away from me, Emmy reached for her purse. "I'm sorry I got… overwhelmed. You can go back to work now."

"Turn around, Maila," I commanded.

"I appreciate the job opportunity," she replied, ignoring me. "I'm sure you'll find someone else quickly."

Fuck this.

Stepping up to her back, I crowded her. Her scent, ethereal and fleeting except for when she moved close, ghosted across my senses. Using my height, my size, I shamelessly caged her against her luggage, but I didn't touch her.

I lowered my voice. "Do you know what I think?"

Her hair twisted up in a sexy style that exposed her neck, goose bumps raced across the exposed skin of her nape. "Step back, Adam."

"I think you never gave yourself time to grieve." I traced an invisible line from her hairline to the top of her shirt collar.

A shiver she couldn't hide had her crossing her arms, but she didn't step to the side to escape me. "What are you doing?"

"I think you're hurting." Skimming my finger over her shoulder and down her arm, I leaned to her ear. "And I think you're running again." Letting my lips touch her neck once, I inhaled her aloofness and the intoxicating scent of memories. Then I laced my fingers through hers. "But you don't have to do it alone. Let's go to Miami together. Let's open an AES office there. Let's make it what you want."

A sob I was expecting, one I was purposely aiming to induce in her vulnerable state because I was a ruthless asshole, shook her small frame. "Do not do this again, Adam Trefor."

Shameless, putting every ounce of coercion I had into my tone, I pushed harder. "Make this your decision. Take the reins. Take control, Maila. Make a decision for you. Not for your country, not for your father, not for your brother." Bringing our joined hands to her chest, I pressed them against her heart. "Do it for you."

"For me?" The whirlwind that was the teenage Emmy Nilsen I knew spun and threw her indignant anger at me like a flashbang. "This is about you," she accused with disdain.

"No, it isn't." This was about everything she'd lost, and I'd triggered it today by giving her another bullshit assignment. I'd driven her to this breaking point, and I wanted to undo every goddamn second of it, but I had to work the problem before I could get to the solution.

She wrenched her hand from mine. "I know what you're doing, and it's bullshit, Adam."

Without thought, without hesitation, I gripped the back of her neck. "Was it about me when I brought you into AES? Was it about me when I flew halfway around the world to find you?

Was it about me when I washed the blood of your first kill off you?" My anger ramping up, my voice turned lethal. "Was it about me when I told you to wait for me seven years ago?" It wasn't a fucking question, it was a demand, and I didn't wait for another one of her excuses. "This has always been about you, because it has always *been* you, Maila." I gripped her neck harder. "*Always.*"

Her muscles poised for defense, her body stiff, she stared at me with eyes I knew better than my own. Then she fucking broke me. "If it was always about me, how come you didn't wait for me?" Her voice dropped. "You slept with other women, but I waited for you."

My jaw tight, my hand locked, I fucking froze. "What?" She'd never thrown my past in my face.

Her throat moved with a swallow. "You were never going to put me in the field any more than I was going to be your first."

Trying to calm down, I sucked in a breath, then another. I knew where she was going with this, but I didn't want to have this conversation. I didn't fucking *do* conversations. I was an action man. The Teams trained me well, and now, even though I sat in more fucking meetings than I ever wanted to, I didn't converse. I laid out parameters, metrics, fees and plans of action. I disseminated information, I didn't exchange it. That shit I left for Zulu, Conlon and November.

This shit right now?

I didn't do this.

But if I wanted my endgame, I needed to man the fuck up.

"You're right," I admitted. "I wasn't going to."

She nodded, taking the point she'd already earned. "But now you're offering me up an entire AES branch, as my *decision*?"

I tipped my chin.

"Why?"

"Because I learn from my mistakes."

"Simple as that?"

Nothing about her or us was simple. "No. But I can't undo the past four weeks, and frankly, I don't want to. They've been the best of my life, but I realize now how unhappy you've been, and my part in that, so I'm changing it. The offer stands."

"With strings?" she smartly asked.

"As much as I want to put a thousand fucking disclaimers on this about your safety and not sending you out in the field, I'm going to let you make those decisions for yourself from now on. I want to protect you. It's what I do. I'm not talking about the Navy or AES, I'm talking about you specifically. You hold every piece of me that's worth a damn, and I can't fucking breathe if I think about a world without you. So yes, I want to protect you, every minute of every day, but I also realize I can't smother you."

She studied me for a beat. "I know why strategically it makes sense to have an AES office in Florida, but why do you want one?"

I fucking frowned. "Did Conlon talk to you about this?"

She looked surprised. "No, why?"

"Never mind. I want an office in Miami if it makes you happy."

"AES isn't my company."

AES was technically mine, but everything I was I owed to her. "When I marry you, it will be."

"Now you're asking me to marry you?"

Unable to gauge her now locked expression and her tone, I shook my head. "If I was asking you at this moment, I would be on one knee and I'd have a ring in my hand." A ring I'd already had for two weeks but hadn't wanted to pressure her with after just moving in together.

"And here you said you weren't romantic."

I wasn't. "The Falcon's fueled. We can be in Miami in three hours."

"And what?" She looked almost incredulous. "Start over after having only started four weeks ago?"

"If that's what it takes."

For one impossible fucking moment, she stared at me.

Then she smiled.

My woman fucking smiled at me. "The beast," she said quietly, color infusing her cheeks.

I couldn't fucking help it, I smiled back and nodded in confirmation. "The beast."

"*Alpha*," she whispered, still smiling.

That was it.

With a fucking roar, I picked her up and slammed my mouth over hers.

Then I kissed the hell out of her as I walked us into the bedroom.

EPILOGUE

Maila

I GLANCED OVER MY SHOULDER.

Leaning against the SUV in a T-shirt and jeans with his hands in his pockets, Adam's eyes were locked on mine as if he expected me to look back at him. He tipped his chin in encouragement.

I can do this, I silently chanted.

Nodding at him, I looked forward again.

Then I walked the final paces to the cemetery plot that held my family.

Kneeling down in the early morning, dew-kissed grass I whispered, "Hi Momma, hi Daddy, hi Billy."

A bird sang.

My eyes welled and I reached forward, placing my hand over Billy's name on the family headstone. "I'm sorry, Billy. I should've been here."

Another bird returned the first bird's song.

I laughed through the tears. "If that's you, Billy, singing forgiveness through those birds, I appreciate it, but we both know I should've been here seven years ago." Inhaling, I smoothed my hand over his etched name in the cool granite. "For whatever it's worth, I came here first thing after we got in last night. Actually, we came here," I corrected. "Adam's just giving me space to say hi first."

The bird sang a beautiful song of life and the second one joined in as a third added another melody.

Tears slid down my cheeks. "I hear you," I whispered. "All of you." And suddenly, I knew. It was right to come back home. Opening this office, as much as I could help Adam with that, it was right. Being here with him—I was where I was supposed to be.

The grief, the pain in my heart I carried everywhere, it was still there. But I was also here, in the present, and I wasn't afraid of falling and never being able to get back up because I didn't feel so desperately, completely alone anymore.

I glanced over my shoulder.

His eyes still on me, Adam met my gaze as he pushed off the SUV.

My stomach fluttered and I looked back at my family. "I love him so much," I whispered.

A strong hand landed on my shoulder. "I love you back, beautiful." Adam tapped the top of the headstone over Billy's name with his fist. "Hey man, miss you." His gaze cut toward my parent's names. "Vice Admiral, Mrs. Nilsen." Squatting next to me, Adam kissed my forehead. "Mind if I speak to them a moment?"

"No, of course not." I rose. "Daddy, Momma, Billy, I love you all. I'll see you soon."

Adam's large hand grabbed mine and squeezed. "Meet you back at the SUV."

"Okay." I turned and soft morning sunlight fell over my face and I briefly closed my eyes. A warmth I hadn't felt in seven years spread through me as I walked back to the fancy black Escalade that Adam said was a loaner from his and Billy's Marine buddy, André Luna, until he could get to a dealership.

I was about to open the passenger door when a slick black muscle car drove through the cemetery and pulled up behind us. The driver door opened and a muscled surfer I hadn't seen in years got out.

Blond hair, green eyes and a smile as wide as the ocean, Talon Talerco grinned at me. "Rumor has it a little firecracker and a badass Alpha came rollin' into town last night and I had to see for myself."

"Talon." I smiled, walking over to him. "What are you doing here?" Last I heard, Billy's Corpsman buddy, Talon, was up in Daytona.

"Gettin' some love, sugar." Talon held his arms out wide. "Come here, M and M. Give me some of that sweetness before Alpha pounds my face in for huggin' on ya."

I stepped into his embrace.

He wrapped his arms around me. "There, now ain't that better, M and M?"

The scent of beach and coconuts surrounded me as the birds sang louder. "No one calls me M and M anymore."

"I do, sugar. Always will." He pulled back and looked down at me with concern. "Heard about a little scuffle in a sand trap half-way 'round the world. You good?"

"I'm good." I patted his arm that looked bigger than the last time I'd seen him. "You going for reenlistment with these guns?"

He laughed his charming laugh. "Pretty sure Uncle Sam's had about enough of me. Good thing my ladies haven't." His expression turned serious. "Also heard Uncle Sam's spyin' brother had enough of you."

"Is there anything you don't hear?"

He grinned. "Yeah, your sweet voice for too many years. Thought I was your favorite but then you go and break my heart."

I shook my head. "You haven't changed."

"Never." His smile held but his gaze cut over my shoulder and he held his hand out. "What up, Alpha? Patrol says you're here to stay and Vikin's got property mapped out for ya."

"Talerco, good to see you." Adam shook his hand. "And Luna would be right. AES is opening a branch in Miami and

Christensen has a lead on some property for us." He frowned. "Does Christensen know you call him Viking?"

Talon laughed. "Yep, and he hates every second of it." Talon looked at me and winked. "But I wouldn't be me if I held back, now would I?" He glanced back at Adam. "Glad to have you both here. I know you got a busy day, just wanted to say hi to my favorite M and M and give Billy and the old man a shout-out."

I was touched Talon had come to see us and to say hi to Billy and Daddy. "Thank you, Talon."

"Of course, sugar." He leaned down and kissed my cheek. "We'll get together soon." He slapped Adam on the shoulder. "Glad to see you finally locked it down, Alpha. Get 'em young and train 'em, huh?" He laughed.

"Christ." Adam shook his head. "You're lucky we're in a cemetery and it'd be disrespectful to level you."

Talon's laugh carried as he walked toward my family's plot.

Adam opened the passenger door for me. "You ready for our next stop?"

"The office space?"

He nodded. "The office space."

Suddenly overcome, I went on tiptoe and threw my arms around his neck, hugging him tight.

Adam pulled me in close and hugged me back with his strength as my feet briefly left the ground. "What's this for?"

"Nothing." No, it wasn't nothing. "Actually, it's everything. I love you. And thank you."

His arms still around me, Adam looked down at me with the same starkness I'd always counted on. "You don't have to ever thank me."

Yes, I did. "Yes, I do."

He nodded once as if he understood. "Come on, Christensen will be waiting."

I hopped in the SUV and Adam casually pulled my seatbelt out for me as if it were second nature.

"See?" I smiled. "Thank you."

Shaking his head, but with a look of amusement on his face, he clicked the seatbelt home. But then he surprised me and cupped my cheek before covering my mouth with his and kissing me once, hard and fierce. A deep groan rumbled from his chest and spilled into my mouth.

In the next second my fingers were twisted in his hair, both of his hands were holding my face and the kiss went from hot to nuclear.

Groaning again, he abruptly pulled back and looked at me with his Mediterranean blue eyes that were swirling with heat. "After the office, I'm taking you somewhere."

Wet and achy with desire, all I wanted to do was skip the office and climb on his lap. "Okay."

His hands still on my face, his thumb stroked my cheek. "You keep looking at me like that and we're skipping the office."

Words came out of my mouth and I didn't know who I was. "Can it wait till later?" I was never irresponsible, but Adam, dressed casually in dark jeans and a black T-shirt, kissing me in a semi-public place when he'd never kissed me in the New York office—it was making me feel like I didn't want to be responsible. I felt like I wanted to live. In this moment. With this Adam.

His eyes on me, Adam pulled his cell out. Then he dialed and held it to his ear. "Christensen, can we change the meet time?"

Talon walked back from my family's plot and held a hand up as he went to his car.

I waved back.

"Tomorrow," Adam clipped. "Eight a.m.?"

Talon drove off.

"Good copy. See you then." Adam hung up.

My heart leapt with joy. "We get a day off and I get you all to myself?"

For a split second, Adam frowned, but then he quickly covered it. "You always have me all to yourself." He kissed my temple. "And yes, we're taking the day and I'm taking you somewhere." With one more kiss, he closed the passenger door.

I smiled.

Adam

Christ, that smile.

Those lips.

I couldn't get enough of her.

Taking her twice before we'd gotten on the Falcon last night and flown down here, then again this morning in the hotel before she asked to come out here and see her family, I knew I should give her sweet, tight cunt a break, but then she'd asked for the day.

She'd never asked for my time.

In fact, before yesterday, she hadn't asked for a damn thing from me in the four weeks we'd been together. She'd worked her ass off on the bullshit assignments I'd given her, organized shit I'd been meaning to get to for years, then every night she'd let me devour her sweet body in every conceivable way I could come up with.

She took it all.

Me, my dominance and my control, and she'd fit herself into my world.

I was a selfish prick and I was glad she'd walked out yesterday. More glad she'd given me a second chance to prove myself because that's what I'd done all this for.

Her and this moment.

A life for both of us.

A life she'd be proud of.

I wanted to give her the world. I wanted her to have everything I never did, but more than all that, I wanted to prove to her that I was worthy of that first innocent smile she'd given to the broken kid from the wrong side of the tracks.

Today, I was going to prove it to her, starting with the office space I'd seen pictures of, but then she'd looked at me like she'd looked at me last night when I first sank inside her and I wasn't waiting anymore.

I wanted back inside her and I wanted her to be mine.

Permanently.

Nerves edging in, I rounded the SUV and got behind the wheel.

Cheeks flushed, a shy look of excitement in her eyes, she glanced at me with her reserved smile. "Where are we going?"

"You'll see." Hopefully, she'd like it. If not, I'd fucking sell it and buy another one.

"Adam Trefor and surprises—those are three words I never thought I'd put in the same sentence."

I glanced at her as I pulled out of the cemetery. Her tone even, I couldn't tell if she was fucking with me. "You think I'm incapable?"

She laughed.

It was quiet and reserved, but it was a laugh and I wanted to fucking hear it again. "You better not be underestimating me, beautiful."

"First, by the time I was seven I learned to never underestimate you." Her hand landed on my arm and her tone turned serious. "Second, you're the most capable person I know."

Curiosity got me. "What'd I do when you were seven?"

"Besides enlist with Billy then come home and tell me with utter confidence that you were going to be a SEAL?"

"I wasn't lying." I headed east toward the beach, then turned north.

"That's my point. Did you know the actual statistical probability of becoming a SEAL when you enlisted?"

Of course, I'd known. "Six percent of SEAL applicants." I wasn't going to be one of those ninety-four percenters, no fucking way.

"Like I said, I never underestimate you." Her fingers glanced down my arm.

I grabbed her hand and brought it to my mouth. "I appreciate it, but you said *besides*." I kissed her knuckles. "What else made you decide to not underestimate me?"

"Back then or recently?"

I glanced at her and she blushed. I laughed. "Spill it, beautiful, starting with back then." I rested our clasped hands on my thigh.

She looked out the window and I could sense the shift.

"Hey." I squeezed her hand. "What just happened?"

"I'm just..." She shook her head, then inhaled and let it out slowly. "Do you remember when I fell off my bike in front of the house when you and Billy were playing football?"

I remembered. "You skinned your knee."

"Do you remember what you told me?"

I did, but I was surprised she remembered it. Not one of my finer moments. "I told you not to cry." It was a dick move, but even back then I'd hated her tears. Nothing made me feel more helpless than when she cried.

She nodded. "Yes, but you also told me something else."

Stopping at a red light, I looked at her. "What'd I say?" I knew what I'd said. I'd stupidly fucking told her everything would be all right. Then her father and Billy died.

"You said *I'm here, and you're okay.* Then you said *I'm going to take care of you.*" Her piercing green eyes held my gaze. "You're still here, and you're still taking care of me." Her voice dropped to a whisper. "I never underestimate you, Adam Trefor."

The light turned green and I looked back at the road, thankful as hell I was driving because I needed a damn minute. My chest tight, the urge to pull over and consume her overwhelming, I was at a loss for words.

I fucking loved this woman.

Bringing her hand back to my mouth, my lips landed on her soft skin and I forced emotion-rough words past the lump in my throat. "I'll always be here for you, Maila. *Always*."

"I know," she quietly agreed, giving me her trust.

I crossed over to one of the barrier islands and turned north, but I didn't ask her any more questions. She'd already given me more than I deserved. Praying like hell she'd give me one more thing, I pulled into a gated private driveway almost completely concealed by fan palms and a ten-foot-tall awabuki hedge.

Stopping at the gate, I lowered the window and entered the code.

As the gate opened, I glanced at her. "Trust me?"

She hesitated only a fraction. "Yes."

I pulled through the gate. "This morning, you told me you loved the sunrise over the ocean."

"I loved more than that." She glanced at the thick tropical landscape on either side of us.

I took the turn in the driveway and bypassed the four-car garage with guest quarters above it, and pulled directly up to the house. Still holding her hand, I cut the engine.

Then I turned to her. "I thought you might like to wake up to the ocean every morning."

Staring at the modern three-story house for a full beat, she slowly turned to me. "This is yours? When did you..." Trailing off, she looked back at the house.

"I bought it three years ago after AES got its first paycheck."

She looked back at me. "You live here?"

"No, but I'm hoping you'll like it and we'll live here." I prayed like fuck I hadn't overshot this. "It's ours."

Her mouth opened and closed, then she exhaled slow. "You bought an oceanfront mansion three years ago and you don't even live in it?"

"Never slept here," I admitted.

Frown lines creased between her eyes as she continued to take in the house. "Why?"

"I was waiting."

She turned to me. "For?"

"You."

She blinked. Then, in keeping with the woman she'd grown into, she stated the practical. "It's huge."

"Eighty-eight hundred square feet, five bedrooms, nine baths, two-point-three acres," I rattled off the usual stats but then gave her the ones that made me buy it. "Impact glass, hurricane shutters—all of it built to withstand hundred and fifty mile per hour winds."

"Category five," she murmured.

Not quite. "Almost." Category five was anything over a hundred and fifty-seven mile per hour winds, but this place was a damn fortress. "Wait there, beautiful." I got out of the SUV and opened her door.

When I held out my hand, she looked up at me with concern. "What if I'm not a mansion type of woman? It would take me a week to vacuum eight thousand square feet."

"There's a staff."

"A staff," she stated.

"A groundskeeper and a cleaning service that comes every other week."

She stared at me.

I smiled. "Come take a look before you dismiss it, beautiful."

I leaned in to kiss her forehead. "And you're my type of woman. That's all that matters." Taking her hand, I helped her out of the Escalade.

Leading her to the front door, I entered the security code and pushed the door open, but then I let her walk in first.

Not saying a word, she stepped inside the foyer then just stood there.

Closing the door, I came up behind her and wrapped my arms around her. "You like the view?"

"Adam," she whispered, staring at the two-story view of the ocean from the living room before glancing around. "It's furnished."

"It is." I didn't tell her I'd hired a design firm to outfit this place or that I'd been waiting for this moment for fucking years. "Come on, I want to show you my favorite place in the house."

Taking her hand, I led her past the dining area, family room and kitchen to the north set of stairs that led to the master suite. Then I pushed open the door to the room that had two walls of glass overlooking the ocean.

"Oh my God," she barely whispered, walking toward the sliders that opened to the balcony. "There's no railing."

I brushed her long hair over her shoulder. "There is, but it's glass so it doesn't obstruct the view." My cock already hard as fuck, I kissed where her shoulder met her neck.

She shivered and whispered. "I see it now."

Lifting the hem of her summer dress, I dragged my fingers up her thighs. "I want you, beautiful." I'd fantasized about this since I'd bought the place three years ago.

"Anyone on the beach can see us," she barely breathed, but not stopping me.

"Reflective coating on the glass." No one would see but I was so far gone, I didn't give a fuck if they did. I wanted inside this woman. I wanted the world to know she was mine. Pushing her dress up higher, I almost lost it. "Fuck, woman, no underwear?"

"You always take them off me anyway." She lifted her arms.

I pulled her dress over her head and undid my jeans. "Have I told you how fucking perfect you are?"

"No." She braced her hands on the glass and gave me her sweet ass. "Maybe."

Dragging my hands down her back and over her hips, I kissed her neck. "So goddamn perfect, baby." I bit the skin just below her ear and freed my cock. "Spread those gorgeous thighs for me."

Beautifully, naturally submissive for me, she stepped wider.

"Good girl." Stroking the head of my cock through her already wet cunt, I palmed the front of her throat.

Moaning, she arched her back, pushing her hips into mine. "I'm not a girl."

"You're my girl," I corrected, dragging my cock through her heat again, spreading her sweet desire. "You always have been." I shoved into her.

"*Adam.*" Her entire body bucked and her hands fisted against the glass.

Pulling out a few inches, I slammed back in. "Say it," I demanded.

Her tight cunt drenched my cock with a rush of wetness. "*Oh my God.*"

Pinching one nipple then the other, I drove in and out of her again. "Tell me you're mine, beautiful."

Her fingers spread back out against the glass and she leveraged, trying to ride my cock. "I'm yours."

Pulling out then slamming back into her, I fingered her clit. "Tell me you're my girl."

"*Ahhh.*" The moan crawled up her throat and vibrated under my hand.

Gripping her hips and going still, I fought not to fucking thrust. "Say the fucking words, Maila," I ruthlessly demanded.

Her cunt constricting, her body shaking, the words spilled out of her mouth. "I'm yours. I'm your girl. *Oh my God, yes.*" Pushing against my tight grip, she tried to thrust. "I'm all yours. *Fuck me, please, please, please.*"

I pulled the ring out of my pocket and let go of her throat to hold her left wrist against the glass. Then I slid the diamond onto her ring finger and drove deep. "You were always mine." I laced our hands and thrust hard. "Now you're mine forever."

Her gasp filled the bedroom of our home.

Then she fucking fell apart in my arms.

The burner phone vibrated as I stared at the setting sun.

Unknown number.

Answering, I held the phone to my ear, but I didn't speak.

"It's handled."

"Thanks," I replied.

"There'll be questions," he warned.

"There always are." I hung up, removed the SIM card, and broke the phone in half.

THANK YOU!

Thank you so much for reading ALPHA! If you are interested in leaving a review on any retail site, I would be so appreciative. Reviews mean the world to authors, and they are helpful beyond compare.

Turn the page for a preview of VICTOR, the next exciting book in the Alpha Elite Series!

VICTOR

Philanderer

Mercenary.

Marine.

I didn't join the Marines because I was honorable. There wasn't one scrupulous thing about me. If I saw an advantage, I took it. But serving my country turned out to be the best decision I ever made. It led me to Alpha Elite Security.

AES was the most sought after security contractor in the world. Our reputation unmatched, we got the job done—by any means necessary. Which is where I came in. I handled AES's difficult clients, the ones no one wanted to touch. My success rate flawless, I thought I was invincible.

Then my boss sent me a cryptic text. *New client. Sensitive matter. Corporate Espionage.* Except he failed to mention the suspected spy was a terrified brunette. And the client? Her husband. Now I had one objective.

Code name: Victor.
Mission: Infiltrate.
VICTOR is a standalone book in the exciting new Alpha Elite Series by *USA Today* Bestselling author, Sybil Bartel. Come meet Vance "Victor" Conlon and the dominant, alpha heroes who work for AES!

ROMEO

Pilot.
Handler.
Marine.
My first memory was in the cockpit of a plane. My second was of a uniform. All I'd ever wanted was to be a pilot. The Marines gave me wings and I gave them my all.

Half a dozen deployments, countless flight hours—I knew the controls in the cockpit better than I knew my own name. I never made mistakes. But war didn't care how good you were. One surface-to-air missile and my career was over.

Thinking I'd left dangerous missions and adrenaline rushes in my rearview, I was piloting a seaplane in the Florida Keys when a beat to hell, dark-eyed blonde washed ashore. In nothing but a bikini, she asked me for help. Help I couldn't give without an assist from Alpha Elite Security. Except AES wanted a favor in return… one that would put me right back in the line of fire.

Code name: Romeo.
Mission: Rescue.

ROMEO is a standalone book in the exciting new Alpha Elite Series by USA Today Bestselling author, Sybil Bartel. Come meet Roark "Romeo" MacElheran and the dominant, alpha heroes who work for AES!

ZULU

Navy SEAL.

Sniper.

Mercenary.

The Navy trained me to be the best, but the Teams turned me into a deadly weapon. Every mission honing my tactical skills, I never missed a shot. Living for my brothers and the Trident I'd earned, I didn't look past my next deployment.

Then my friend and former teammate made me an offer—private sector, government contracts, combat missions and the chance to fly my own jet. Retiring from the Teams, but not the mission, I joined Alpha Elite Security.

As second-in-command at AES, I demanded precision because I didn't do things the wrong way. Until a mysterious brunette walked through the door, and everything went FUBAR.

Code name: Zulu.
Mission: Exfiltrate.

ZULU is a standalone book in the exciting new Alpha Elite Series by USA Today Bestselling author, Sybil Bartel. Come meet Zane "Zulu" Silas and the dominant, alpha heroes who work for AES!

ACKNOWLEDGMENTS

In November 2020, five impossible months ago as I write this, my only child, my son Oliver, passed away tragically and unexpectedly in his sleep from an undiagnosed birth defect in his heart. My Sweet Boy was only fifteen-years-old.

Oliver was my entire world. Born with an auto immune disease, he overcame every obstacle life threw at him and he not only survived, he thrived during his time here on earth. Intelligent beyond comprehension, he was a straight A student, (with a 4.45 GPA!). He was an incredibly talented cello and piano player, a black belt in Karate and Jiu Jitsu, and a compassionate friend to everyone he met. He had the biggest heart of anyone I've ever known. I was blessed with a gift beyond words the day he was born.

Oliver taught me about unconditional love and perseverance. He showed me what determination looked like, and he showed the world how someone so young, yet so wise, can handle life's obstacles with grace and humbleness. Oliver made me a better person. He brightened every single day. His smile was my joy, and he truly made this world a better place.

I will never understand why he was taken from us, and I cannot imagine a day where the grief isn't so punishing that it robs me of all breath. I would give anything to have just one more minute with him so I could hold him, and tell him I love him. But life, for all its beauty, cruelly doesn't work like that. So this is me, holding my son and telling him how I love him more than words. This is the first book I have written since he passed, and I could not have done it without Scott, my parents, my sister, Peggy, Trina, Chelsea, Liz, Virginia, Olivia, Jaime, Sally and all my family and friends. This book is a testament to my son's perseverance. My new reality, while unfathomable, is me doing my best to honor the memory of my beautiful son.

My Sweet Boy—you were, and will forever be, my most treasured gift.
I love you, Oliver Shane.
I love you more than anything.
XOXO
Mom

ABOUT THE AUTHOR

Sybil Bartel is a *USA Today* Bestselling author of unapologetic alpha heroes. Whether you're reading her deliciously dominant alpha bodyguards or alpha mercenaries, her page-turning romantic suspense, or her heart-stopping military romance, all of her books have sexy-as-sin alpha heroes!

Sybil resides in South Florida with her wonderful family, one furry canine, and she is forever Oliver's mom.

To find out more about Sybil Bartel or her books, please visit her at:

Website: sybilbartel.com

Facebook page: www.facebook.com/sybilbartelauthor

Facebook group: www.facebook.com/groups/1065006266850790

Instagram: www.instagram.com/sybil.bartel

Twitter: twitter.com/SybilBartel

BookBub:www.bookbub.com/authors/sybil-bartel

Newsletter: http://eepurl.com/bRSE2T

Made in the USA
Monee, IL
07 September 2021